Seth's strong hand grabbed hold of her right biceps, and he pulled her into his body, somehow

both upright.

"I've got you," he sai

He was hot and swea
plastered against his

"Oh, indeed," he murmured.

Her heart was hammering in her chest, and not only from the run and the near fall. She'd been physically aware of him since the first moment that he'd almost slid into her under the awning. And waking up in the same room had only exacerbated the tension coursing through her body.

She was needy. Aching with it, truly.

She tilted her head up. He leaned down.

His mouth was just inches away. So close she could feel his warm breath.

He was going to kiss her.

And then he straightened up and stepped away. "We should probably finish up," he said. "I think there's a mile or so left. Ready?"

* * *

If you're on Twitter, tell us what you think of Harlequin Romantic Suspense! #harlequinromsuspense

Dear Reader,

I love road trips. The excitement of picking the destination and then planning the route. The routine of packing snacks for the car; a trip without a bag of red licorice at my side is really not a trip at all. The challenge of shoving suitcases and shoes and way too many things into the trunk because there's nobody to threaten me with a fifty-pound weight limit and that I only get one carry-on bag!

Then there's the drive and all the good things that come with that. Perhaps a glimpse of something unexpected like the field of prairie dogs in South Dakota or the joy of a sunset in Bryce Canyon National Park. Or a back road in northern Wisconsin that led to a little store selling the best jelly and pickled beets one might ever taste.

And what is better than the anticipation of arrival and then finally seeing new things or old friends, depending on the trip?

In *Protecting the Boss*, Megan North is about to take a big-time road trip. She's going to open four boutiques in four different states in less than two weeks. Her bags are packed, and she's got a plan! It does not include security specialist Seth Pike.

But there's danger ahead, just beyond the bend in the road, and it's going to take the two of them, working together, to make it back home alive.

I invite you to come along for the ride! I think you're going to enjoy it.

All my best,

Beverly

PROTECTING THE BOSS

Beverly Long

HARLEQUIN® ROMANTIC SUSPENSE

ISBN-13: 978-1-335-66184-5

Protecting the Boss

This edition published by arrangement with Harlequin Books S.A.

For questions and comments about the quality of this book, please contact us at CustomerService@Harlequin.com.

Printed in U.S.A.

Beverly Long enjoys the opportunity to write her own stories. She has both a bachelor's and master's degree in business and more than twenty years of experience as a human resources director. She considers her books to be a great success if they compel the reader to stay up way past their bedtime. Beverly loves to hear from readers. Visit beverlylong.com, or like her author fan page at Facebook.com/beverlylong.romance.

Books by Beverly Long

Harlequin Romantic Suspense

Wingman Security

Power Play
Bodyguard Reunion
Snowbound Security
Protecting the Boss

Harlequin Intrigue

Return to Ravesville

Hidden Witness
Agent Bride
Urgent Pursuit
Deep Secrets

The Men from Crow Hollow

Hunted
Stalked
Trapped

The Detectives

Deadly Force
Secure Location

Visit the Author Profile page at Harlequin.com for more titles.

My thanks to my good friend
Margaret O'Connor Govett at Girls in Pearls Boutique
for all things boutique related.
Any errors are solely mine.

Chapter 1

Seth Pike had two child-size teddy bears wrapped in clear plastic under one arm and a twelve-year-old bottle of scotch under the other. What he didn't have was an umbrella, which meant he was going to get wet.

The rain, a welcome relief from the heat, was falling hard, practically bouncing up when it hit. Vegas, a mass of concrete and hard-baked earth in August, was unreceptive to Mother Earth's goodness.

He had four blocks to go and it would be a damn miracle if he didn't get his eye poked out by some fool who couldn't control his umbrella in the strong wind that had come along with the rain. He spied the big green awning of one of his favorite pizza places and made a run for it.

He slid the last couple feet, almost ramming into the back of a woman who hadn't been there a second before. "Sorry," he mumbled, managing to stay upright and not drop the scotch or the bears.

"No problem," she said, turning. "I perhaps should

have taken the warning about monsoon season a little more seriously."

She talked fast and her very blue eyes sparkled. She wore a short black dress and black heels. Her bare legs were toned and tanned and he told himself it wasn't nice to stare. With effort, he shifted his gaze upward. A brightly colored scarf was hanging off one shoulder, secured with some kind of fancy knot that only women seemed to know how to do. Her damp hair was a dark brown and hung below her shoulders. She was in the process of gathering it up into a ponytail and then wadding said ponytail into a bun on the top of her head. On one wrist was an oversize gold watch and on the other, at least five gold bracelets, in varying shapes and sizes. There were rings on three of her fingers. None of them looked like the wedding type.

"Whew," she said, giving the bun a pat. "That's better."

With her three-inch heels, they were almost at eye level. She had the darkest eyelashes he'd ever seen.

She smiled at him and for the first time, looked at the things he was carrying. "So the bears enjoy scotch?"

He pointed at their pirate suits. "Strictly rum drinkers."

"Of course. Love a good piña colada myself."

He inclined his head toward the dark window behind them. "There's a nice bar twenty feet behind you. Unfortunately, they're only open for dinner."

"I'm free later. Maybe I'll come back," she added, her tone unconcerned. "Congrats on being much smarter and carrying your alcohol with you."

He shook his head. "The bears are for my business partner who is expecting a set of twins in a couple months and the scotch is…"

"To ensure that they all get a few hours of sleep?" she said, finishing his sentence.

"No. For my other business partner, who is getting married early next month."

"I see. Well, good wishes to them all. Does it rain like this every day?"

"Only for a couple weeks out of the year," he said. "Where are you from?"

"California. Near Carmel."

He'd spent a few weeks driving Route 1 along the coast a few years back. "Nice place," he said.

"I suppose," she said, not sounding convinced.

"First time in Vegas?"

"Third."

"What brings you here?"

"Business," she said.

She was the queen of one-word answers. "Not the gambling."

She laughed. "My business is enough of a gamble."

That made him curious. But before he could ask, she glanced at her watch and said, "I think I'm going to have to make a run for it."

Wait. It almost came out of his mouth. But that was crazy. "Good luck," he offered instead.

She gave him a dazzling smile. And took off fast. In the opposite direction of where he was going.

And seconds later, his own steps back to his office were slower, even though he was getting really wet. She'd taken her energy and maybe some of his with her.

When he got to the Wingman Security offices ten minutes later, he was still thinking about the woman. About how fast she talked. About the color of her eyes.

He opened the door, waved at Jane behind the reception desk, who was on the phone, and quickly walked down the hallway to his office. He shoved his purchases into the credenza behind his desk. He had a lot of work to do before tonight's party. His first appointment after lunch was due in fifteen minutes.

He took a seat behind the desk, which was almost entirely covered by piles. Files to review, security-related white papers to read, personal bills to pay and his laptop computer.

He glanced up when a shadow passed by his door. "Hey," he said.

Royce Morgan stepped into view. "Sorry, didn't realize you were back. You're soaked," he said.

Right down to his underwear. "Get any sleep last night?" he asked.

Royce shrugged, not looking that concerned. "Couple hours. Grace and I got some quality bonding time in the middle of the night."

Royce's seven-month-old daughter was teething. "Is she your date for tonight?"

"Yeah. Jules doesn't get back from New York until this weekend."

How Jules managed motherhood and being the CEO of a large pharmaceutical company was beyond him, but she seemed to do it effortlessly. Royce had really lucked out there.

As had his other two partners. Trey Riker had married Kellie McGarry last fall and his tux was ready in his closet for when Rico Metez and Laura Collins got hitched next month.

Then he'd be the only bachelor left at Wingman Security.

Fine with him.

"Don't let her drink too much," he said.

Royce shook his head. "She has to be at least two before she can have a cocktail."

Seth laughed. Royce was a supergood dad. Not that any of them had had any doubts.

"You got a date for tonight?" Royce asked.

"Nope."

"Still between prospects?"

That's how he'd explained his dating situation a few weeks ago when he, Royce, Trey and Rico had gone out for a few beers. "I'm not looking," he said. "I think it's good if one of us stays single. We don't want to cut ourselves out of a key demographic."

"Which is?"

"Single woman looking for protection. They aren't going to want one of you married types."

"You don't tell single clients that, do you?" Royce asked in response, perfectly serious.

Seth knew his partners thought he could be a little blunt sometimes. He preferred to think of it as being a direct communicator. "Not unless they ask," he said.

"Marketing strategies should always be a secret."

Seth held a finger up in the air. "I knew I should have gone to business school. All I cared about was trying to keep my ass from getting shot out of the sky."

Royce laughed and disappeared from view down the hallway. Five minutes later, Seth's desk phone buzzed. It was Jane, telling him that his appointment had arrived. He checked the name again on his phone calendar.

Abigail Chevalier. Some thirty years ago, her mother and Kellie McGarry's mother had been sorority sisters. That connection was enough that she'd been able to land a spot on Seth's calendar with barely twenty-four hours' notice.

When he got to the lobby, his potential new client was staring out the window. She turned as he approached. She was short, with short blond hair tucked behind her ears, and very pregnant.

"Would you like a chair?" he said quickly.

She shook her head. "It's easier to stand at this point. More room for the baby, you know?"

He didn't know. And maybe that's why he was uneasy. Or maybe it was because there was something about Abigail Chevalier that seemed familiar. But he was pretty confident they'd never met.

He led her back to his office and pointed at the chair. "Sit or stand. Your preference." He went behind his desk and sat. "What can I do for you, Mrs. Chevalier?"

"Please, just Abigail. I've only been married for four months so I'm still getting used to the name. My maiden name of North was a little easier. Anyway, I'm rambling. I do that when I'm nervous."

"Don't be nervous," he said.

"I need security."

She'd chosen to stand, but because she couldn't be much over five feet, he didn't have to look up too far. "For yourself?" The idea that a pregnant woman might need security spiked all kinds of protective emotions in him.

"For my sister, Megan North. She was supposed to meet me here but she's running a little late. Her meeting at the bank ran long."

"Why does your sister require security?"

"Megan and I are not just sisters, we're also business partners. We've purchased an existing small chain of high-end women's boutiques. Four locations in total. The Vegas store is right across the street from here."

"Oh, yeah," he said. He knew the place. Hadn't paid too much attention to it, but it had interesting window displays at times of sexily dressed mannequins. And he recalled a story where his partner Trey had picked out a red sparkly dress for Jules Morgan when she and Royce were undercover in Vegas. Rumor had it that Royce's jaw had dropped. "Four locations," he repeated. "Where are the others?"

"Sedona, Arizona. Albuquerque, New Mexico. Colorado Springs, Colorado. In Vegas, we were able to purchase the building, and in the other locations, we're renting space. We're rebranding the properties and reopening all four as North and More Designs."

"Very exciting," he said.

"Yes. But I'm due in five weeks and my doctor isn't crazy about me traveling, and that's all my new husband, who is very French and very protective, had to hear. He insists that I not go. But that means that Megan is going to have to do the openings herself."

It sounded like a good reason to hire an assistant, not necessarily a security specialist whose bill rate was $2,500 a day. "Wingman Security might not be—"

"There was another potential buyer in the mix," she said, interrupting him. "We beat their bid and we understand they're not too happy about it."

Probably not. Nobody liked to lose. But still. "You're anticipating that they'll transfer this unhappiness into action against your sister."

"Not her," she said. "I don't think they're that crazy. Thank goodness. But possibly against the properties and the events associated with the reopening of the properties. They've been the losing party before and while it was never proven, most of us in the industry think they had some responsibility for a fire that consumed their competitor's warehouse."

Well, that put a different spin on things. "Reopening four stores in four states," he said. "Over what time period?" He had to be here for Rico's wedding.

"The next twelve days. We'll be done by the end of the month."

That would work. Rico's wedding was the first weekend of next month. "Has the travel been booked?"

"Hotels, yes."

"Air travel?" That's what he'd meant.

"All travel will be done by car. Megan doesn't fly."

He felt the first shiver of unease. Flying was like breathing to him. But he didn't want to disappoint Kellie McGarry by refusing to help a family friend or turn away good business. "I'll get somebody started on the contract," Seth said. He got up from his desk at the exact moment his intercom buzzed. "Yes," he said.

"Megan North is here to see you."

"Oh, good. She made it," Abigail said.

"Thanks, Jane," he said. "Bring her back, would you?"

Abigail Chevalier waved her index finger to get his attention. "I probably should have mentioned this," she said, her voice a mere whisper, "but Megan isn't too happy about this."

And before he could ask why, in walked the brunette he'd stood in the rain with.

Megan suspected she looked every bit as stunned as Seth Pike. "Hello again," she said, working hard to sound nonchalant. She barely made eye contact, instead focusing on her younger sister.

"Hi, Abigail," she said, taking one of the empty chairs. She wasn't surprised to see her sister standing. "How are you feeling?"

"Fine," her sister said. "No different from when you asked me two hours ago." She said it without angst. She knew Megan worried. And tried to be a good sport about it. She was sweet like that.

But under all that sweetness was a rip current of manipulation, Megan had realized, when two days ago, her sister had no trouble using Megan's concern to her advantage to get Megan to agree to hiring security.

Megan had been excited to be away from Carmel, away from the craziness that had permeated her life for the last few months. The craziness that nobody else had heard, seen or believed, especially the police. The craziness she hid from Abigail.

The way her life had been going lately, she should not have been the least surprised that it was Seth Pike she'd shared a dry spot with earlier that afternoon. Coincidences, both alarming and not, seemed to abound lately.

"Mr. Pike," she said, extending her hand to him. He was still standing by the side of his desk. His shirt and pants were drying but he looked as if he could use a good iron. "Good to see you didn't melt."

"Oh, I'm not that sweet," he said.

No, but he was a bit of eye candy. Lean and tall, but not too tall. Probably just under six feet. His dark brown hair was cut short and he had very light brown eyes. His skin was tanned.

"Ms. North, I presume," he said.

"Please, just Megan. After all, we have history."

Abigail looked at Seth, then Megan. "Do you two know each other?"

They both shook their heads. Megan turned to her sister. "Earlier today, I got caught in the rain. As did Mr. Pike."

"Seth," he said.

"As did Seth. We shared a canopy before I had to dash to the bank. Which, by the way, went well."

"Good," Abigail said.

"Now that I see the two of you together, the resemblance is definitely there," he said.

She was six years older, seven inches taller, and had dark hair. But she understood. Their eyes were the same shape and almost the same color. They both had their mom's smile and their dad's long fingers. "Most people don't see it," she said.

"I have always taken some pride in not being most people," he said.

There was a pregnant, no pun intended, pause in the room. Megan looked from her sister to Seth Pike. "So, did you two get the details all worked out?" She tried hard to keep the irritation out of her voice.

"I think I've got the basics," Seth said. "You and I will need to work out some of the finer logistics. Which should not be as painful as your last root canal," he added.

Ouch. Maybe she wasn't doing that good of job of keeping her feelings at bay. "Of course," she said.

"Two rooms have already been booked," Abigail said. "Our assistant did that weeks ago when I thought I'd still be able to go."

"Excellent. If you'll give me your email address, I'll send over the contract this afternoon." Seth pushed a piece of paper her direction and held out his pen.

Once the contract was signed, it would be too late. This was her last chance to put a stop to this nonsense. She could find another way to give Abigail peace of mind.

She stood up. "Actually, Seth. I—"

Chapter 2

"Oh, good," Seth interrupted. "You made it." He waved his partner in. Earlier, Trey had mentioned stopping by to say hello. Now his timing was impeccable, because Seth had a feeling that Megan North was about to pull the plug on the whole deal and all he knew was that he didn't want that. "Trey, this is Megan North and her sister, Abigail Chevalier. Ladies, my partner, Trey Riker."

Trey shook both women's hands. "Kellie's mom mentioned that you were expecting, too," he said to Abigail.

"I can't believe you're having twins," Abigail said.

"We're still sort of in shock," Trey admitted. "But stoked."

Everyone laughed.

"And Kellie is feeling good?" Abigail asked.

"She's a trouper," Trey said. "Doc says both babies are over three pounds right now. Due date is two months away."

Seth was happy for his friend. Trey and Kellie were lucky to be alive. Kellie's diabolical former boss had tried to kill them, and only because they were both supersmart and resourceful, they were here to tell the story.

"It's been a while since we've seen the McGarrys," Abigail said.

"Actually, that's why I wanted to stop in. We're having a little party tonight, a combined baby shower for Kellie and me and a wedding shower for Rico, another partner, who is getting married soon. We'd love to have both of you join us. It will give you a chance to catch up with Kellie."

Seth saw the quick look of distress in Megan's eyes. "It won't be pizza," he said, reminding her that she'd let the cat out of the bag that she had a free night, "but I can promise the food will be good."

"That sounds like so much fun," Abigail said.

Megan turned to her sister. "Are you sure you're up to it?"

"Absolutely. Where and when?"

"Here, and any time after six," Trey said. "And please, no gifts. I know this is a last-minute invite and I don't want you worrying about that."

"I guess we'll see you then," Megan said.

"About that contract?" Seth asked. "Should I email it over?"

Abigail nodded. "We're just so grateful that you were able to see us on such short notice and that you're available for the assignment."

He looked at Megan. She was staring at her sister.

Finally, she turned to him and very deliberately picked up the pen that he'd previously offered. She scribbled down her email address. "Yes, so grateful," she echoed. The pen dropped back onto his desk with a *thud.*

"I'll walk you out," Trey said. Both women moved toward the door.

And just that fast, Seth was alone. The room seemed

dimmer somehow, as if the sun had slipped behind a cloud.

He was going on a road trip with a beautiful woman. Hadn't seen this one coming. And didn't feel bad that he'd used circumstances to stack the deck in his favor when it had appeared that Megan might back out at the last minute. Could claim that he'd done it to preserve the $30,000 fee. Their business was successful, but that wasn't pocket change and would certainly help the monthly financials. But he hadn't really been thinking about that. Had been solely focused on the fact that he'd let Megan walk away from him once and he wasn't going to do it a second time.

He didn't profess to believe in fate but then again, he generally didn't disavow the possibility, either.

The dynamics between the two sisters were interesting. He wanted to know more. They'd certainly have time to discuss it. The distances between those cities were all one-day drives but in places, there wasn't much to see.

An hour later, Rico Metez walked by his office, whistling. For some reason, the man had started whistling after falling head over heels in love with Laura Collins and her four-year-old niece, Hannah, whom Laura had now officially adopted. Rico was going to become a husband and a father at the same time. And he couldn't wait.

"Why are you whistling?"

"I'm just happy, man. Hey, Jane showed me the contract."

"I know you normally take care of those things, but it was kind of a rush job and I wasn't sure when you were returning to the office. I will be back for your wedding."

"I saw that and the rest of it all looked good, too," Rico said. "Ten days on the road and then finishing up the assignment with two days in Vegas. You want me to look in on your mom at Everpark? I know they watch their residents really closely but just in case."

"I'm going to run out there tomorrow morning before the assignment starts. If something comes up while I'm on the road, I've got you, Royce and Trey all listed as emergency contacts."

"And we'd all step in just this quick. Your mom is amazing."

"No argument here."

Rico smiled. "I'll see you at the party."

"I can hardly believe you and Laura are finally getting married." He knew Rico would have done it last fall, but Laura had really wanted to wait until everything with Hannah was all straightened out and that had taken a while. "By the way, Trey expanded the guest list."

"No problem. We have enough food for twenty more guests. Who?"

"The new clients, Abigail Chevalier and Megan North. They're sisters. Megan is the one I'll be traveling with."

"I was talking with Trey about them yesterday. Sad situation with their parents, isn't it?"

He had no idea what Rico was talking about. "What?"

"They were killed in a small plane crash."

He could hear the concern in Rico's tone, knew that the man was trying to be sensitive given that he'd lost his dad in the same way. "Recently?"

"No. Something like fifteen years ago. Kellie's mom and Mrs. North were close friends and Mrs. McGarry tried to keep tabs on Megan and Abigail after the crash. But as the years went by, the visits were more sporadic and it was mainly a social media post here or there that kept them updated on each other's lives. I got the impression from Trey that Mrs. McGarry was pretty impressed that Megan had done such a good job raising Abigail."

"Raising?"

"Yeah, Megan is six years older. She was twenty and Abigail was fourteen. She gave up college to come home and take care of her little sister."

He understood about helping family. He'd move heaven and earth and whatever else was in his way to help his mom, who had sacrificed so much for him. And he didn't generally like to talk about it, either. In the early days of Wingman Security, he'd worked two jobs once it became apparent that it would be better for his mom to relocate somewhere where her home wasn't so isolated. Sure it had been hard. But family helped family.

But she'd really been just a kid herself. He was more confident than ever that there was more to Megan than a pretty face.

"I'm sorry I didn't get to meet either of them. What's your take on the sisters?"

"They're very different in looks but I could tell they were sisters. Abigail seems very sweet."

"Megan not sweet?"

"I don't know yet. She talks fast," Seth said. "Dresses pretty stylish. I suppose that goes along with owning a boutique." He paused, unwilling to share that she'd knocked him off his stride. His partner would never let him hear the end of that. "Not my type," he added, shaking his head.

Rico frowned at him. "I thought this was a work assignment, not a date."

"Of course," Seth said. "Just making conversation."

Megan rarely had trouble deciding what to wear. She loved clothes. Occupational hazard. But she wasn't sure what one wore to an office party that seemed to be less about babies and weddings and more about the friendship of the four Wingman Security partners. She felt terribly awkward, as if she were crashing a private event. It didn't matter that she had an invitation.

More of a command performance.

But it would be good to see Kellie again, who was closer in age to Abigail. Megan had been closer to Anthony McGarry, who she understood was now some renowned spine surgeon. She'd always felt sorry for the McGarry kids, in that they'd lost their dad when Anthony had been in high school and Kellie had been just a little girl.

Of course, ultimately they'd been the lucky ones because they'd still at least had their mom. Odd how circumstances changed.

She hadn't unpacked her clothes for the one night in Las Vegas, believing that she'd be staying in, ordering room service. Now she opened her large suitcase and pulled out a light blue silk dress with delicate cap sleeves. Then she slipped her bare feet into silver sandals. Changed out her gold jewelry for silver and was ready to go. Was halfway out the door when she remembered her umbrella. Definitely didn't want to be caught in another torrential rain without it. She stepped back inside the room and scooped it up.

When she walked out of the hotel and onto the Las Vegas Strip, there was no rain, just a light breeze. It was still very warm. Probably in the low eighties. There were lights and noise and all kinds of people on the sidewalks. She thought about walking the seven blocks to the Wingman Security offices but decided that her sandals weren't necessarily made for that. She asked the valet for a cab and within minutes, she was on her way.

And arrived too soon, because Vegas was made for people watching. She paid the driver and got out, glancing quickly across the street at the boutique. The Vegas store would be the last store to reopen. Remodeling efforts were still underway, but she had confidence in their general contractor and knew the place would be ready by the time she returned. There would be new fixtures, new flooring, new paint, new artwork and a cool coffee bar to support her and Abigail's upscale vision. Right now, it was still chaos and the big windows were lined with brown paper so that people passing by couldn't get an early look.

She bent forward and gave a sniff to the sweet-smelling flowers that were in big planters, spaced every six feet along the wide sidewalk that ran between the building and the street. Just a few blocks off the main drag, this area was much quieter. Not deserted in any manner, thank goodness. That would be bad for business. But a shade calmer, befitting the vibe they were trying to create in their stores.

She pulled open the door, felt the blast of air-conditioning and turned back to get one more breath of warm, fragrant summer air. And when she did, she caught the quick movement of somebody stepping inside a door across the street. Not her building, which housed her boutique and several other small businesses, but the one next to it. Moving so fast that she couldn't even tell if it had been a man or a woman.

Like they didn't want to be seen.

Had somebody followed her here? Was she being watched at the hotel? Had they flagged down a cab and chased her here?

Or had someone somehow discovered that she was returning to this office tonight?

Or was she simply losing her mind? Because that's what it seemed like.

It was more of the same that she'd been experiencing for months. Footsteps behind her. Doorbells ringing in the middle of the night and no one at the door. Hang-up phone calls from numbers that she couldn't trace. Muffled conversation beneath her open second-story bedroom window.

The overwhelming feeling that she was being watched.

She debated running across the street and searching the other building. Knew the idea had big holes. She was ill-equipped for action in heels with no means to protect herself.

And more importantly, she really wasn't brave enough. Because whatever it was, it felt sinister.

It was twenty minutes to seven when she finally arrived. Cocktail hour was well under way but Seth hadn't had a drink yet. And when the elevator door opened and she stepped out, in something pale blue and silky and several inches above her knee, he thought that was why his throat was suddenly dry.

And maybe the music and the crowd of people in the lobby explained the humming in his ears and his general feeling of light-headedness. He crossed the room fast.

"It…uh…looks…uh…different," she said as he reached her.

Her voice was shaky. And did she seem a little preoccupied? Maybe even upset? Had something happened?

"Everything okay?" he asked.

"Yes, of course," she said, not meeting his eyes. Her hand was clenched so tightly around the handle of her umbrella that her fingers were white.

Something definitely wasn't right. "No rain expected tonight," he said, deliberately staring at her clenched hand.

She tapped the wooden nub at the end against the ceramic tile flooring. Nervously. "I'm going nowhere without my umbrella. Ever again."

"Ever is a long time."

He watched as she drew in a breath. Then another. Saw her fingers relax. "True," she said.

He reached for the umbrella. "Why don't I take that and stow it back here," he said, motioning to the credenza behind Jane's desk.

"Thank you," she said. "I may need some of these," she said, casually looking around at the array of small tables, "when we reopen the Vegas store."

"I'll make sure Jane gets you the contact information for our vendor." He had to admit that it looked good. Jane had arranged for small high-topped ones along with some leather bar stools to be brought in, to provide adequate seating for dinner. They were scattered throughout the lobby and in other areas. Strands of lights had been hung and candles lit.

"Were you waiting for me?" she asked.

He hadn't been. Not really. But like before, her presence had changed the room. "Abigail arrived just a few minutes ago," he said. He pointed across the room where Abigail was chatting with Trey. "I thought you might come together."

She waved to her sister. "I'm at the hotel, but her husband's parents live in Vegas and she's staying with them."

"I thought he was French."

"He is. They are. It's a fish-out-of-water tale. They're here for just a few years. Mr. Chevalier is technically retired but he's mentoring some high potentials in his old securities firm. I imagine they'll be back in France within two years. But them being here was actually a stroke of luck for Abigail and me. We'd been looking at properties and she saw the Vegas store on one of her visits. While it wasn't being run well, we could see its potential. One thing led to another, and well, you know the rest."

"I imagine you're excited about being an aunt."

She looked him right in the eye. "I'm scared to death."

It might have been the first really honest thing that she'd said to him.

"Why?"

"There's a thousand things that could go wrong. Preeclampsia. Placental abruption. I mean, I know medicine is very advanced but still, bad things happen. Abigail isn't concerned. That's good, of course." She stopped. "Whatever you do, don't repeat this conversation. It bothers her that I worry."

And she didn't want her sister bothered about anything.

Which is why she'd agreed to hiring security even though she clearly wasn't happy about it. "I think it's going to be okay," he said.

"Oh, sure," she said, not sounding convinced. But Abigail was approaching and Megan gave her a big smile. "Did you get some rest?"

"I did. And such a stroke of luck that we got invited. Otherwise, I was going to have to learn to play *belote*." She turned to Seth. "It's a French card game."

"We speak poker here," he said. "I see you got something to drink."

Abigail held up her water. "Trey took care of me."

"What would you like?" he asked Megan. "We've got a bartender here. I imagine a piña colada is within the realm of possibility."

"White wine will be fine," she said.

"You two go ahead," Abigail said. "Trey was going to find Kellie and meet me back here."

Seth motioned Megan to precede him down the hall. They'd set the bar up in the break room. There were three choices of white wine, all equally good. They also had red wine and craft beers and all kinds of liquor for mixed drinks. Hagney, a friend of Kellie McGarry's from when she'd been a cocktail waitress at Lavender, was bartending.

"That one is perfect," Megan said. "Thank you." She took the wine and turned.

Hagney's eyes met his and the message was clear. *Wow.*

Indeed. "Business," he mouthed. Then turned quickly back to Megan. "I'd like you to meet my partner Royce Morgan." He led her back to a conference room where Royce stood in the corner, swaying back and forth. Grace, oblivious to the noise, was sleeping on his shoulder. He'd never seen his partner look so comfortable and confident.

"Royce, this is Megan North. She's a new client."

Royce smiled, shifted the baby slightly so that he could shake Megan's hand. "Thank you for choosing Wingman Security."

Seth wondered if she'd correct Royce, insisting that she hadn't chosen them but rather, they'd been pushed on her. But she just smiled. "You're welcome. How old is your little girl?"

"Seven months. Her name is Grace."

"She's beautiful," she said.

"Takes after her mom," he said. "Who is traveling on business, so Grace and I are plotting big things that could involve banana pudding."

"However is she sleeping through this?" she asked, taking a sip of wine.

"I have no idea. It's crazy, really. At two in the morning, a dog barking three blocks away can awaken her."

"I'll bet you always get to the crib first," Seth said.

"Maybe," Royce acknowledged, not at all embarrassed that Grace had him tied around her little finger.

Seth saw Trey and Kellie across the room and waved

them over. "And you met Trey earlier and, of course, you know Kellie."

Kellie and Megan hugged. "So good to see you again," Megan said. "Congratulations," she added, smiling at Kellie.

Kellie smiled back. "It's good to be out. We spent the day babyproofing our house."

Seth rolled his eyes. "I can just imagine the ingenious tips this guy had up his sleeve."

Kellie, who looked like a million bucks at seven months pregnant with twins, winked at Megan. "Trey has a bit of MacGyver in him but it's served me well in the past, so I'm not complaining. I'm on my way to find Abigail in the lobby."

"Go," Seth said. He motioned to Megan. "Come on. We'll find Rico. He's the fourth partner." He led her to yet another conference room and got the man's attention. "Megan North, this is Rico Metez and his soon-to-be wedded wife, Laura Collins, who is incredibly nice and defies all those wives' tales about redheads and their tempers."

"Good of you to come tonight," Rico said.

"Nice of you to extend the invite," Megan said.

"Rico was just telling me about your assignment, Seth," Laura said, her green eyes bright. "I'm a little jealous," she added, turning to Megan. "Your boutiques sound very exciting."

"I understand you've got some excitement of your own in the near future," Megan said.

Laura smiled. "We're grateful that Seth will be back in time for the wedding. Awkward when one of the best men is absent."

"Wouldn't miss it for the world," Seth said. "You two planning to honeymoon in Colorado at the cabin?"

"Of course," Laura said. "Hannah is coming along but

Jennie and Paddie, friends of Rico's since he was a child," she added for Megan's benefit, "have offered to keep her for a few days to give us some adult time."

"Good plan," he said. "We'll catch you later."

He led Megan down the hallway and used his key to open his now-dark office. He turned on a lamp and soft light filled the room. He left the door partially open. "I need just a minute away from the noise," he said. "And I wanted to make sure we got our schedules coordinated for tomorrow before the night gets too late."

"I'm still getting used to the idea that I need to coordinate with you," she said. "I hope you don't think I'm rude but I'm really not confident that security is necessary."

"That's the funny thing about security. You really don't want an event to occur just so that you can prove you're getting your money's worth."

"I suppose not," she said. "I'm curious as to what kind of threat you might be anticipating."

"I'll be ready for anything."

"That sounds rather..."

"Confident," he supplied.

"I was thinking smug."

He couldn't help it—he laughed.

"I'm planning on leaving late afternoon. A rental car is getting dropped off at the boutique for me," she said.

"A rental? How did you get here from Carmel?"

"Abigail drove her car. But she's staying on in Vegas for the next two weeks. Thus, the rental."

"Can you give me the contact number? I'm going to want to be added as a driver."

"*I'm* driving. So that won't be necessary."

He'd hit a hot button. It was rather fun to rattle her cage. Her perfect chin got a little sharper and her nose went into the air ever so slightly.

"It only makes sense that both of us be able to drive. I mapped out the best routes today between the various cities."

"I've already done that."

"Okay. Then you know that there are many days that we'll have a couple hundred miles to cover. It's a lot of driving for one person."

"I'm driving," she repeated.

He let out a loud sigh.

"Oh, fine." She opened her purse, pulled out her phone and scanned through her contacts. Then turned slightly to lean over his desk to write the number down on a notepad, giving him a truly excellent look at her backside.

Yep. Perfect, coming and going.

Chapter 3

When she finished writing down the information, she turned, but not before her eye caught the photo on the credenza behind Seth's desk. Him, younger and in a flight suit, standing next to a plane. Her throat felt suddenly tight. "I didn't realize you were a pilot," she said.

"Air force for eight years. That's where I met Royce, Trey and Rico. Flew an F-16."

"They're all pilots, too." She felt suddenly sick.

"Nope. Royce worked security, Trey was a plane mechanic and Rico was tactical communications."

"Do you fly still?"

"Is the pope Catholic?"

Probably because she showed no reaction, he added, "Yes. I have a Beechcraft Bonanza housed at the North Vegas airport."

"I'm not terribly familiar with airplanes. Is that a nice one?"

He smiled. "Nice enough that I'll need to keep working for a while in order to pay for it. But on a nice day, cruising along at 175 knots, I can barely remember that."

"Right." They needed to talk about something else.

"You know, I never wanted to be a pilot," he said.

Okay. That didn't make sense. "I'm not sure I understand."

"My dad was an air force pilot. Killed when I was two."

That sucked the oxygen out of her lungs. "In combat?"

He shook his head. "Training exercise. That doesn't make it any easier."

"Of course it doesn't," she said quickly, irritated that he'd think she thought that. She would be the last person to ever think that. But that was none of his business, either. "I'm sorry for your loss."

He nodded but said nothing, as if he might be waiting for her to say something else. But really, she knew that words meant little, gave little respite. It dawned on her that he might already know about her parents—after all, his partner Trey had undoubtedly heard the story from Kellie.

But she didn't talk about it.

Ever.

"Listen, I'm not sure how this…um…security assignment works," she said. "What you will be doing, I mean."

"What I won't do is try to stand out in any way. The best security is one that is there but not too obvious."

"Well, if fitting in is your goal, you probably need to know that there is one black-tie event."

"Really." He paused. "I was hoping I could pack my tux."

She knew sarcasm when she heard it. But the idea of him in a tux was a nice one. Sometime this afternoon, he'd changed out of his wrinkled shirt and pants into nicely pressed gray silk trousers and a blue-and-gray button-down long-sleeved shirt. He looked really good.

"We…uh…should probably rejoin the party," she said.

He immediately pushed the door wide open. "Of course."

People were filling plates from the lavish buffet that had been set up in one corner of the lobby. They sat with Abigail at one of the high-topped tables. The food was delicious, and then it was present time for Kellie and Trey and for Laura and Rico. Both Seth's bears and the scotch seemed to be big hits.

It was really fun. Certainly not how she'd intended to spend the night in a city where she knew no one. But once people had settled in for an after-dinner drink, she stood up. "It's getting late," she said to her sister. "I'll share a cab with you."

"No need," Abigail said. "Evan is flying in tonight and he's going to pick me up on his way from the airport. I just got a text from him. He should be here in ten minutes or so. We can drop you off."

"Your new husband, who has not seen you for six whole days, is not going to want his sister-in-law around. Even for ten minutes. I'll take a cab."

"I'll go with her," Seth said, looking at Abigail. He turned to Megan. "I'm your security."

She shook her head. "Store and event security. And that starts tomorrow."

He shrugged. "Details," he said, dismissing her objection. "At Wingman Security, we aim to under-promise and over-deliver."

"Let him," Abigail said. "Please."

"Fine," she said. It wasn't that big of a deal. The ride would be shorter than the argument they might have about it.

"We can go down to the lobby together," Abigail said. She grabbed Megan's hand. "Let's go say goodbye to Kellie."

Once they had done that and were back at the elevators, she saw that Seth had put on a sports coat. He'd also retrieved her umbrella and he passed it to her before pressing the elevator button. There were several others leaving at the same time, which prevented conversation in the elevator. Once they were in the downstairs lobby, it was just minutes before a car pulled up outside and her brother-in-law got out. Abigail saw him and exited the building so fast that Evan didn't even make it to the front door.

She watched as they kissed like the pair of newlyweds that they were. Her new brother-in-law was handsome, educated and rich. And definitely not good enough for Abigail. But who would be? "They almost didn't get married," she said.

"Sounds like a good story," Seth said.

"They'd been dating for almost a year when Abigail unexpectedly got pregnant. He immediately wanted to get married but she told him no four times. I honestly thought he'd give up asking."

"She didn't want to get married."

"She didn't want to be an obligation." Said she'd had enough of that in her lifetime. Megan didn't tell Seth that last part. It would lead to all kinds of questions that she really didn't want to answer. "But he finally convinced her that it was love, not obligation, that had him all but begging in the streets."

"And you like him?" Seth asked.

"I do. And I'm pretty sure that he thinks that she's the moon and stars all rolled into one. And I think he'll be a good dad."

"That's important," he said simply. He opened the door and flagged down a cab.

The vehicle traffic was even heavier than it had been earlier and the cab inched along at times. Definitely a city that came alive late in the evening. And there were lots of people not in cars. The crosswalks were filled with pedestrians. They waited long minutes even when they had the right of way to turn. "Where do all these people come from?" she said.

"Everywhere. The appeal of Vegas is far-reaching."

"Are you a gambler?"

"Hard to live here and not try your luck once in a while. My mother lives in town and she likes slot machines, so we go sometimes. But most of the time, I prefer to bet on things where the odds are better."

"Did your mother ever remarry after your father died?"

He shook his head. "No. I wish she would have," he said. "She *should* have."

Like Mrs. McGarry, his mom had been left to carry on alone. Would either one of her parents have wanted that?

"So, have you always lived in Carmel?"

She was grateful for the change in subject. "All my life," she said. The cab slowed to pull in to the circular drive of the opulent Periwinkle hotel. It was jammed with cars.

She looked behind them. There was a break in the traffic. "This is fine," she said to the driver. She opened her purse to pay but Seth beat her to it, handing the man cash. When he opened the door, she slid across the seat of the cab. Her purse strap slipped off her silk dress and the small bag fell to the ground. She bent at the same time he did to pick it up.

Just as bullets tore into the roof of the cab, ripping the metal.

"Stay down!" he yelled. He put one hand on her head to reinforce his words and the other around her to move her out of the street. The cab took off, door still open.

Fifteen big steps had them inside the circular drive, behind a half wall. Arriving guests had abandoned their luggage and flocked inside. Hotel valet staff were crouched down, scanning the street.

"Are you okay?" he demanded, checking her. She was pale but there was no blood. She had not been hit.

"Were they shooting at us?" she asked.

It sure as hell had felt like it. "I don't know," he said. "Who have you pissed off, Megan?"

Her head jerked up. "No one," she said.

"I was kidding." Sort of. Random shootings occurred. But not that often in the high-rent district that the Periwinkle occupied. It was bad for tourism. He heard the sounds of approaching police. Response time would be fast here.

"What's the name of the competitor that you bested?" He'd thought he was going to have plenty of time to get into this but gunshots had a way of expediting conversations.

"J.T. Daly's. But they're a big operation. I really don't think that they would be all that upset about not getting our four stores. And I certainly don't want to publicly malign them without proof."

He understood that she was warning him to be careful with any unfounded accusations he might make. "I won't skewer them but I think it's worth a mention to the police."

Once the police arrived, both he and Megan gave a statement. He was pretty sure the shots had come from behind them, to their left, and gave that information to the cops. "I think you'll be able to get a slug out of the cab's roof," he added. That made the cops happy. In a succinct manner, Seth also explained about J.T. Daly's and how the retailer might have a bone to pick with Megan. The cops made no comments but dutifully took notes.

The process seemed to take forever. Hotel management

hovered nearby and when the police were done with them, the night manager apologized profusely and offered to send food or alcohol to Megan's room. She declined both.

He thought a double on the rocks would be nice. He generally had real steady nerves—most pilots did. But the vision of what those bullets might have done to her skull wasn't a good one.

"Thanks for getting me out of the street," she said. "I'm not great in those situations—I tend to freeze. And that might not have been good."

"You did fine," he said. She had. She'd stayed low, moved quickly and thus far, hadn't cried.

"I'm hoping that's the most excitement we have for the next twelve days," she said. They were at the bank of elevators. She extended her hand. "Good night."

He ignored her head. "If it's all the same to you, I'd like to make sure that you get to your room safely."

"I'm sure I'll be fine," she said.

He pressed the up button. When the door opened, he motioned her in and then quickly followed. She pressed the seven.

When they got to 710, she waved her card in front of the electronic reader and it immediately clicked. He held up a finger. "Let me go first," he whispered.

Before leaving the party, while Megan and Abigail had been saying their goodbyes, he'd stepped into his office and gotten his gun. He wore it in his shoulder holster, carefully hidden by the sport coat that he'd put on.

Now he pulled it, ignoring the gasp behind him. He swung in through the door, grateful that she'd left a light on. It took him just seconds to ensure that the main room, bathroom and closet were clear.

"You had that gun the whole time," she said after he'd motioned her in.

"Yes." And his first instinct had been to pull it earlier but he had known that it was much more important to get her to safety. "I didn't show it earlier because I wasn't confident in the ensuing chaos that somebody wouldn't take me for a bad guy and decide to shoot me in the back."

"Do you always have a gun?" She sounded shocked.

"I provide security services. I have a permit to carry it and I know how to use it. And while Las Vegas is as safe as any other city, I usually don't go out at night unless I'm armed."

"I guess that's good. I mean, that you have a gun."

He studied her. "You have no idea why anybody might be shooting at you?"

She shook her head.

His gut told him that she was lying. And his gut was rarely wrong.

"What are your plans in the morning?" he asked.

"Why?"

"Just trying to figure out if you're planning on leaving the hotel. I'd prefer it if you didn't."

"I'm afraid that's not possible," she said. "I have commitments at the boutique."

It wasn't much but evidently all he was going to get. He shouldn't be surprised. Earlier tonight, she'd also not been very forthcoming about her parents dying in a plane crash. He'd given her the perfect segue when he'd talked about his own father's premature death in a plane accident. But she'd said nothing.

He was usually good at reading people but she was better than most at hiding her emotions. Her pretty face gave him no hint of what she might be thinking.

"I guess that's good night then," he said.

"Yes," she said, "I'll see you tomorrow."

"Lock the door behind me," he said. With any other

business associate, he would have extended his hand. But he kept it to himself. He'd felt her silky smooth skin when he'd wrapped an arm around her and shepherded her behind the hotel's half wall.

Another feel and he might not want to let go.

Megan flipped the bolt lock and barely made it to the couch before her legs gave out. She'd been shot at. With real bullets.

It was so unbelievable that she felt as if she must be having a dream. A nightmare.

If Seth hadn't been there, she had no idea what might have happened. But he'd responded like a machine, not pausing, just acting. And when he'd started asking questions, she'd desperately wanted to tell him the truth. Even at the risk of seeing disbelief in his eyes.

Seth had asked her who might be shooting at her. She'd given him nothing. It wasn't an outright lie. She really had no idea. But given the other things that had happened over the last several months, she could not ignore the possibility that the attack had not been random.

The idea that somebody had followed her to Vegas, had traveled hundreds of miles, was so objectionable that it made her skin crawl. It made her think that the person had to be very determined.

But that in itself made no sense. She didn't have any enemies. She lived a peaceful, quiet life. Who could be that angry with her?

It gave her a headache. And tomorrow they would begin reopening the four stores that had been closed for months. She couldn't afford being tired or off her game.

She was going to have to move on. Not forget it and certainly not ignore any other odd circumstances or take unnecessary chances with her safety, but for now, she was going to have to set it aside.

She undressed for bed and pulled on a nightgown. She slipped between the cool sheets and decided that she would think of something else.

Seth Pike.

Handsome. Fast thinking. Quick acting.

She hoped he didn't make a big deal about driving. He'd been insistent about getting his name registered with the rental car company. But she did not intend to hand over the wheel.

Bad things happened when you gave control to others. Her parents had made that mistake. Did it make it better or worse that it had been to someone they trusted? To someone *she* trusted? Loved?

She closed her eyes.

It had been a beautiful clear day. Everybody had said so.

And every day, she comforted herself with the image that her parents' last hours had been full of sunshine and beauty. And she tried never to think how horrific the final moments might have been. How worried they would have been about her and Abigail.

They'd have had no way of knowing what the future held for their daughters. She liked to think that they'd have been happy with her decisions. Even proud now.

She'd done everything within her power not to let them down. She wasn't stopping now. She started making her mental list of all the things she needed to do the next day. Felt a measure of peace. Work had always been her salvation. And Abigail her joy. It was a life that most would be very content with.

And she was. She certainly didn't need Seth Pike messing that up.

Six hours later, Megan woke up when her alarm went off at five. She stretched and glanced out the window. It was not yet light out. Still, she forced herself to swing her legs over the side. She ran most mornings, tried to get in at least five miles. She had a treadmill at home and while she was on the road, she intended to make good use out of the hotel fitness equipment.

She brushed her teeth, washed her face and put on her workout clothes. Then she pulled her long hair back into a low ponytail. Once she'd tied her shoes, she made sure she had her hotel key card in her shirt pocket and then flipped the bolt lock.

She opened the door, turned and almost fell over Seth Pike. She let out a little squeal. He was sitting on the floor, his back up against the wall on the same side as her door. He opened his eyes and turned his head, as if he was scanning the hallway.

"Keep it down," he said. "It's pretty early yet."

"What are you doing here?" she hissed.

He shrugged and stood up. "Morning," he said. He ran his eyes from her head to her toes. "So you're the type that gets up and heads to the gym."

It wasn't a character flaw. "I run."

"I see," he said, not sounding thrilled. "Let's go."

"I wasn't anticipating company at the gym."

He nodded and ran a hand over his head. "Yeah, but I got a streak going here and I don't want to break it."

His clothes were again wrinkled, like they'd been after the rain. With his innocent act, he reminded her of a mischievous little boy.

Except she wasn't fool enough to fall for it. She'd seen him in action last night, immediately after the shooting and then again when he'd very competently inspected her hotel room, looking quite at ease with a deadly looking gun in his hand.

"You're not exactly dressed for the gym."

"Maybe I'll just watch this morning."

He was not going to watch her run. Just the idea made her warm.

He fell into step next to her. But then stopped suddenly. He was staring at her shoulder. At the lovely green and purple. "What the hell is that?" he asked, his voice deep.

"It's a bruise," she said. She hadn't expected company, hadn't thought to keep it covered. Yesterday, when they'd first met, her scarf had been strategically arranged to cover her upper arm. Last night, her dress had sleeves that had done the trick.

"I know that," he said. "But how did you get it? Not from last night," he said. "It's not a fresh one."

"No. Two weeks ago, I rolled my car and hit my shoulder pretty hard."

"Tell me you went to a doctor," he said.

"Of course." She'd been taken by ambulance. "It wasn't broken, just badly bruised. It's getting better every day."

"Right," he said, starting to walk again. "How did the accident happen?"

"Another car blew a stop sign," she said. "Hit the passenger side. My car was totaled."

"Any serious injuries?"

"No. Thankfully. And the other driver got the ticket. Look, if you're coming to the gym with me," she said, wanting to make sure he understood, "you have to do something. Keep yourself busy."

"Don't worry about me," he said.

She was starting to think that Seth might be something to worry about. It had been a long time since she'd dreamed about a man. But she certainly wasn't going to tell him that. "Fine," she said, starting to walk fast.

He kept up with her no problem. "How did you sleep?" he asked.

"Fine," she said.

"That's two fines. I think this is going really well."

"I don't think so," she said. She stabbed the elevator button. The gym was on the top floor. Once they were inside the space, she took two deep breaths, then turned to him. "I'm sorry," she said. "I don't normally wake up bitchy. But you surprised me."

He shrugged, not looking concerned. "Well, then we're even. You surprised me, too. Wasn't expecting the door to open at five o'clock."

"You were in the hallway all night?" she asked.

"Yes," he said.

As if that were perfectly reasonable. "Because you were worried that somebody was going to try to get in or that I was going to try to get out?"

"Maybe a little of both," he said.

"We have no idea if somebody was actually shooting at me. Maybe they were aiming at you."

"No way. Everybody loves me," he said.

"Then it was probably just random."

"Very possible. I'll follow up with the Vegas police this morning to see if they know any more."

She'd been planning to do that. But it wouldn't make sense for both of them to call. "You have to be exhausted. You couldn't have gotten much sleep sitting up in the hallway."

"I got enough," he said. "Had a nice conversation with the night manager around three when he tried to remove me. Evidently, they picked me up on camera. It's not comforting that it took them that long."

The elevator doors opened and she stepped out. "What did you tell them?"

He didn't answer right away. He was looking around, to the left, to the right. There was only one other guest using a treadmill. Finally, he turned to her. "That you'd dumped me and if I couldn't change your mind in the morning, I was going to throw myself over the Hoover Dam."

"You didn't," she said.

"Maybe," he said. He walked over to a rowing machine that faced the elevators. "I'll give this a go."

She told herself not to watch him, to just run her miles and forget him. But that was hard to do. Even in his dress shirt, she could see his muscles flex as he pulled on the rope. She was getting all hot and sweaty and it had nothing to do with her pace.

She ran for forty minutes before slowing the machine down to a walk. After another minute, she stopped it and grabbed a towel from a nearby shelf. She wiped her face, then draped it around her neck. He was already off the rowing machine.

He was watching the man who'd been on the other treadmill approach them. When the elevator door opened, she stepped in. Then felt a hand on her hip. She almost let out a yelp but realized in time that it was Seth, simply edging her in the direction of the corner. Then he placed himself in front of her, between her and the man.

By the time they got off on their floor, leaving the poor man by himself, she was strangely irritated. "Don't you think you're carrying this a bit too far? The man was just jogging. Not a threat to me."

"Can't be too careful," he said. They were at her door. "In that spirit, give me your room card. I'll open your door."

She decided it wasn't worth arguing over. It wasn't going to take him long. It was just a bed and a small bath.

He handed her back her key when he was finished. "I need to go home and get showered and changed."

"That's fine. We're not leaving here until four." That had been clearly stated on the contract. "You have the whole day."

He continued to stand there. "What time are you headed over to the boutique?" he asked.

It was none of his business. But she didn't say that. The man had slept in the hall. Not her fault, but still. "At eleven. I've got back-to-back meetings with our general contractor and our architects."

"You have our office number?" he asked.

"I do."

"And my cell?"

"Already in my phone."

"And you would call if you needed something?"

"I'm not going to need anything," she said. "But yes, I would," she added, because she had the feeling that he was seconds away from insisting that he spend the day with her. She needed some space. Some time to get her head together. She couldn't start a big road trip with somebody who had her off her stride. "I'll meet you in front of the boutique at 4:00 p.m."

"I could swing by and give you a ride later this morning."

"Evan and Abigail are picking me up," she said.

"Oh, okay."

He didn't sound convinced but she wasn't giving in. She couldn't be concerned that he wasn't completely satisfied with the plan. Probably he wouldn't be satisfied with anything that wasn't his plan. He might be providing security but he wasn't calling the shots. "Is there anything else?" she asked, her voice deliberately curt.

He shook his head. "Naw. I should probably get going.

I can tell you're busy," he added, letting her know that he knew he was getting the brush-off.

She refused to feel bad about that.

Chapter 4

He waited until he heard the bolt lock turn and then he left. Not 100 percent happy to do so, but knew that he'd pushed her about as far as he could. Contrary to what his partners might believe, he did have a restraint gene.

Now his best bet was to get coffee and a shower, in that order. As he walked to the elevator, he checked his cell phone, making sure he hadn't missed a call when he'd been in the hotel gym. Late last night, once he'd made the decision to spend the night outside Megan's room, he'd called his good friend Bobby Bayleaf. With more than twenty years as a Vegas cop, the man would have access to the information that Seth wanted.

But there was nothing on his phone yet. No surprise there. It wasn't even six o'clock. He took the elevator to the third-floor lobby and then the escalator down to the ground floor. Walked to the coffee shop that was four doors away. He got a large coffee and an egg, cheese and bacon sandwich on a muffin. His car was still back at the

Wingman Security offices and he started walking, eating his sandwich on the way. By the time he reached the parking lot, he'd finished both the coffee and the food. Felt a little more human.

Knew that he likely looked rough after his night in the hallway. On the other hand, Megan had looked like a million bucks when she'd practically bounced out of her hotel room. Hair in a cute little ponytail, nicely coordinated workout outfit, new-looking shoes. He'd been impressed.

And then he'd seen the bruise. And having had his share of bruises in his youth from his many fistfights, he'd immediately assumed that she'd been hit. And the idea of that, of her being physically attacked, had made his empty stomach roll.

He'd felt a little better once she'd explained that it had come from a car accident but he'd still felt bad that she'd been hurt.

He opened the door of his old Jeep and drove the twenty minutes to the house where his mother had lived for the last thirty years before she'd moved in to the assisted living center a few years earlier. She'd been reluctant to totally leave the house. He'd been more reluctant to let her stay, a mile from the nearest neighbor, after she'd fallen and broken her leg and lain in the yard for four hours before help had happened by. In an effort to compromise, he offered to leave his city apartment and move in to the house if she'd agree to move in to Everpark. That way, they still both had their independence but the house would be there for her if she ever wanted to come back.

Now she came for Sunday dinners that they cooked together and seemed okay with that arrangement.

Once at the house, he started more coffee and stepped into the really hot shower. Ten minutes later, he was finished and pulling on clothes. Then he pulled a suitcase off the top shelf of his closet. Started packing. Mostly dress shirts and dress pants. Things that he could wear a sport coat with so his gun would be hidden.

He grabbed some other essentials, remembering at the last minute to add some workout clothes. *You're not exactly dressed for the gym.* If Megan thought that was going to stop him, she had a few things to learn. Seth had in the past, and likely would in the future, looked like an idiot. He never cared.

But nor did he want to stand out unnecessarily, especially when he was working a job. Which was why the last thing he packed in his bag was his tux for Rico's wedding. He folded the plastic suit bag it was hanging inside, hanger and all, hoping that it wouldn't wrinkle too badly. He glanced at his watch. It was fifteen minutes before seven. He dialed his friend. "Morning, sunshine," he said.

Bobby Bayleaf, who was big, black and had played tackle in college, offered up a string of profanity that ended with Seth sticking the sun where it wouldn't shine.

"Now, now," Seth said. "Isn't your department working on better relationships with its citizenry?"

"You're not citizenry. You're the guy on the bus who used to pick fights with me, even when I got big enough to pound on you."

For a long while, he'd solved a number of problems with his fists. But then he'd started to fly and everything had changed. "I was just preparing you for your future," Seth said. "Listen, do you have anything on the shooting last night?"

"Nope. I talked to the detective who snagged the case. Officers canvassed the area where the shots were thought to come from but nobody saw nothing. And there weren't any other shootings in that area. They're writing it off as an isolated incident."

Was that what it was? Hard to know. "And what about Megan North?"

"Found her in Carmel, California, just like you said I would. No police record with the exception that her name came up in connection with a traffic accident that occurred recently where the other driver got a ticket for blowing a stop sign."

"Okay. That's it?"

"There was just one other thing. I was able to find a report where she'd made a 911 call, indicating that there were intruders in her apartment complex."

"In her apartment?" Seth clarified.

"No. In the complex. She lives on the second floor and she said that there were people having a threatening conversation under her window."

"A threatening conversation? Two people threatening each other?"

"I don't think so but there's not a lot of detail. The cops responded to the 911 call, evidently had a conversation with Megan but didn't see anybody. I think you're going to have to ask her if you want more information."

That would go well. She'd want to know what the hell he was doing looking into her background. "Okay. I'll do that."

"I'll be in touch if I hear anything else about the shooting," Bobby said. "Other than that, I guess I'll see you when you get back from your shopping trip."

That's what Bobby had called it when Seth explained the assignment the night before. The idea that anything he was doing being in the same sentence as *boutique* had seemed to tickle Bobby.

"When I get back, I'm going to take some money off your hands in cards," Seth said, ending the conversation.

He put his luggage into his vehicle and drove back to

the office. He had work to do before leaving town. When he got there, he studied his desk. Then the two tall windows behind his desk.

He liked those windows. They had a western exposure that offered spectacular views of sunsets. But there was something wrong with them this morning.

They didn't face Megan's boutique.

He started gathering things up, taking them to the small conference room. It was all cleaned up; no one would ever guess that there'd been a party there the night before. He spread everything out on the table. He'd been there about an hour when Trey walked past his door. "Morning," Trey said. "What are you doing in here?"

"Clearing off my desk," he said.

"How much did you have to drink last night? Because that's not your desk."

"Funny guy," Seth said. He had his chair at just the right angle that he could see the front door of Megan's building. He was confident that Megan had not yet arrived.

Trey walked over to the windows. He sipped the coffee that he carried. "I'm glad we were able to help Abigail and Megan. That means a lot to Kellie. They both seem very nice." He turned to look at Seth. "And Megan is really gorgeous."

"I guess," Seth said. "But she may get me killed."

The amused look left Trey's face. "What?"

"Last night when I took her back to her hotel, shots were fired in our direction as we exited the cab."

"Holy hell. Did they get the shooter?"

Seth shook his head. "Nope. And Megan said there was absolutely no reason that anybody would be shooting at her."

"You didn't believe her?"

He'd wrestled with that question during the night. "I don't know. For one thing, the reason I was hired was because of concern about a competitor—J.T. Daly's—wanting some revenge for North and More Designs besting them. But it doesn't feel right. I did some research on them. By and large, they are a reputable company. There was a suspicion that they might have been involved in a questionable fire of another competitor but it wasn't proven. And even if it's true, burning down an empty warehouse is different than taking potshots at the executive team."

"So if not them, then who?" Trey asked.

"I don't know. And Megan claims not to, as well. But she said a few things that were kind of odd and it makes me think that there's a story there."

"You going to initiate a background check on her?"

They did that sometimes with new clients. A clause in their standard contract gave them that right. Bobby had done the quick check on her recent criminal history but Wingman Security had contacts who could dig deep. With a few clicks of his computer, he could initiate a background investigation that would tell him everything from her grammar school teachers to her shoe size.

He'd know everything there was to know about Megan North. "I'll think about it," he said. "She has meetings today at the boutique. Made it clear that my services were not needed until we leave town late this afternoon."

"Yet you're going to sit here all day and watch the street."

Seth shrugged. "I'm going to sit here until about two and then I'm going to go see my mom. And then swing back about four to get Megan."

"I'm going to be here all day," Trey said. "Kellie has

a girls-only baby shower. Come get me when you leave and I'll work out of this space."

"I appreciate that," Seth said.

"Here's what you'll appreciate even more. I'm calling in a pizza order at noon." Trey turned to walk out the room.

"I would marry you if Kellie hadn't beaten me to it," Seth said, calling after him.

Trey's pithy response echoed back into the quiet conference room, making Seth smile. He really had the best partners in the whole world.

A half hour later, Seth saw a car pull up and park in the no-parking zone in front of the boutique. He recognized it as the same one that Evan Chevalier had been driving the night before. He got up to get a better look but stayed back from view. Megan got out of the back seat. Her dress was a pale-yellow-and-white print that reminded him of his favorite lemon dessert. Her hair, which she'd worn long yesterday, was pulled up and in some kind of fancy bun on the top of her head.

Evan Chevalier got out of the car, walked around the front, and opened the front passenger-side door. He helped his wife out. Then Abigail and Megan waited while Evan opened the trunk. The first bag he pulled out was a big suitcase that would never have fit into an overhead compartment. It was a rich-looking buttercream. The second was a matching garment bag that zipped up the front and had a wide leather strap. Classy. It was going to make his black same-as-everybody-else's look almost shabby.

Seth smiled when he saw the last thing that Evan removed from the trunk. Megan's umbrella. She *had* said that she was going nowhere without it. Now she reached for it and tucked it under an arm. They were expecting rain today but it likely wouldn't start until the afternoon.

She reached for her other bags but Evan waved her away and grabbed for both.

He watched as Megan unlocked the door and held it for her sister and brother-in-law. Then disappeared.

Seth waited. Shallow breaths. Knowing that he was crazy but really unable to stop himself. He did not believe those gunshots last night were random. Regardless of the story that Megan was spinning.

He didn't breathe easy again until Evan came back outside five minutes later, got into his car and drove away. He sat back down to work. Twenty minutes later, a cab pulled up. Out got two men, both with gray hair. One was carrying a cardboard tube, like what an architect might use to carry around rolled blueprints. The other carried a laptop computer.

Old school, new school.

Old school knocked on the glass door. Megan opened it and shook both men's hands. She was smiling. Then they were all inside.

She was safe. She knew these people. He sat back down. Tried to work. Fifteen minutes later, he dialed her number.

"Hello," she said.

"Hey, how's it going?"

"Fine."

"Yeah, uh, I was just checking on the time that I should pick you up? Was it four?"

"Yes. At the boutique," she said.

She sounded fine. Certainly not under duress. Maybe a little puzzled that he'd forgotten.

"Great. I'll be there." He hung up.

He got busy. He had a lot to do. When Trey came in with pizza later, he pushed the paperwork aside. After his first piece, he sighed. "This is great. Thank you."

"All's well across the street?" Trey asked.

"Yeah. Megan and Abigail are inside meeting with two men. Architect. General contractor. Something like that."

"You want me to make up some excuse and go knock on the door, just to make sure everything is okay?" Trey asked.

"I already called her."

"I knew it," Trey said. "You can be such a mother hen."

Seth accepted the criticism. He didn't care about things or that many people. But those he did care about, he protected fiercely.

Megan, by virtue of signing that contract, fell into that category. That's all this was.

By two, his desk was clean. He left an out-of-office message on his desk number and also on his business email. Told Trey he was leaving and waited until his partner was settled in the conference room. Then he got in his Jeep and drove to Everpark to see his mom.

When he arrived, she was sitting on her porch. Everpark was massive and provided all levels of care. His mom, at almost seventy, required no nursing care and maintained her own small stand-alone condo. But there were neighbors close by who kept an eye on one another. They also played cards frequently, and on nice days could be found on the Everpark golf course. She had access to a dining room, where she could have a meal once in a while when she wanted company.

It gave Seth peace of mind. "Hi, there," he said. "It's pretty hot to be out here."

"Yesterday's rain cooled it off a bit, I think," she said. "I wasn't expecting you. I just had lunch."

"No worries. Trey and I had pizza at the office. Hey, I got an assignment yesterday that's going to take me out of town for a while so I wanted to see you before I left."

"Is it taking you somewhere fun?"

"Sedona, Arizona, and Albuquerque, New Mexico. Also Colorado Springs. I'm providing security services for an executive who is opening a line of women's boutiques."

"Are you looking forward to it?"

Oddly enough, he was. Megan was sort of fun to spar with. Of course, he didn't want to get shot at again. But now he'd be more vigilant. He wouldn't be caught off guard again. "It will be fine. But you know you can always call me if you need anything."

"You. Any of your partners. I've got the whole list. But I'll be fine."

She likely would be. After her fall, she'd remained fiercely independent. But she was alone. "You need anything done around here before I go?" he asked.

She shook her head. "I also know how to call maintenance," she said gently.

"Well, you let me know if they don't respond and I'll break some arms for you."

She kissed his cheek. "I can always count on that."

He stayed another hour, had some tea and some really great chocolate chip cookies, and finally, stood to go. "I'll call you," he said. "I'll be on the road for about ten days and then back in Vegas for a couple to finish up the assignment."

"Don't worry about me. Go. Be safe. I'll be anxious to hear about your trip when you get back."

"I love you," he said.

"I love you, too."

He drove back to Wingman Security and parked his Jeep. Before he got out, he called Trey. "I'm back," he said.

"Okay. The two guys left about a half hour ago. Then

Abigail's husband came and picked her up. No sign of Megan."

"Okay. I'm on my way." He hung up, made sure his vehicle was locked and walked across the street. He tried the door of the building. It was locked. Good girl.

He knocked and cupped his hands around his eyes so that he could see inside. A wide corridor ran down the middle of the building. The boutique was off to the left and there was a furniture…no, that wasn't right…an antiques store to the right. It looked like there might be other storefronts toward the back but the corridor was too dark to see much.

He pounded on the door. Hard.

And within seconds, Megan exited from the boutique. Looking…gorgeous. When she opened the door, he stepped in. "Thanks," he said.

"No problem."

He walked in a few steps and looked inside the open door of the boutique. "Wow." Walls had been torn down to the studs and the old tile floor was half ripped up. A stack of hardwood flooring sat in the corner.

She laughed. "I know. It doesn't look like much now but we made a lot of progress today. It will be ready by the time we get back to do the opening here. I'm confident. The same team has been working on our other three stores and I saw pictures today that were awesome. Can't wait to see these places in person."

She looked excited and happy. And now that he was close, he could see the multiple necklaces around her neck and her gold earrings that dangled down, almost reaching her shoulders.

His fingers itched to reach out, to touch. Give them a little jingle-jangle. But he resisted. He caught a whiff of her perfume and breathed deep. He'd expected something light and floral, but it had a sharper edge and he liked it.

"So your day went well?" he asked.

"Of course," she said, as if she couldn't imagine anything else. As if bullets hadn't been flying the night before.

"So that means no one has shot at you today," he said. "Yet," he added, deliberately goading. He wanted her sharp, aware.

"That's right." Her voice remained pleasant but there was a flash in her deep blue eyes that she wasn't quite so successful in hiding.

"These your bags?" he asked.

"Yes." She walked over and grabbed the handle of the large rolling bag.

He'd used restraint before but now, he just had to say it. "It's kind of weird, you know. That we met under the awning of the pizza place."

"What do you mean, kind of weird?"

She knew exactly what he meant. "Weird in that you were already headed for my office later that afternoon."

"Yes. I suppose it was," she said.

No supposing about it. But he didn't press her on it.

"Let me get that," he said. He grabbed her bag in one hand and his suitcase in the other. She carried her garment bag, her umbrella, and a purse that was on one shoulder and crossed over her body to rest on her hip. It was yellow like her dress with a big white daisy for the clasp. Her shoes were white sandals with a high heel that did very nice things for her calves. And, of course, he was pretty impressed by her pink painted toenails that were clearly visible.

She was perfect in a cotton-candy kind of way. Except

he didn't think she was fluff. And that made her such a fascinating contradiction.

She had one weakness, for sure. Her love of her sister. Hard to hold that against a person.

She opened the door and they were on the sidewalk. She locked it behind them. "We've got a big drive ahead of us to Sedona." She pulled out her cell phone. "Looks as if I missed a call. I had my phone on vibrate. But they left a message. It's probably the car rental company. I thought they'd be here by now."

She put the phone up to her ear to listen to her message. But almost immediately, he sensed a change, knew that something was wrong. Her shoulders tensed, her jaw became rigid. Her eyes… Was that panic? Distress?

"What?" he said, looking around. He felt open and exposed and motioned for her to get closer to the building.

She held up a hand. He could tell that she was starting the message again. And at the end, she drew in a deep breath. "Well, that wasn't the car rental company," she said finally. "At least I assume not," she added, and then laughed with what sounded like nervousness.

"Who was it?" he asked.

"I don't know," she said.

"What was it about?" He could feel his patience rapidly evaporate. He was worried about her. Her face had lost all color. "Maybe we should go back inside," he said.

"Sure." She unlocked the door. Held it so that he could pull their luggage in. Then she leaned up against a wall. She was very still. Very quiet. She was staring straight ahead.

"I'd like to help," he said. "But you're not making it easy."

She nodded, as if in a trance. "That was a message from someone claiming to have information about the plane crash that killed my parents." She looked up at him. "Yes, my parents were killed in a small plane crash. Sort of like your dad. And I probably should have said something last night when we were talking about your dad. But their crash was different. They weren't flying the plane. They were the only passengers."

He wasn't going to tell her that he'd known about their deaths. "What about the pilot?" he asked.

She shook her head. "He survived the crash."

She spoke so slowly, so distinctly, that he could almost hear a drumbeat between each word. "So he was able to tell you what happened."

"Not really."

They weren't getting anywhere quickly. "Can you tell me what you do know about the crash?"

"It was a clear day. They'd been flying in the morning and had taken a break over the lunch hour. The crash happened shortly after they took off in the afternoon. Witnesses said they were banking for a turn and suddenly the plane went nose-down. They were able to issue a Mayday call but this was a small airport, with no air traffic operators on duty. The distress call was picked up by a regional airport but by the time help could be summoned, the plane had already crashed. The NTSB found no evidence of mechanical malfunction, although—" she paused "—I'm not sure how they could have. The plane was ripped apart."

He knew what that plane had looked like. Probably had been a debris field that stretched for hundreds of feet.

"The finding was pilot error," she said.

That was generally the finding if there were no mechanical issues. "What did the pilot have to say about that?"

"Not much. He couldn't dispute the findings. He suffered a serious head injury, along with other very serious injuries, and has never been able to provide much detail."

None of what she was telling him was super surprising. Commercial aircraft almost never crashed but with smaller airplanes, those in the general aviation category, it was a different story. There were plane crashes literally every week and, unfortunately, way too many fatalities. And more times than not, the reason was pilot error. It was no different than a guy who might miscalculate how slick a wet Vegas street was and slam into the back of a line of stopped cars. Pilots, many with limited time in the air, made bad decisions, generally as a result of not being familiar with the plane, the terrain they were flying over, the weather conditions, or the airport they were landing at or taking off from.

"And now somebody is calling to tell you that there is more information. Can I hear the message?"

"I guess." She picked up the phone. Put it on speaker. Played the message.

It was a man's voice. He spoke quietly, as if there might be the potential that he'd be overheard. There was no obvious regional or ethnic accent. "Your parents were killed. It wasn't an accident. You better wake up and start smelling the roses."

"Play it again," Seth said.

She did.

"Again," he prompted, thinking he might have picked up a little background noise the second time.

"No," she said. "We've heard it enough. The words aren't going to change."

He didn't want to push her. She looked very fragile. "You don't recognize the caller's voice?" he asked.

She shook her head.

"Is it possible that it's the pilot? You said he had head

injuries. Maybe he's… I don't know, maybe he's delusional."

"It's not the pilot," she said.

"How can you know that for sure?" he asked. It was the most likely person to have information about the crash. The only person who had been there.

"I would recognize his voice," she said.

"Are you sure?"

"I would think so," she said. "Given that I almost married him."

Chapter 5

Seth scratched his head. “Come again?” he said.

She sighed. She so rarely ever talked to anyone about this. “We were engaged. At the time of the accident.”

“How old were you?”

“Twenty. We’d been dating since I was seventeen.”

“But suddenly you had responsibility for Abigail.”

“She was fourteen. It was devastating for her.”

“You’d lost your parents, too. And your fiancé was flying the plane. Couldn’t have been a walk in the park for you, either.”

She said nothing.

“So what happened between you and…the guy?”

“He recovered. A couple surgeries, so much physical therapy. But he was young and healthy and he worked really, really hard.”

“Who ended the relationship?”

It was a very personal question but she wasn’t surprised. She got the feeling that Seth considered very few topics as off-limits. "I did."

"Because you couldn't forgive him?" he said.

"Sort of," she said, looking at her shoes. "Not for the crash. That was an accident. He adored my parents."

"What then?" he asked.

"I couldn't forgive him for continuing to fly planes."

Now, it seemed, Seth had nothing to say. He just stared at her.

"Seth Pike speechless," she said gently. "Why do I think that doesn't happen very often?"

He shrugged. "You gave him an ultimatum and maybe he came back with the only answer that he could have. A pilot, somebody who loves to fly, can't just give it up."

"I understand. But for me, that was the wrong answer."

"It might have been easier for him to give up a kidney. Or both kidneys. Throw in a spleen."

He didn't say it unkindly. More so just knowingly.

"We should go," she said.

"What was your fiancé's name?"

"Logan Lewis."

"And you're a hundred percent confident it's not him?"

"Yes."

"Maybe you should call him. See if he's gotten a similar message."

She had not spoken to Logan in over ten years. Once their engagement had ended, there had been the intermittent card or brief conversation for the first couple of years, as if neither one of them could completely cut the cord. But then even that had stopped. Her college roommate had married his best friend. And while Megan was still friends with Didi, and made a point to see her when she was in New York, where the woman had moved after college, by some tacit agreement they never discussed Logan.

What would he say if she called him out of the blue?

But perhaps not out of the blue? Not if he'd gotten a similar message.

But surely if there was something new, Logan would have called her. He'd been a nice guy. That was likely to still be true. While she and Didi never discussed it, she was confident that he'd moved on, probably had a wife and kids and a pretty house in the suburbs.

"I don't want to call him."

"Where does he live?"

"I have no idea."

He stared at her. "Would you know how to reach him if you wanted to?"

She nodded. "We have a mutual friend. But I'm not going down that route."

He didn't argue. Instead, he reached for her phone. "There's a number."

"I suppose that's why I didn't give it a second thought before I listened to the voice mail."

"You're sure you don't recognize the number?" he asked.

"It seems sort of careless, doesn't it?" she said, her tone thoughtful. "In this day and age when everybody has caller ID, to call from a number that displays. I'm sure there are ways to block that."

Yes. He knew a bunch of ways. And most any idiot who did some research online could figure it out, too. "Let's do a reverse lookup."

Using his own phone, he brought up the website and entered the number. It took just seconds. "Marta's Deli in Los Angeles. Does that mean anything to you?"

She shook her head. "No. I mean I've lived in California for my whole life and I've certainly been to Los Angeles a bunch of times. But I don't recall that business. Of course, I might not remember a deli. I've had a lot of turkey sandwiches in my time."

Again he used his smartphone, this time to pull up the home page for Marta's Deli. It was simple with a clean design and some nice photos of food. He clicked on the About Us tab and found a picture of Marta. "Do you know this woman?"

Again, she shook her head.

He pulled up the address. "Recognize this street?"

She shook her head. "It's a big city."

"Call the number," he said.

"What if someone else answers? I don't know who to ask for."

"Tell whoever answers that you got a message from this number but you couldn't understand it and you're trying to reach whoever left it."

"This can't be right," she said. "Why would someone from there—a place I've never been to or even heard of—call me and leave a message like that?"

He shrugged. "Call," he said. "Leave your phone on speaker so that I can hear."

It rang three times before it was answered.

"Marta's Deli. How can I help you?"

It was a woman's voice.

"Hello. My name is Megan. I'm calling because I received a message from this number but I'm having difficulty understanding it. I was wondering if you might be able to help."

"A message?" the woman said. "From me?"

"Uh, no. It was from a man. I wasn't able to catch his name."

Seth nodded at her. She was doing very well.

"I'm sorry," the woman said. "I don't think I'm going to be able to help you."

"Is there someone else who might be able to?" Megan asked. Her voice rose at the end.

"Stay calm," Seth mouthed. Always easier to get ants with sugar.

"I just...want to make every effort," Megan said. "It sounded as if it might be important."

"I'm sorry. I can't help you. I own the place and there's no men working here today. We don't let customers use our business phone. So I'm pretty sure you're mistaken. But...um...good luck." The woman hung up.

Megan looked at him.

"You did a good job," he said. "She sounded pretty legitimate. I suppose it could be some technical glitch with the phone, and an incorrect number is displaying, but that seems far-fetched. We could do some research on that."

"No. We're not doing that." She put her phone back into her purse. "I don't want to spend any more time on this. It was...a stupid message."

"Don't delete it."

"I don't see why not."

"You can't ignore this," he said. "You should probably report it to the police."

"No," she said quickly. "I'm not doing that."

"But—"

"No," she interrupted him. "In today's world, I suspect there are many, many crank phone calls or emails or text messages every day to multiple people. That's all this is. It wasn't a threat."

Maybe not an explicit one. "'You better wake up and start smelling the roses,'" he repeated. "If it's not a threat, is it a clue? A call for action?"

"I know what it is. It's somebody just trying to…" She paused. "Trying to unsettle me."

"'Unsettle,'" he repeated. It was a very odd word choice. And it reminded him of his conversation with Bobby Bayleaf. Megan had reported a threatening conversation below her apartment window. Had that *unsettled* her?

But he didn't really want to throw that in her face. Didn't want her to know that he'd been checking up on her. "Megan," he said, then stopped when two cars, the first, a new-model black sedan and the second, oh, my goodness, a spanking-new BMW B7 with metallic blue paint, pulled in to the no-parking zone. Both drivers got out and tried the door of the building. Seth motioned to Megan that he'd get it.

"Rental car delivery for Megan North," one man said.

"Great." Megan stepped up and was smiling and acting as if the odd phone call had never happened. "Do I need to sign anything?"

The second man pulled a form out of his breast pocket and handed it to her. Then he handed her a key fob. "Just drop it off at our branch at the airport when you bring it back."

They left and got into the boring black car. Seth watched it pull away from the curb.

"This is our rental car?" he said.

"If I'm going to drive, I like it to be in something that responds well and—" she stopped, looking a little embarrassed "—something that looks good."

"You're a car chick," he said, honest awe in his voice. Just because he drove an old Jeep, it didn't mean that he couldn't appreciate the finer things in life. "You know, I'm free the Saturday after next. How about you and I get married?"

She rolled her eyes. "We should get going. We've got a big drive ahead of us."

He reached for the bags. He was willing to sideline the conversation about the strange phone call. It did not mean that he'd forgotten it.

She opened the trunk and Seth loaded their luggage. It was full by the time he got finished.

She got in the driver's side, adjusted her mirrors, and found the headlights and windshield wipers. While she was doing all that, he was programming their next stop into the GPS.

She pulled out, signaled, made a nice neat turn and accelerated smoothly. Absolutely nothing to give away that her stomach was in knots.

Who would play such a cruel trick on her to leave a message like that? Who disliked her so much? Was it more of the same that she'd been dealing with these past weeks? Was somebody trying to make her lose her mind?

She wanted to tell Seth everything. She really did. But would he believe her? Would he think she'd been imagining things? He absolutely couldn't believe she was imagining the message. He'd heard it. Did that mean that the person responsible for this had become careless and would soon expose himself? Or more aggressive, maybe upping the stakes by taking a chance that others would hear the message?

She could not ignore that there could be another possibility. Was there new information about the crash? It had been fifteen years. That seemed rather a long shot.

"It's just super odd that after all these years you'd get a voice mail like that," Seth said, proving that she wasn't the only one rehashing the call in her head.

"Yes, odd."

"From a number that claims it is impossible that the call came from there." He moved his seat back to make room for his long legs. "Like I said, the website seemed pretty legitimate. What did you think about what Marta told you? What kind of vibe did you get?"

"'Vibe?'" she repeated.

"Gut reaction," he said.

"I got the feeling that she didn't know what I was talking about. So I think that's the end of that."

"After what happened last night, I'm going to repeat my suggestion that you should at least make a police report."

She turned to give him a quick look before focusing on the road again. "There is no reason to think the two things are connected."

"Agree. But two odd things."

His words hung in the air. "Listen, Seth. The next twelve days are going to be exhausting. I do not have time to make a police report or to be available for any of their follow-up questions."

He didn't say anything for at least five minutes. Finally, he sighed. "I'm only agreeing to this because there wasn't an explicit threat. If something like that happens, all bets are off."

"I'm not a fool," she said.

"I never thought you were," he said. He leaned back in his seat. "If you want me to drive, just let me know."

"I'm fine," she said. "But I will turn on some music. Keep myself awake."

"Sounds good. It's roughly an hour and a half to Kingman, Arizona. That would probably be a good place to get some dinner. Maybe a nice steak."

"I wasn't planning on stopping," she said. "We could

just get something in our rooms once we arrive." That's what she usually did when she traveled.

"Nope," he said, acting as if he had every right to make that decision.

"I'm not crazy about steak," she said.

He gave her a look that made her think she might have two heads. "I'm starting to get nervous. What is it that you like to eat?"

"Salads. Seafood. Some pasta. All very normal foods." She paused. "With the exception, of course, that every once in a while, I love a bat wing fried in whale blubber."

He smiled. "I've always preferred my bat wings to be poached."

"I only poach eggs."

"A purist," he said.

She supposed it was a little unreasonable to expect him to miss dinner. He was in good shape with plenty of muscles and he likely could burn through a couple thousand calories without blinking an eye. "Fine. Find a place and tell me when I should turn."

"On it," he said, picking up his phone again.

She settled in for the drive. Ninety minutes later, she saw her first sign for Kingman.

"That's the exit you want," he said.

From there it was a couple rights and one left before she pulled in to the Purple Onion. It was a rather nondescript brown wooden building but the parking lot was full of cars, which was always an encouraging sign. She found a place to park.

Seth straightened up in his seat and opened his door. Once out of the car, he motioned for her to precede him into the restaurant.

It was dark inside and the booths were a burnt-orange

leather. “I expected purple,” she said over her shoulder as the hostess led them to a table.

He didn’t respond. Once they were seated, he picked up the menu. She did the same.

Her stomach grumbled and she knew that he’d been right to insist that they stop. She found a couple things that would be fine and settled on shrimp and roasted tomatoes over linguine. He already had his menu at the edge of the table.

The waitress approached. “Good evening. My name is Clarice and I’ll be taking care of you tonight.”

“Evening, Clarice,” he said. “My friend here was hoping that you’d have your bat wings fried in whale blubber on special tonight.”

Megan kicked him under the table, making solid contact with his shin. He didn’t even flinch.

“Uh…” Clarice stumbled. Nobody had prepared her for that question.

“Please,” Megan said, delicately waving her hand. “Just ignore him. He just took his meds so things will get better.”

“Right. Are you ready to order?” Clarice asked tentatively.

Megan ordered her pasta and he got a sixteen-ounce New York strip. They both got salads.

Once Clarice walked away, Megan leaned forward. “You know that she’s on her way back to the kitchen to talk about the weirdo in her station.”

“And the chef will immediately look up bat wings fried in whale blubber to see if it’s the latest thing offered by places that really got it going on.”

She looked around. “You don’t think the Purple Onion with the orange booths has it going on?”

He shrugged. “The decor could use some work. But it

smells good in here, it looks clean and there were a bunch of excellent reviews."

"I'm glad we stopped," she said. "Fortunately, we can sleep in a little in the morning. The first event is a luncheon at noon with the Women's Art Club. Then we do a fashion show."

"Fashion show, huh," he said. "That sounds...great." He reached for the cracker basket at the end of the table and offered her a breadstick.

She took it. It was empty carbs, which she stayed away from, but tonight, sitting at this table with handsome Seth Pike, she felt as if she needed something to do. They were definitely not on a date—this was work for both of them. But still, he was funny and charming in an odd way and it made her realize that she was missing all that kind of interaction from her life.

It was her own fault, of course. After her relationship with Logan ended, she'd had offers. Just hadn't felt inclined to accept any. Had chosen to focus on raising Abigail. She'd never regretted it for a minute. Had also had to work very hard to learn her craft, to get to a point where it was a natural step for her to have her own stores, to offer her own designs.

"If the fashion show isn't exciting enough, in the evening, there's a cocktail party for local officials, some of the neighbors, our employees, the contractors who worked on the store. Basically, everybody who has been involved."

"Black tie?"

She shook her head. "Not until we reach Colorado Springs."

"So much to look forward to," he said.

She smiled. "You're a liar. But that could come in handy the next day. A few appreciative looks from you and I see the potential for big sales. You manage a *wow, you look terrific in that* and I expect that we'll exceed our sales goals substantially."

"This is worse than I imagined," he said, his tone very serious.

The waitress picked that moment to return with the salads. She set them down. "Can I get you anything else right now?"

"This is fabulous," Seth said. "You got them here so quickly, exactly what we wanted."

The server almost beamed. "Thanks," she said.

Megan could barely keep a straight face. "And I was worried."

They ate their salads. And then Clarice returned with their food, which looked really good. Megan so rarely took the time to eat a real dinner that this was luxury.

"Did you enjoy it?" she asked, once he had finished.

"Perfectly cooked," he said. He glanced at her half-eaten pasta. "Did you like yours?"

She nodded. "Just full," she said. As good as it had been, she hadn't wanted to overeat. They had a long drive still ahead of them. "I'll get the check," she said.

"But..." He stopped. "I suppose that makes sense," he said.

It did. It was part of the contract. His meals were covered. If he paid for it, it would simply be billed to her later. It was a good reminder that as comfortable as she felt talking to him, this was still very much a business situation.

Ten minutes later, they were back in the car. She pulled out of the parking lot and looked at the time. It was seven thirty. They still had a three-hour drive ahead of them.

It went fairly quickly. They didn't talk. She had thought he might close his eyes and rest but he stayed alert, watching the road. The terrain got hillier and the highway was a bunch of sharp twists and turns as they made their way into Sedona. She was grateful when she finally pulled in to the hotel's parking lot.

It was crazy. This was the first day and she was already tired.

They unpacked the trunk and carried their luggage in. The lobby was brightly lit but empty with the exception of a lone man sitting on one of the couches, reading a newspaper. The woman behind the desk smiled at them. Her name tag said "Lana" in big letters and "Anderson" underneath it, in smaller type. "Good evening," she said. "Checking in?"

"Yes," Megan said. "Two rooms. One for Megan North and one for Seth Pike. I'll be paying for both with this." She slid her credit card across the counter.

"How many keys for each room?" the clerk asked.

"Just one," Megan said, before Seth could pipe up.

He didn't correct her. But he did step up to the counter. "We need the rooms to be connecting," he said.

"Of course, Mr. Pike," Lana said. The tone of her voice had been pleasant with Megan but it had warmed when addressing Seth. *Oh, please*, thought Megan. She gave Seth a look to see if he'd noticed but he seemed oblivious.

"In town on business or pleasure, Mr. Pike?" Lana asked, her fingers typing as she talked. She was probably twenty-five and she wasn't wearing a diamond on any finger.

"Little of both," Seth said, noncommittal.

Lana stared at him. Then picked a business card off the stack on the counter. "If you have any questions about Sedona while you're here, don't hesitate to ask." She wrote a telephone number on the card. "Here's my cell. That's the easiest way to reach me."

Seconds later, she slid across two different key cards. "Ms. North, you're in 402. Mr. Pike, 404," she said. "Free continental breakfast is from six to nine in the space just to our left. If you need anything," she said, looking at Seth, "just ask. I'll be here all night."

Oh, good grief. "Thank you," Megan said. She reached for both keys. When they were in the elevator, she handed him the one for room 404. "I hope Lana remembers who has which room. That way, she won't wake me up later when she knocks on my door by mistake."

"I have no idea what you're talking about."

He had to be lying. Lana hadn't been subtle.

"None of my business what you do," she said. "As long as you're available tomorrow."

He held up his key card. "Not to worry. As for tonight, I'm going to be sleeping. I didn't get all that much last night."

She saw that their rooms were the first two to the left. "Well, good night."

"Can I take a quick look at your room?" he said.

She was exhausted and really didn't think she could stand up much longer. The drive, maybe because of the strange car or the strange road, had taken more out of her than she was willing to admit.

"Sure," she said, and handed him the key card when he reached for it.

He opened the door and walked in. She followed. It was a basic hotel room. The bath off to the left, the closet to the right. Then there was one queen bed and a dresser with a flat-screen television on it. At the rear of the room, there was a desk and a chair and a door on the right side of the room, near the windows. The only thing perhaps a little unusual was that it didn't have any of the standard cheap carpeting. There was wood flooring.

And she remembered that downstairs, in the lobby, there hadn't been carpet, either. Just lots of tile and wood. It was rather nice.

Seth walked over and unlocked the connecting door. “Is this going to be a problem for you?”

Seth was a little nosy, maybe a little opinionated, but he wasn’t a danger to her. She was confident of that. “No, that’s fine.”

“You can keep it closed. Just don’t lock it,” he said.

“Got it,” she said.

“What time to you want to have breakfast?” he asked.

“I don’t generally eat breakfast.”

“That’s going to change,” he said. “Most important meal of the day, you know.”

Her parents had loved breakfast. Loved making it for the family. “I don’t need a nutrition lecture,” she said.

“Good, because that’s the extent of what I know.”

“Fine. Let’s say eight.” She would be up way before that but could do some work on her computer in her room.

“Okay. I’ll be outside your door then.”

Seth undressed for bed in the dark and slid into the tightly-tucked sheets wearing just his boxers. He stretched out. And thought about Megan doing exactly the same thing, just feet away. Wondered what she slept in.

He suspected something silky and perfect, just like her. Even after what had been a long day, she’d still looked beautiful as he’d studied her under the harsh lighting in the hotel lobby. She’d been busy paying the bill and it had given him a chance to really examine her.

She’d gotten her dig in about Lana. Was it even possible that she’d been…jealous?

That was ridiculous.

But not a bad idea to fall asleep on. He closed his eyes and breathed deep. He willed his muscles to relax.

And didn’t wake up until he heard Megan’s scream.

Chapter 6

Seth rolled out of bed, grabbed the gun that he'd placed in the nightstand drawer and moved to the connecting door. He opened it, prepared for the worst.

But still, when he saw her on the bed, jumping, one hand up to her mouth, the other pointing wildly toward the corner of the room, he wasn't sure what to think.

"Snake," she said.

He looked. Yep. She was right. About four feet long with dark brown stripes against a lighter cream background. Ugly skinny thing, with a triangular-looking head.

"Shoot it," she said.

A gun going off in a hotel in the middle of the night was guaranteed to cause some commotion. He put his gun down on the night table. "I think we need another plan."

She'd stopped jumping but she was shaking so much, he was afraid she was going to fall off the bed and really hurt herself. Her arm wouldn't be the only thing bruised. "Maybe you should sit down."

"No."

"Okay, then." He glanced around the room. His eyes landed on the umbrella. It was leaning up against the wall, maybe four feet away from the snake.

He judged the distance, the angle. Thought it was about right.

He grabbed the handle of the umbrella and when he got close enough, slid the other end of the umbrella toward the middle of the snake. Got the two-inch nub at the top firmly under the snake's middle and hefted his arm upward. The snake flew through the air, into the bathroom, landing in the bathtub. He closed the door fast and grabbed the damp towel that she'd left hanging on the closest door. He stuffed it under the bathroom door.

"It's not getting out of there," he said. "You're safe," he said, turning to look at her.

Now she had one hand up to her mouth. "I think I'm going to be sick."

Her bathroom wasn't an option. He grabbed the empty wastebasket from next to the dresser and took it to her. But she didn't reach for it.

She was scaring him a little. She was so pale. "Come on. You're made of stronger stuff that that. Don't be such a girl," he goaded.

Her head jerked up; color came back into her face.

Yes, much better.

"We're leaving," she said.

"Right now? It's the middle of the night."

"I don't care. This place has snakes. We have to go now."

He walked over to the phone. "How about we talk to a manager. I'll call down to the front desk." He paused. "Maybe you should put a robe on."

Her pretty skin took on a pink hue and she crossed her

arms in front of her chest. It was a little too late for that. He'd gotten a pretty good look and he'd been right about her pajamas. White. Silky. The ensemble hit her midthigh and was tight enough in all the right places. She didn't sleep in a bra.

She inclined her head toward the chair by the window. "My robe is over there," she said.

He picked it up and tossed it to her. She hurriedly put it on. When she was tying the belt, she said, "Maybe you should put some pants on."

"Tit for tat," he said. The air in the room seemed to sizzle. "I will but let's get you off the bed first," he said.

She shook her head.

"You have to sit down, at least."

She did, stretching her long legs out in front of her. He suspected there was no way she was going to let them dangle over the side.

He pressed a button on the phone. It was answered on the second ring. "Ms. North, what can we help you with?"

"It's Seth Pike calling. We need to see a manager up here. Pronto. Ms. North has a snake in her room. I've tossed it in the bathtub but we're going to need somebody to do something else with it." He hung up. "I'll be right back," he said.

It took him just seconds to pull on pants and a shirt but when he came back, he got the idea that he hadn't been fast enough, that any amount of time alone in the company of a snake was too long.

"Can you check the closet?" she asked.

He'd taken a quick look in her closet when he'd first inspected her room. But he was willing to do it again. "Sure." He opened the sliding doors, first one direction, then the other. "All clear," he said.

"Could you look under the bed?"

He got on his knees, lifted the bed skirt and looked down. Saw that the bed frame was solid and rested on the floor. But still, he dutifully looked on all four sides. "Clear," he said.

There was a knock at the door. "I'll get it," he said. He didn't want her answering the door in the middle of the night. But he didn't expect an argument. He wasn't sure she was ever moving from the bed.

He looked through the peephole. It was Lana. He opened the door.

"Our night manager stepped out to get a bite to eat," she said. "I've called him but I thought that I'd see what I could do." She looked down at the towel on the floor, up against the bathroom door. "Is it in there?"

He nodded.

"I'm terribly sorry about this," she said. "What happened?"

He motioned with his hand. "You should probably ask Ms. North that," he said.

Megan didn't wait for Lana to repeat the qucstion. "I woke up and decided to use the bathroom. I turned on the lamp next to my bed and…and I saw the snake."

"I just can't believe it," Lana said. "I've worked here for four years and we've never had something like this happen."

"I'm not making it up."

"Of course you aren't," Lana said. "Do you mind if I take a look at it?" She seemed genuinely excited about the possibility. And she'd seemed to have lost all interest in flirting with Seth.

"Maybe you should wait. I don't want it to get out," Megan said.

"I'll be careful." Lana used her fist to knock on the door several times.

Seth didn't know much about snakes but a kid couldn't grow up in the desert and not pick up a few things. He'd always been told to stomp on the ground, that the vibration would scare the snake. He figured a knock on the door would achieve the same effect.

When the desk clerk opened the door, he got close enough to see that the snake was still in the bathtub. He expected Lana to do a quick look. Instead, she studied the thing. Finally, she closed the door and put the towel back into place.

"It's a Sonoran lyre snake," she said. "They're called that because the markings on their head remind you of a lyre harp."

"I associate harps with something nice and peaceful. That's not what it reminded me of," Megan said.

"It wouldn't kill you," Lana said. "I mean, you don't want to get bit but its venom is not deadly. Probably would make you sick, though," she added, almost as an afterthought.

"How do you know so much about snakes?" Megan asked.

"I'm a geology major. Rocks and snakes sort of go together."

"No wonder I hated science classes," Megan said.

"We'll get it out of here," Lana said.

"I want a different room," Megan said.

"Yes, well, unfortunately, we're sold out. Probably most of the hotels are. There's a big festival this weekend."

That didn't bode well for them easily finding another hotel. And he really didn't want to sleep in the car. But he understood that Megan would be skittish about staying in the room. "How about we switch rooms. I'll sleep here and you take the one next door."

"You could have a snake in your room, too," she said.

She wasn't being totally reasonable but he understood. She'd woken up after just a few hours of sleep and had the pants scared off her. In a few hours, after a good night's rest, this could even be funny. But not right now.

He just wanted a solution that didn't involve changing hotels. Plus, he didn't want to have the conversation in front of Lana, who was looking way too interested.

"Can you excuse us," Seth said. "Maybe step out for just a second?"

"Of course," Lana said. "I'll just be in the hall."

Seth waited until she'd closed the door behind her. "I really don't want to move out of the hotel. But I get that you're a little freaked out right now. How about we share my room? You can take my bed and I'll take the chair. That way, if there is a snake in my room, too, I'll be handy. And we'll take your umbrella as our weapon of choice."

"But..." Her voice trailed off. She looked at the clock next to the bed. Just after three. "I guess that could work," she said.

Seth opened the front door. "We're going to both bunk in my room tonight. I want confirmation once the snake has been removed. Knock on my door," he said, "regardless of the time."

"Of course, Mr. Pike," Lana said. "I'm so very sorry this happened. We'll be back when the night manager returns."

"Snake is in your capable hands now," he said. He closed the door.

Megan was still on the bed.

"Need me to carry you?" he asked.

That got her moving. He barely had time to turn on the lights in his room. Once there, she stood near the dresser. Without her even having to ask, he made a point of checking the closet and under the bed. Then it was a good look into the bathroom. "All clear," he said.

"Thank you," she said.

"No problem," he said. He grabbed an extra blanket from the shelf in the closet and walked toward the chair.

"You should let me take the chair. I'm shorter," she said. "I'll fit better."

It was true. His neck was going to be killing him in the morning. He sat down and covered himself up. "You can get the light," he said, and closed his eyes.

He heard nothing for a long minute. Figured she hadn't moved. But then the whisper of steps, the rustle of covers being tossed back. She'd taken the opposite side of the bed from where he'd been sleeping.

He heard the *click* of the lamp. He did not think that she'd taken off her robe.

Not that he hadn't already seen everything.

And just the thought of that caused his body to heat up and harden. He shifted and the chair creaked.

"Everything okay?" she asked.

"Just dandy," he said. He was going to have to count sheep, ugly, skinny, smelly sheep for a good long time, before he'd be relaxed enough to nod off. "Couldn't be better."

When Megan woke up, she realized that Seth was already awake. And dressed, in different clothes than he'd slept in. He'd certainly been quiet about it.

"Hi," she said.

He put down a magazine about Sedona that had been in both their rooms when they'd checked in. "Coffee is made," he said, gesturing to the small pot on the shelf above the mini fridge.

"Thank you," she said. "But I'll wait. I don't usually

drink it until after I've run." She glanced toward the window and saw that it was just getting light. A look at the bedside clock told her it was just before six, a little later than she usually woke up. But then again, her sleep had been disrupted.

But oddly enough, she'd had no trouble falling asleep. And she hadn't dreamed of snakes. "Did they confirm that they'd removed the snake?" she asked. She hadn't heard anything.

"Yeah. About twenty minutes after we got settled in here."

"What do you think they did with it?"

"I imagine they took it outside and let it go. It's probably telling all its snake buddies what a crazy night it had inside the hotel."

"I'm determined to put it out of my mind," she said. "And in that vein, I think I might run outside today," she said.

He rubbed his chin. "Like I just said, they probably let the snake go nearby. And there are probably others. This is Arizona."

She certainly wouldn't be crazy about seeing another snake but she didn't want to give up the opportunity to see Sedona. She'd always heard about the great hiking and running trails in the area. "I know. And I guess this is as good a time as any to apologize for my highly emotional state last night. I think it was waking up out of a sound sleep and seeing the snake in my room. Outdoors, where those things can be expected, I won't have that kind of reaction. I'm embarrassed about last night," she admitted.

He waved it away. "It would have put anybody off their game. And you calmed down pretty fast."

"That's because I was well on my way to having a heart attack and that would have really put a damper on things."

He laughed. “True.”

She got out of his bed. Stood there in her robe, feeling off balance. Maybe she should have taken him up on the coffee. “I…uh…will get dressed in my room.”

“Want me to check the closet?” he asked, his tone teasing.

“I think I can handle it,” she said.

“Okay. Meet you in the hallway in five,” he said.

She walked back into her room, shutting the connecting door between the two rooms. Then, very carefully, looked around. She knew the snake had been removed and she really wasn’t expecting to see another one but still, it never hurt to be careful. Then she opened her closet door. All clear. She looked into the bathroom. Tub was wonderfully empty.

She opened her suitcase and pulled out a good running bra, black yoga pants and a pink shirt. She dressed quickly, not wanting him to have to wait on her. She put on socks and slipped her feet into running shoes. Then she checked to make sure she had her phone and her key card to get back into her room.

She opened her door. He was standing in the hall, one foot resting against the wall. He wore gray sweatpants and a white T-shirt. His running shoes looked as if they’d gotten some use.

“You don’t have to do this,” she said, feeling as if she had to protest. The idea of running with him was fun but given that she’d taken his bed last night, maybe he’d be happier just getting another hour of sleep.

“I’m not opposed to a good workout,” he said. “And it’s been years since I’ve been in Sedona. But I still remember a place, near Oak Creek Canyon.”

When they walked out of the hotel, the morning air

was cool, probably around seventy. After the heat of Las Vegas, it felt blessedly cool. They drove for a few miles before Seth pointed. "We can park here," he said.

She locked the car and put the fob in her pocket. She stretched, loosening the muscles in her legs. Then they started off slow, but a half mile into it, picked up speed. Seth had no trouble keeping up and she suspected that he was probably holding back some. Which irritated her, and she pushed herself harder.

The trail led them between big cliffs of red rock and past waterfalls and abundant vegetation. It was stunningly beautiful.

She was hardly even thinking about snakes.

Three miles or so into the run, her running shoe hit loose rock. She slipped, lost her footing and knew she was going to fall.

But Seth's strong hand grabbed hold of her right biceps and he pulled her into his body, somehow managing to keep them both upright.

"I've got you," he said. They came to a jarring stop.

He was hot and sweaty and she was basically plastered against his right side. "Oh," she said.

"Oh, indeed," he murmured. He loosened his grip on her arm but didn't remove his hand. "Okay?" he asked. "Damn, you'll probably have a bruise on this side."

Her heart was hammering in her chest, and not only from the run and the near fall. She'd been physically aware of him since the first moment that he'd almost slid into her under the awning. And waking up in the same room had only exacerbated the tension coursing through her body.

She was needy. Aching with it, truly.

She tilted her head up. He leaned down.

His mouth was just inches away. So close, she could feel his warm breath.

He was going to kiss her.

And then he straightened up and stepped away. “We should probably finish up,” he said. “I think there’s a mile or so left. Ready?”

Not really. Her legs felt wobbly. But she wasn’t going to admit that. “Of course,” she said, taking off.

He ran alongside but didn’t say anything else to her. Once they were back in the car, he remained quiet all the way back to the hotel. When they reached her room, he finally spoke. “How much time do you need to get ready?”

“Why?”

“Like I said last night, I’m all about breakfast.”

Great. Another thirty minutes of staring at each other in silence? She wanted to tell him no thanks but remembered that he’d been a really nice guy the night before. So what if he’d…rejected her this morning?

Rejected was perhaps too harsh a word.

He’d hung on to his common sense and she’d lost hers somewhere on the path. She should be happy with him. Not feeling oddly irritated.

She unlocked her door. “I’ll be ready in forty minutes,” she said.

“You want to use my shower?” His face colored. “I can use the one in your room,” he added quickly.

“I assumed that’s what you were offering.” If he didn’t want to kiss her, he certainly didn’t want to shower with her. “I’ll be fine. Snake cooties never hurt anyone.” She closed the door behind her and started taking off her clothes. Then she realized she was just a big talker when she turned on the water in the shower, let it get as hot as it could and let the water run for a good five minutes, washing away any remaining dust from the snake. Then she turned the temperature down to normal and stepped in.

Thirty-nine minutes later, she opened her door. Again, Seth was standing in the hallway. She caught the whiff of a smile before his face cleared.

"What?" she demanded, still irritated with him.

"Nothing," he said.

"Tell me," she demanded.

"I was just thinking that you're a really good advertisement for your business. You always look very put together. A complete package. Clothes. Jewelry. Shoes," he added.

She loved all of those things. Today she wore a lightweight apricot-and-white flare dress with some beaded necklaces and her favorite strappy brown high-heeled sandals. Her legs were bare, in deference to the hundred-degree heat that was expected today. "Actually, North and More Designs will sell everything that I have on."

"I predict that you're going to be wildly successful," he said. "But then again, I can barely match my shirts to my pants."

He'd done pretty well so far. Today, he wore tan slacks, a blue-and-tan button-down shirt and a blue sports coat.

He started walking. "I'll bet you're looking forward to breakfast."

Oddly enough, she was. Fifteen minutes later, she looked up from her bagel and saw Lana and a man she didn't recognize approaching at a fairly good clip. And her heart started to beat fast, as if it was keeping time with their steps. Seth, like a watchdog attuned to any change, put his fork down.

"What?" he asked.

She kept her hands by her plate but discreetly pointed with her index finger. "Company."

He turned his head to look, then stood.

"Good morning," Lana said. She was businesslike.

"Morning," Seth said. He looked at the man.

"I'm Jase Hall," the man said. "The manager of our hotel. Lana and Harry, our night manager, filled me in on your incident last night. I was very sorry to hear about it and want you to know that there are no charges for either room for last night."

"That wasn't necessary," Megan said. She'd thought they might comp her room but letting them both stay for free was very customer friendly.

"I know that but I want to do it." He looked at Lana. "Actually, that's not the only reason I wanted to talk to you. I've got something that I'd like to show you."

"What is it?" Seth asked.

"Hotel videotape. I think you're going to find it very interesting. You're welcome to come, too, Mr. Pike. Please, finish your breakfast and when you're ready, my office is just behind the registration desk."

Megan watched the two walk away and waited until they were out of earshot before leaning toward Seth. "What do you think this is?"

He shook his head. "I don't know but I've got a feeling it's not going to be good."

She had the same feeling. She pushed her food away and felt mildly ill as the coffee in her stomach started to churn.

She waited for Seth to lecture her on the importance of breakfast. He said nothing.

That didn't make her feel any better. He was obviously thrown off by the manager's odd request.

He finished his food quickly and poured his coffee into a to-go cup. He offered her one and she declined.

They walked to the office just as Lana, her purse on her shoulder, walked out the door. She didn't see them. Seth gave his name to the clerk at the registration desk and the young man waved them back. The manager's office was small, maybe ten feet by ten feet, so there was barely room for his desk and two office chairs. But Jase Hall didn't invite them to sit down. Instead, he motioned for them to come behind the desk.

"I was very concerned to learn that we had a snake in the building. Of course, this is Arizona and we do have snakes, so it's not an impossibility. But I thought it warranted another look. So I pulled the video from all the entrances and from the hallway outside your room." He pushed a couple buttons on his computer. "I want you to see this."

His screen came to life. Megan saw elevator doors open and someone stepped out, wearing white pants and a white lab coat. They had their head down and a white baseball cap on their head. Either their hair was stuffed up inside or it was very short. It was hard to tell if it was a man or a woman but Megan thought male, once the person started to walk down the hall.

He was carrying a sack of some kind.

And it didn't take her long to figure out what was in the sack. Outside her door, the person knelt down, fiddled with the sack and out came the snake. It had to be nudged a bit with a boot before it slithered under the door of room 402.

The person didn't return to the elevator. Instead, he kept walking to the end of the hallway and went through the door marked as stairs.

"Do you have him exiting the building?" Seth asked.

The manager pushed some buttons and pulled up a

new screen. Again, the face was averted, as if he expected that there were cameras. He opened the door and walked through it to the parking lot.

The manager pulled up another screen. "Here's him walking across the hotel parking lot onto the public sidewalk. I lose him once he clears the hotel grounds."

She felt sick. She couldn't even think.

"What do you have of him coming into the hotel?" Seth asked, still evidently able to think.

"That's where it gets odd. We don't. I have reviewed every piece of footage from last night and I can't find where he enters the hotel. We know he's in the hallway at approximately 2:20 a.m."

She'd awakened at three. That meant that the snake had been in her room for over a half hour before she'd realized it. She walked around and sat in one of the chairs. She didn't need to see any more.

"So I've looked at all the entrances, going back to the time that the two of you checked in. There's nothing."

"That can't be right," Seth said.

"I've spent the last two hours looking at the tapes. I'm very sure," the manager said.

"So he had to be in the hotel before we arrived," Seth said. "I want a list of all your guests last night."

The manager leaned back in his chair. "Mr. Pike, I hope you understand but I'm not handing that information over to you so that you can badger my hotel guests. This appears to be a very targeted attack…" He stopped. "Let's just say, a very bad joke of some kind."

He'd pulled back from *attack*. Probably didn't want to heighten the tension already palpable in the room.

Too late.

Seth appeared to be considering the manager's words.

"Last night, when we checked in, Lana Anderson was at the desk. She also responded to our call, asking for the removal of the snake. You both mentioned an assistant manager. Was there anyone else working at the registration desk or in the office last night?"

The manager shook his head. "Just Lana and Harry Givens, our night assistant manager."

"I'd like to talk to both of them," Seth said.

"Why?"

"By your own words, you indicated it appeared to be a targeted attack. I want to know how somebody would have known that Ms. North was in that room."

Now Jase looked as if his shirt collar was too tight. His face was getting red. "If you're suggesting that the information came from either of them, you're barking up the wrong tree."

"How do you know that?" Seth asked.

"Because I already asked both of them. It is against our policy to provide any outside caller or any visitor with the room number for any of our guests. We can transfer a call to a room but we will not provide the room number. That's hotel management 101," he said dismissively.

"May I speak with both of them?" Seth repeated, his voice tight.

"They've left for the day," the manager said. "They were here all night."

"I'd like their home numbers," Seth said. Since he already had Lana's, he obviously didn't want the boss to know that.

"No. We protect our associates' privacy just as much as we protect our guests."

Seth snorted, as if he wasn't putting much stock into

the hotel's ability to protect the guests' privacy. "I'd like to have a copy of that video," he said.

"No, I'm sorry," Jase Hall said. "It's hotel property."

Seth turned to her. "We need to report this to the police."

He was right. What if the next time they let loose a more venomous snake? "Okay," she said.

He seemed surprised that she'd given in so easily. He'd likely been prepared for a fight since she'd been so reluctant to report the odd voice mail to the police. But now he wasn't wasting any time. He turned back to the manager. "Please don't do anything with those tapes until the police have had a chance to respond."

"I regret that you feel it necessary to involve the police. But I certainly understand that it is your right. And we will, of course, cooperate with the police in any way possible."

Jase Hall clearly wasn't happy. She understood. It was going to take him time and energy to deal with questions from the police. He'd likely known that was a possibility before he'd shown them the tapes and had already weighed that out against the possibility that a disgruntled guest would post all over social media that she'd found a snake in her room.

Seth stood up. He motioned for Megan to precede him out the door. When they were in the lobby, his concerned eyes searched her face.

"How are you doing?" he asked.

"Peachy," she said.

"You want to call the police or do you want me to?" he asked.

"I will. I suppose it's not a 911 call but rather one to their nonemergency number." Somehow that seemed to diminish the episode, which was still making her head pulse.

"That sounds right," he said. "Let's call from my room," he said.

She glanced at her watch. "It would be nice if they could respond quickly. We've only got a couple hours before we need to head over to the luncheon and then the fashion show. Then I need to be at the store for a couple hours and then off to the evening reception. Unfortunately, we don't have a lot of flexibility with our schedule."

He didn't answer. She understood. There was no reason to discuss it until they knew what the police response would be. They rode the elevator in silence and once back in his room, she used her phone to find the nonemergency police number in Sedona. She put the phone on speaker so that Seth could hear.

She got transferred twice but finally got a chance to tell her story. The woman on the other end took down the details without comment. She asked for a callback number and when Megan provided it, she said that a responding officer would contact her in advance of coming to see her.

"My schedule is only free for the next couple of hours," Megan said.

"I'll add that information to the report," the woman responded in a way that made Megan think "not my problem."

"Thank you for your help," she said. She hung up and looked at Seth. If and when the police arrived, she suspected that he was going to want to be there. And if she told them everything, he was going to be very surprised. And likely a little pissed off.

He'd been genuinely nice and helpful the previous night and she'd repaid him by lying.

Well, maybe not lying, but certainly not being forthcoming about the troubling things that had occurred over the past several weeks.

It wasn't right.

"I think I need to tell you something," she said.

Chapter 7

Seth took a seat on the couch and she sat on the bed, her back resting against the headboard. She didn't look relaxed, however, and he had a feeling he wasn't going to like what she had to tell him.

But he wanted to hear all of it. The image on that computer screen had made him mad as hell. It hadn't been chance or bad luck that she'd ended up with a snake in her room. It had been deliberate.

And even if the snake wasn't deadly, a snakebite was never not serious. And what if she'd awakened and it had been in bed with her? She might have had a damn heart attack. The manager might have wanted to pass it off as a bad joke but it was no laughing matter.

"I haven't been exactly truthful with you."

"Okay," he said.

"I dismissed the cab shooting as random, that it couldn't be anything else."

He said nothing.

"I don't know if it was anything else but I should have been more forthcoming about what's been going on in my life. Odd things have been happening."

He kept his eyes steady and his mouth shut. He wasn't going to interrupt.

"A couple times, I've thought I was being followed as I walked home from work. I live about six blocks from my office in Carmel so I walk to and from work most days. I have for years. And have never had any issues. Even when I walk later at night. It's very safe."

No place was safe anymore but that wasn't the point.

"But just because it's very safe and I've never had any problems in the past, I don't take it for granted. I'm careful, aware of my surroundings. And usually make a point to look behind me a couple times, just to make sure that nobody is approaching from behind. One evening in June, I left later than usual, about eight. But because it was June, there was still some daylight left so I wasn't too worried. However, I noticed a man walking behind me. Light-colored hair, slim build. I couldn't tell his age but he moved as if he was pretty agile. After I turned around, he moved to the other side of the street, always staying about fifty yards behind me. When I went inside my apartment, he kept walking. I felt uncomfortable but told myself that I was imagining things. I ate something and showered and decided to go to bed. I turned out my light, lay down for maybe five minutes and just couldn't relax. I got up, leaving the lights off, and I looked out the window. And I saw the same man, still across the street. He was looking up, at my apartment."

"What did you do?"

"I called the police."

"Good," Seth said.

"They came and by that time, the man was gone. The

officer who took the report was pleasant but I could tell that he thought there were bigger fish to fry somewhere else. He told me to call again if I saw something similar."

"Did they investigate, talk to people in the area?"

"I don't think so. But I felt better that I'd reported it. And I kept watch but didn't see anybody again for almost three weeks. So by now it's early July and I'd gone to watch the fireworks with a friend from work. It was after ten when we walked home but we were together so I wasn't concerned. We were still at least a half mile from my apartment when we crossed under an overpass. Once we were through, I had this sudden feeling that I was being watched. I looked over my shoulder and didn't see anyone. Then I happened to look up. The blond man was standing on the overpass. I could see him under the light. I grabbed my friend's arm, to have her take a look, but by the time she turned, the man was gone."

"Did you call the police?"

"No. Maybe I should have but really, I could just imagine their response. Our fireworks attract a huge crowd so now there's crazy traffic everywhere and it's likely that many people driving have had too much to drink. The police department would have been stretched very thin that night. Me catching a brief glimpse of somebody on an overpass was not going to be met with much concern. Plus, my friend couldn't even back up my story."

He understood but still, it was always better when everything was reported.

"That week I started to get hang-up calls on my office phone. I rent space in a building and expenses for basic utilities, like electricity, gas and telephone, are shared by the tenants. As a result, there is a small information services team, which maintains our phone and internet connections. I asked them if the calls could be traced. I was told no."

He suspected there might have been a way but it would likely have involved some work and it might have simply been easier to tell her it was impossible.

"Then my door buzzer started ringing at odd hours of the night."

"Door buzzer."

"I live in an eight-unit apartment building. Our last names are on the door buzzer unit that is outside the main door of the building. Multiple times, usually sometime between two and four in the morning, the buzzer would ring, waking me up."

"Who was it?" he asked.

"I have no idea. I can't see the front door from my apartment building. When I would answer the buzzer, there would never be anyone there."

"Cameras?" he said.

"No. I asked the landlord but he thought that was an unnecessary expense. I think he was afraid of the technology. The man doesn't even have a cell phone."

"Idiot. Obviously doesn't understand he has a responsibility to his tenants to not be a Luddite. Cameras are basic security tools."

"Well, I went even more basic and spent several nights in my car, down the street from my apartment, watching my front door. It was low-tech and yielded no results with the exception that I was exhausted at work. Fortunately, the door buzzer episodes ended after a couple weeks."

"Then it was over?"

"No. Something scarier happened about two weeks ago. It had been very hot for weeks. But the heat had broken and we had a wonderfully cool evening. I went to bed and left my windows open."

He opened his mouth.

"My apartment is on the second floor and there's no balcony or fire escape access," she said. "I'm not stupid."

He closed his mouth. He had an idea of what was coming based on what Bobby Bayleaf had told him.

"I woke up because I heard voices below my window. It was two people. A woman and a man. I didn't recognize either of their voices. They both had an accent. I… I swear to you that they were talking about the best way to kill someone. I heard the woman say *her* a couple times. The man favored strangulation because it was a quiet, clean death. The woman was concerned about DNA and she thought a gunshot was much better."

Good Lord. "What did you do?"

"I called 911. The police came very quickly, without lights or sirens. But still, by the time they'd arrived, there was nobody there. This time I know they talked to other people in my apartment building but nobody else had heard or seen anything."

"So let me summarize to make sure that I've got it. On two occasions, you saw a blond-haired man watching you. You had a series of telephone hang-ups. You had middle-of-the-night door buzzers. You overheard a man and a woman talking below your window about killing someone. We were shot at the other night as we exited the cab. You get a strange call on your voice mail about a plane accident that happened fifteen years ago. And somebody lets loose a snake under your hotel door."

"Kind of a jumble," she said.

"Is there anything else?" he said.

"Well, actually yes. The night of the party at Wingman Security, I took a cab from the hotel. But as I was entering the building, I happened to turn around and I caught a glimpse of somebody across the street, who hurried out of view when I turned."

"Blond guy?"

"I don't know for sure."

He remembered thinking that she'd seemed a little off when she'd stepped from the elevator. He really wished she'd said something. He and his partners could have torn the building apart.

"I think that's it," she continued. "But given that several of those things have happened within the last forty-eight hours, I think somebody wants my attention. And they have it."

"They've got mine, too," he said, his voice hard, maybe harder than necessary when he saw her wince.

"I am sorry I didn't tell you," she said.

He waved a hand. "Based on your two confirmed sightings of the blond-haired man, do you think that's the same person who put the snake under your door?"

"I can't say for sure but I think it could be. The build, sort of slim and not too tall, seems right." She paused. "Both times that I saw him, he was wearing a flannel shirt and jeans."

"A flannel shirt on the Fourth of July?"

"Weird, I know. It was a stifling hot day, too. I was in a tank top."

He could just imagine her in a tank top. Reluctantly, he let the image go. "But on the hotel video, it looks as if he's wearing white jeans, similar to painter's pants, and a white lab coat."

"And the hat makes it impossible to see whether his hair is blond." She glanced at her watch. "It's almost nine o'clock. I can wait here until ten thirty for the police but if they haven't shown up by then, we need to leave for lunch."

"Talking to the police is more important than lunch," he said.

"Listen, I get that this is serious. If it's the same guy who was watching me outside my apartment and from the overpass, that means he drove a couple hundred miles to yank my chain some more."

"And that doesn't concern you?" he asked.

She drew back. "It scares the hell out of me. But I can't dwell on it. I reported the other things to the police and I'm going to report this. I don't know what else you'd have me do. I'm not stopping the grand opening events."

"I'm not asking you to. I simply want your head in the game."

"I imagine you think this makes your job more difficult," she said.

"I'm not concerned about that," he said.

"I'm sorry that you're getting sucked into my drama."

"I'm not complaining."

"You've...you've been great," she said.

He felt about a hundred feet tall.

"Maybe there will be a really good dessert at lunch," she said.

He smiled. "Tell me where lunch is again?"

"At the Women's Art Club in Sedona."

"Can't wait," he said. "Love a pretty tea sandwich."

She laughed. "Do you even know what a tea sandwich is?"

"Yes. A sandwich made out of...tea leaves."

"That's right," she said, her tone deliberately placating. "Once lunch is over, we'll go to their auditorium, where we'll do the fashion show."

"Just gets better and better." He glanced at his watch. "I think I'm going to call Lana." He picked up his phone.

"Oh. Well, I guess you can have the room, then. I'll

just...wait in the lobby," she said, moving quickly from the bed.

That was confusing. "I don't need privacy. You can listen."

"I'd rather not."

He stared at her. "I'm calling her to ask what she might know about somebody knowing that you were in room 402."

She said nothing. Then finally she said, "I thought it was something personal between you and Lana."

And she hadn't liked that idea. "There's nothing personal between us."

"She gave you her number."

"I didn't ask for it," he said.

"But you didn't refuse it, either," she countered.

He gave her a slow smile. "That's true." He wanted to tell her that the idea of spending time with Lana paled in comparison to being with her but he didn't want her to think that he was a freak. It looked as if she already had one stalker.

He was a little frustrated that she hadn't trusted him with the truth from the get-go but he understood. He was just glad that she'd finally come clean. Now that he knew there was a threat, nobody was going to get close enough to harm her.

He pulled Lana's card from his pocket. Dialed the number. Put the phone on speaker.

"She's probably sleeping," Megan said.

"I doubt it. You don't jump immediately into bed when you get home from work, and I suspect she doesn't, either. She probably needs a couple hours to wind down."

"I could never work nights."

In the air force, he'd flown a lot at night. You got used to being up when everybody else was sleeping.

"Hello," Lana said, her voice cautious.

"Hi. It's Seth Pike, from the hotel."

"Oh, hi, Seth." Her tone sounded guarded.

"I know you're at home and I don't want to bother you but I've got a couple questions about the video that we watched in your manager's office. I'm assuming you also saw it."

"I did."

"It seemed to me that the person carrying the snake deliberately picked out room 402, as if he might be targeting the person in that room. We had just checked in hours earlier. My question is how would someone have known who was in that room?"

Silence.

Seth waited. "Lana?"

"I have no idea," she said. "I certainly didn't give out the information."

He hadn't suggested that. It seemed to him that Lana might be a little defensive. "I'm sure you didn't," he said. "But can you help us think of any way that information could have been available to someone?"

"Listen, I worked all night and as you know, it was sort of an eventful night. I'm going to bed." She hung up.

Seth put his phone down.

"I don't think that's the call she was anticipating when she handed you her card," Megan said.

"Probably not. Listen, while we're waiting for the police to show up, I'd like to look at your luggage."

"My luggage?" she repeated.

"Yeah. That's that bag on wheels and the thing with the strap that goes over your shoulder," he added.

"Thank you," she said sarcastically. "Why?"

"We need to make sure that you didn't lead Snake Charmer to your door. That he didn't somehow plant a device on you that made it easy for him to know exactly where you were. People are sneaky. Not that long ago, somebody planted a tracking device in Kellie McGarry's boot and let me tell you, it caused a problem. So, we're going to check. The luggage and all—" he waved his hand "—your things."

"Things as in all my clothes."

"Yeah. And by the looks of it, you've got a fair amount of those."

She licked her lips. Made no move to answer or to get her luggage. After a long moment, she said, "Fine."

"I've noticed that when you're really irritated and maybe feeling pushed into a corner, that *fine* is your go-to word. But it's a tough one. Open to interpretation. Fine day? Fine weather we're having? Fine way to whittle away—"

"Stop," she said.

"What?" He pretended to be shocked. "Fine, let me open my luggage for you, Seth?"

"Yes. Fine, let me open my luggage, my life, my world."

He smiled. "Now we're communicating."

They walked into her room. He helped her put the big suitcase on the bed. Then stepped back while she unlocked and unzipped it. She carried the leather garment bag to the bed. Opened it, too.

"You'll need to take everything out," he said. "Unless you want me to."

"No," she said quickly.

She was a neat packer. Dresses in one pile. Shirts in another. Workout clothes rolled. Dainty piles of lace that she pulled out and shoved under the dresses.

When the case was empty, he examined it. Took his time. Saw or felt nothing that gave him any indication that she'd been bugged.

"I'm going to need to actually look at the clothes," he said.

"I'll check my own underwear," she said.

"Okay. But pay special attention to your bras, especially if you wear underwires."

"Really, Seth. Is there no topic that is off-limits to you?"

"Nope. Not when people are shooting at me."

He could plainly see the look of indecision that crossed her face. Then she scooped up her underwear and tossed it toward him. He caught it and pulled it close to his chest.

"Examine away," she said.

He said nothing. Just got busy. But he did sneak a look at the tag on her bra and silently congratulated himself. He'd been right: 34C.

"What?" she demanded.

"Nothing," he said. "This is all very nice, by the way."

She rubbed her forehead. "Two days ago, I just didn't see this moment coming."

"Yeah. I thought this was going to be one of my easier assignments. And now look at me." He held a yellow lace thong in his right hand and a pale blue one in his left. "Are the boutiques also selling this underwear? I mean, I just want to know if I need to be prepared for a stampede."

"No lingerie for sale," she said. "Can we just get this over with?"

He gently set down her lingerie. "I reluctantly move on."

He unzipped her garment bag and carefully looked through all the clothes. Got through them fast. Spent enough time on the leather garment bag to know that it was clean. Pulled out four pairs of shoes from the bottom compartment of the garment bag. "I'm going to need to lift up the lining," he said.

"We've come this far," she said.

She was being a good sport. He did not find anything odd with her shoes.

"Computer?" he said.

"I have excellent virus protection and security software."

"Good. Not looking for that," he said. He held out his hand. Once she handed it over, he used his pocketknife to unscrew the back cover. Examined it. Didn't see anything unusual and put it back together.

"Okay," he said. "I'm starting to feel pretty good about the fact that it's not on you."

"What about you?" she asked.

It was a good question. "You looking for a chance to go through my boxers? I mean, I've got a couple different colors but really, they're pretty damn boring in comparison."

"That's not why I asked," she said.

"Okay, but I don't generally make the same offer twice. But just so you don't think that this isn't an equal opportunity inspection, I'm going to do exactly the same with my things. You want to come watch?"

She shook her head. "I'll just put my things away while you go do that."

Seth went back to his room and opened his suitcase, grateful for a few minutes away from Megan.

Who was…awesome. Amazing. Gorgeous. Funny. Strong.

The adjectives just kept coming. From that first moment he'd set eyes on her, he'd known there was something very different about her. Something that made him want to stop, enjoy, enjoy some more.

And then when she'd come to Wingman Security, both that first afternoon and then that evening, for the party, he'd been even more intrigued. Wasn't generally a big proponent of fate but it did seem a bit wild that circumstances had thrown them together.

When they'd been running, she was a joy to watch. Her body was firm and graceful and it had been a total turn-on to run alongside her. And when she'd slipped, his heart had skipped a beat until he'd known that he'd been fast enough and she was safe.

And then he'd almost really screwed up. He'd been this close to kissing her. Had stopped. Told himself that it was wrong to complicate their relationship and give her any reason to be wary that he wasn't 100 percent professional. But the real reason was that she was all wrong for him.

She'd ended a serious relationship with someone that she'd obviously cared about—because he wouldn't stop flying. There was no future for them because he sure as hell wasn't ever going to stop.

But the physical attraction was pulling at him, making him needy. He'd been so damn nonchalant when he'd been holding her underwear. It had taken every acting skill he'd had.

He heard her phone ring. In three steps he was back in her room.

She picked it up. "This is Megan North."

She listened for a minute then said, "That will be fine. I'll meet you in the lobby. Thank you for calling." She put her phone down.

"The police?" he asked.

"Yes. They should be here in about fifteen minutes."

"Let's get to the lobby."

Once there, she took a seat on the couch and Seth wandered off to a far corner, cell phone in hand. He stood where he could see her at all times.

It was only ten minutes before an officer wearing very dark blue pants and shirt came through the door. Megan gave him a little wave and he veered in their direction. When he got closer, Seth guessed him at close to forty and married, given that he wore a wedding ring. That did not stop him from giving Megan a look that Seth recognized: sincere appreciation.

"Ms. North?" he said. When she nodded, he pulled a card from his breast pocket. "Officer Indeego."

They shook hands. She turned in Seth's direction. "This is my associate, Seth Pike. I'd like him to stay while we talk."

"Fine. Maybe over there," he said, motioning to an empty table in the area where they'd eaten breakfast. All the food had been cleared away and there were no other guests lingering nearby. Someone from the hotel staff was restocking paper products but didn't seem terribly interested in them.

"What can I help you with?" the officer asked once they were all seated.

"I want to make a report," Megan said. She launched into her story, succinctly summarizing all the events she'd previously shared with Seth and then describing the snake incident.

When she was finished, Officer Indeego remained silent. He'd been taking notes and it appeared that he was reviewing them. He looked up. "You said there's video of the person letting the snake loose outside your door?"

"Yes. Jase Hall, the manager of the hotel, has it. He showed it to us this morning. His office is behind the registration desk."

"I know Jase," he said. "Our kids play on the same baseball team."

Seth didn't know if that was good or bad. Jase Hall would likely be inclined to be cooperative with someone that he'd see at the ballpark, but would he also be comfortable asking Officer Indeego to keep the investigation to a minimum to avoid any bad press for the hotel?

"The initial report indicated that you're only in Sedona for a couple days," Office Indeego said. "Is that correct?"

"Yes. I'm here to do a grand opening of a store. We have a couple private events today and tonight, and then I'll be at the store tomorrow. Then late tomorrow, I'll be leaving for Albuquerque."

"The number I called you at earlier is the best number to reach you at?" the man asked.

"Yes."

He stood up. "If I have any questions or have anything to share, I'll contact you."

It was probably as good a promise as they were going to get. And Seth realized it was likely they weren't going to hear from the officer again. He would have a discussion with Jase Hall, would probably look at the videotape and then wouldn't do much with it. It was an isolated incident and nobody had been hurt. In any police department, it would get very little attention especially because Megan was moving on.

No longer his problem.

But still, Seth felt it was the right thing to have done to report it to law enforcement. Now there was a record of it. If nothing else, another set of eyes on the videotape, proving that it existed. "We asked Mr. Hall for a copy of the videotape but he wouldn't provide it, indicating that it was hotel property. I didn't want to force the issue as long as we can be assured that it will be secured by the police department in the event that we need to view it again or use it as evidence," Seth said.

"Okay," said the cop.

It wasn't a resounding *yes, I'll make sure of that* but again, it was probably the best they were going to get.

Megan glanced at her watch and he knew they were cutting it close to get to the luncheon on time. "Thank you, Officer Indeego," he said. Seth extended his hand.

The cop returned the shake and in turn, shook hands with Megan. Then he turned and walked up to the registration desk. Seth wanted to wait, to see if he actually talked to Jase Hall, but knew that wouldn't endear them to the cop. Plus, they needed to go.

But before that, they needed to do one more thing. "We need to get our bags out of our rooms," he said.

She pursed her lips. "We're staying here one more night."

"We're staying in Sedona, but we're not staying here."

Chapter 8

"That's what I was doing while we were waiting for the police," Seth said. "Calling hotels. Lana was right in that the town is pretty booked up but I was able to find two rooms." Most hotels kept a few rooms back for emergencies. His offer to pay a premium for the space must have qualified as that.

"You didn't say anything to the manager about us leaving. Or to Officer Indeego."

"That's right. We're not going to say anything. Not going to check out. That means that you'll get charged for the room so Wingman Security will cover the cost of the second set of rooms."

She was looking at him rather wide-eyed. "Do you really think all of this is necessary?"

"I have no idea. But I'm not feeling too kindly toward this space. My gut is telling me to go. And in general, I've got a good gut. There's no risk to leaving. If Officer

Indeego needs to contact us, he's going to use our cell phone numbers. There could be risk to staying. It seems like an easy decision."

"But..."

"Let's review what we know. Last night, in a hotel that was reserved by your assistant, a person released a snake that slithered under your door."

"Do you have to use the word *slithered*?" she asked, swallowing hard.

"Slipped? Ducked in?"

"Just go on," she said.

"The hotel has Snake Charmer on video in the hallway and exiting the hotel but, according to Jase Hall, nothing that shows him arriving last night. So either he arrived looking different and Jase is easily fooled, which is possible, or he was in place before that. There are a whole lot of hotels in Sedona, so that seems unlikely to have happened by chance."

She let the words settle. "So what you're saying or implying, at least, is that Snake Charmer got the information about where we were staying from the person who made the hotel reservation?"

"I'm saying that we shouldn't discount that possibility. How well do you know your assistant?"

"Very well. She's worked with Abigail and me for years."

"What's her name?"

"Why?"

"Because I think it makes sense to take a look at her. If there's nothing there, great. She'll never be the wiser."

"That's not necessary. We did a background check."

"I'm sure you did. Criminal background, probably. Maybe even a financial check, since she was in a trusted position. All that's good if you've hired a criminal. But not so effective when you've hired somebody decent who is later *motivated* to do something not so decent. And those motivations come in all sizes and shapes. Too much debt. Bad family. Alcohol or drug dependencies. Gambling addictions. Our background checks don't look at numbers and statistics. We talk to people, we watch, we look at online activity. We look at their environment."

"It sounds intrusive."

"Wingman Security can be very discreet."

"I hate the idea."

He shrugged. "If we rule her out, then we don't need to think about her anymore."

He could easily find out their assistant's name. And if he was going to do this, she didn't want him operating behind her back. "Fine. Gillian O'Day."

"Thank you. Who else would have access to your itinerary?"

She considered the question. "Abigail, of course. But she would never do anything to harm me."

"We'll assume she's clear," he said.

"Thank you so much," she said, sarcastically. "I suppose it's possible, maybe even likely, that she's told her husband. But really, I think you'd be barking up the wrong tree."

"That's very possible," he said agreeably. "But there are other ways that people get information. Maybe somebody hacked into the assistant's computer? Or your brother-in-law's?"

She couldn't immediately dismiss that. Everyone was getting hacked all the time. "I suppose that's possible."

"I'm going to order background checks on Gillian O'Day and Evan Chevalier." He picked up his phone.

"Not wasting any time," she said.

"Nope," he said, his tone pleasant.

She rubbed her temples. "I'm sorry. I really do not need to be a bitch about this. I know that you're just doing your job. Doing what we hired you to do."

He stared at her. "That's right. It's my job."

The air seemed very still and even though they were in the middle of a busy hotel lobby, it seemed as if they were very alone. "Then I'll back off and let you do it," she said. "But are we going to book double hotel rooms for the rest of the trip? That's going to get pretty expensive. It will eat into Wingman Security's profit margin."

"We won't double-book. We'll be able to cancel the other existing reservations and replace them. But we're going to keep that to ourselves. I'll work on finding us new hotels in Albuquerque and Colorado Springs later."

"I guess I'll get my suitcase then."

"If the maid hasn't been in yet, we'll put signs on our doors asking not to be disturbed. That should avoid the problem of housekeeping realizing that we're gone."

"You're really very good at this," she said.

He waved a hand. "Child's play."

Ten minutes later, their suitcases were in the trunk and they were pulling out of the parking lot. She pulled the directions to the fashion show up on her phone.

It took them about fifteen minutes. The destination was a big old house, three stories high, surrounded by lovely gardens. Next to it was a law office and then a yoga studio. Across the street were houses with little kids playing in the front yard. It was clearly a street that was zoned both commercial and residential, but the businesses kept their signage discreet and their properties blended in.

He was just about to open his car door when Megan's phone rang.

"It's Abigail." Emotion flashed in her eyes and he was pretty sure it was fear.

"Hi," she said, snatching up the phone. "Everything okay?"

She must have gotten immediate reassurance because the tension in her face relaxed. "Oh, I'm doing well," she said after a minute.

She listened. Then, "Yes, it's…fine. He's…an easy traveling companion."

Was he a dog or a maiden aunt?

"We're just on our way to the luncheon and fashion show at the Women's Art Club. I'll send you a text later and let you know how it goes."

She listened. "Love you, too. Talk to you soon," she said before she ended the call.

"You didn't tell her about the snake?" he said, choosing to let her description of him go. For the time being.

"Of course not," she said.

"Because you don't want to worry her."

"Because…it's been reported to the police and it's in their hands now. And you're doing your thing so it seems as if we've got it covered."

She sounded tired. "Very true," he said.

"I sure as heck am not going to tell her that you're doing a background check on Evan. You better be discreet."

"We are. Shall we?" He reached again for the door.

"Just a second," she said.

He settled back into his seat.

"We need to talk about how we're going to play this," she said.

"Play?" he repeated.

"You know what I mean. People are going to want to know who you are and what you're doing."

"We tell them that I'm providing security. One, it's the truth so it won't be hard to remember. And two, it sends a clear message to anybody who wants to screw with you that you're no longer alone in this. And I understand that while you see me as…merely a comfortable traveling companion, that others might actually see me as somebody they don't want to go up against."

Her cheeks turned pink. "I didn't mean to insult you."

"Not insulted. It takes a great deal more than that."

"Well, fine. Of course, they'll see you…as something. You're six feet of muscle and you have a gun."

Better than *comfortable.*

"But they're going to wonder why I need security. Especially if you act as if I'm the president, you're Secret Service and you're just waiting to take a bullet for me."

"That could have happened the other night," he said, feeling compelled to point out the obvious.

"I know that," she said, her voice almost a hiss. "Listen, I can't become the story. Because if I do, then Abigail finds out and that would be horrific. The boutique openings are the story."

He could feel his back teeth grinding together. "She's not a child," he said. "I suspect she could handle the truth."

"After the baby is born," Megan said. "I'll tell her everything. After that."

He looked out his window. Settled himself. "I'll do the very best I can not to smother you. But you need to do your best to cooperate a hundred percent and to not question or hesitate if I tell you to do something."

"Fine."

Oh, they were back to that. "Here's a couple basic commands." He held up his hand.

"I know that one," she said. "Stop."

"Halt," he corrected. "Stay in place."

He raised an index finger. "One." Added his middle

finger. "Two." And finally, his ring finger. "Three. On three you go. No hesitation."

"Go where?"

"Proceed. Whatever it is that I'm telling you to do, it's your sign to move. Give it everything you've got."

"Got it. On the count of three, go," she said.

"It sounds easier than it is in real life sometimes," he said.

"I'll do the best I can," she said. "Now, I'm not going to count to three, but it really is time for us to go."

Once inside the Women's Art Club, they met Mary Trove, the president of the group. She was early sixties, trim with short gray hair and dressed in all black. "We're so delighted to have you here, Ms. North and Mr. Pike. Tickets have sold out for the show. All 175. In fact," she said with a smile, "just this morning I heard that there was some ticket bartering going on. A few people got contacted about the possibility of selling their tickets for a nice profit."

That made the hair on the back of Seth's neck stand up. Somebody was trying to get into a *fashion show* at the last minute. What was the likelihood of that? Could it have anything to do with Snake Charmer? "Did they make a deal?" Seth asked.

"I don't think so," Mary Trove said. "Nobody wanted to give up their seat."

He didn't feel much better. She couldn't possibly know about everybody who'd been contacted. Maybe one of them had indeed taken the cash.

"Lunch is in our dining room." Mary Trove waved her hand in the direction of a large room at the end of the hallway. When they stepped through the doors, he saw a small group. He quickly counted. Fourteen, not including him and Megan. All women. He relaxed a little. Not because a woman couldn't be every bit as dangerous as a man but he was fairly confident that the person on the video had been a man.

For fifteen minutes, they mingled. Mary Trove introduced them to every attendee. Then they were finally in seats. Salads were already on the table and soon, a young woman in a white shirt and black pants carried out plates of chicken and rice.

"No tea sandwiches," Megan said softly from the corner of her mouth.

"There's always tomorrow," he answered.

The food was decent and he finished his. Megan ate about half. It was likely all she had time to do. She was busy answering questions about the store and the outfits that they'd be wearing. She was totally charming.

At one point, a woman three chairs down leaned forward. "Mr. Pike, what is your role in the fashion show?"

"I'm handy to have around. Lifting and toting are my specialties," he said easily.

"I've got an extra ticket for my next trip to the Bahamas," said a woman who had to be at least seventy. "I have very heavy suitcases. Say the word and it's yours."

That cracked up the table and he realized that the luncheon hadn't been nearly as painful as he'd been expecting. They finished up with chocolate cream pie and then it was downstairs into the auditorium. They had forty-five minutes to get set up.

Megan tested the audio and the video. He found all the exits, counted the rows and the numbers of chairs in each row.

"What are you doing?" she asked, looking up.

"Orienting myself to the room. I want to be able to negotiate the space in complete darkness. If I know how many rows and how many chairs in a row, I can run my hand across the backs of the chairs and know immediately where I'm at in the room. And how many steps away I am from the exit."

He could read her face. *Overkill.* "Has this habit paid off for you in the past?" she asked.

"The ability to navigate quietly and quickly in the dark saved my life in Afghanistan when an unfriendly with a big-ass gun and a bad attitude had a different idea."

"I see. Count away," she added, looking back at her notes.

And as the time grew close, he watched as every single person came through the door. While not forgetting Megan's belief that a blond-haired man had followed her twice, he focused on body type, knowing that hair and clothes were easy to modify. Height and weight were much harder to change. He was looking for somebody who was roughly five-eight or -nine and about one hundred and fifty pounds. Unfortunately, by the time the doors shut and the seats were full, at least 25 percent of the 175 ticket holders fell into that category. And most of them were women. The three men who fit the description all had dark hair.

He wanted to stop Megan, to ask her to take a closer look, but she had already kicked off the show. So he watched the crowd. And felt his heart start to beat faster when one of the three men in question reached into his suit coat pocket and pulled out a…

Phone. He was taking a picture. It was likely his wife on the runway.

There was a woman wearing a press lanyard around her neck taking pictures, too. He suspected Megan photographed well. The crowd was captivated as she introduced each model, explained what the woman was wearing, talking about fabric, its swing and stretch and how it might travel. Then there were the accessories: earrings, bracelets, necklaces, belts and scarves. For some of the pieces, she shared an anecdote about how the design had come together. For others, she talked about things like style and trend and classic lines. The models were all ages, with the youngest being in her teens to the oldest probably in her seventies. And they were all shapes, too.

She was brilliant, he thought. She was making sure that every woman in the crowd could see herself in an outfit from North and More Designs. The models looked as if they were having a great time, as did the crowd.

Finally, the hour show came to a close. Megan thanked the crowd for their generous donation to the charity and they funneled out. Then she spent a few minutes with the person with the press credentials.

Mary Trove hovered in the corner, stepping up immediately when the reporter stepped away. She hugged Megan. "That was wonderful," the woman said. "I had very high expectations and you exceeded them. Thank you so much."

"It was my pleasure," Megan said.

And he thought she was likely telling the truth. Finally, she turned to him. "I'm going to step backstage," she said. "I want to thank the models."

"Okay." He took a step that direction.

"You can't come," she said, smiling. "They're going to be changing clothes."

Him barging into the dressing room was probably not the kind of news coverage she was hoping for. But his job was to provide security. At all times. Everywhere. "How long do you need?"

"Five minutes," she said.

"Fine," he said, using her word when she wasn't thrilled

but had decided to go along. "I'll stand outside the door," he said. "Yell if you need me. At five minutes and five seconds, I'm coming in."

She was back in four and a half minutes. "Not willing to chance it?" he asked under his breath. There were still people milling around.

"Not one bit," she said.

They walked back to the car and got inside. Megan started it and turned the air-conditioning on high. Still, it was stifling hot after sitting in the sun for a couple hours. He felt like a piece of wilted lettuce and she looked…as good as ever. "Nice job," he said.

"Want to buy a dress?" she asked, her tone joking.

"I'm giving consideration to my color palette right now. I'll get back to you."

"I always have an order form available," she said.

It was fun to tease her. But they still had serious things to think about. "Can you check your phone and see if the police have called with an update or any questions?"

"Sure." She opened her purse. "No," she said. "Nothing."

In his gut, he was fairly confident that the responding officer wasn't going to do much. They'd seen him at the registration desk, could assume he'd had a conversation with Jase Hall and hopefully watched the video, but beyond that, how much time was he really going to invest in the case?

"Now what?" he asked.

"Now we drive over to the store, where the manager will be having an all-staff meeting in—" she looked at her watch "—about twenty minutes. I imagine you know the drill. Last-minute instructions, making sure everybody has a handle on procedures and practices, and a basic pep talk. My job is to add the final rah-rah."

"A cheerleader, then?"

"I've carried my share of pom-poms. All through high school for football and basketball. I had a crush on the quarterback, who was also the starting forward on the basketball team."

He could see her in a short skirt and tight sweater. And every corny movie he'd ever seen with a sexy cheerleader was flashing through his brain at warp speed. "And did he have a crush on you?"

"He did."

It was pretty crazy to be jealous of a teenager and something that had happened when she was in high school. "Did the romance survive graduation?"

She smiled. "It didn't even survive spring of my senior year. Once basketball season ended, my allure evidently faded. He asked my best friend to go to prom."

"Idiot," he said.

She shrugged. "Best thing that could have happened. I'd have probably stayed home and gone to the junior college because that's where he was headed. Instead, I left home and went to school in Savannah for fashion management. That's where I met Logan."

"I've spent a little time in Savannah. Nice place."

"I loved it," she said. "I mean, I enjoyed my program and learned a lot, but it was the city that I really missed when…I left."

"Do you regret that?" he asked. "Not finishing?"

"I finished my degree. At night. One class a semester. Took five years, but I did it. I knew it was important for me to do that but, quite frankly, it paled in comparison to the importance of…other things."

"Raising Abigail?"

"Nothing was more important than that."

She pulled out of their parking space and eased the

car into traffic. Fifteen minutes later, they were parked in front of North and More Designs. The sign looked brand-new. The store looked…well, not like very much. There was brown paper in the windows, just like in the Vegas property. "You're not still under construction here?" he asked, pointing.

"Oh, no. I've seen photos—it's ready to go. We didn't do as much remodeling here since we're renting this space. More cosmetic than anything. The paper will come out of the windows tomorrow, in time for the grand opening. Let's go," she said.

She was excited. He didn't blame her.

Once they were inside, he was quickly introduced to Jasmine Pajo, the operations manager who had responsibility for the Sedona store, as well as the Albuquerque and Colorado Springs stores.

"This is Seth Pike," Megan said. "He's providing security services."

"Good to meet you, Seth. I'm hoping we need crowd control services," Jasmine said, her dark eyes dancing. She was a stunning black woman wearing something that he wasn't sure if it was an oversize shirt and loose pants or a long dress, but it was a swirl of oranges and reds when she walked.

He sucked at fashion.

"The team is all here," Jasmine said. "In our combination break room–slash–conference room, which might have to triple up as inventory storage because we're about bursting at the seams with merchandise."

He glanced around. There was a lot of merchandise but they'd done a good job of keeping space free to walk around. And while the racks were full, they weren't so crowded that a shopper couldn't easily see what was there. When he commented as much to Megan, she smiled.

"We made a decision early on that we'd only have front-facing racks where the clothes hang facing out, versus having racks where hangers are lined up side by side and you can't really see the item until you pull it from the rack. We can display less but it makes for a prettier store and a nicer shopping experience for our guests."

Megan greeted everyone as they entered the break room. He counted heads. Nine women and one man. They were gathered around a table in the middle of the room. There was an open seat at the head of the table and one in the middle.

Megan took the one in the middle. Classy. All the way. He took a spot leaning against the back wall, where he could see Megan and the door.

They spent a little time on introductions and Seth basically tuned them out until he heard something that got his interest. One of the women had worked for J.T. Daly's, the competitor that North and More Designs had bested. He glanced at Megan but could read nothing on her face to suggest that she was remotely concerned about her new employee's work history.

When it was his turn, he kept it simple. "Seth Pike. I'm consulting with Megan on security."

Nobody asked any questions. He supposed that was a sign of the times. Now people just assumed that security was as necessary as lights and running water.

The meeting went for about an hour, with Megan doing the final ten minutes. She was enthusiastic, optimistic and supportive. She closed by reminding them to attend that evening's cocktail reception as honored guests. It was a perfect rah-rah speech.

And she got a round of applause when it was done. The group filed out. Six of the ten would work tomorrow, with the other four having shifts later in the week.

Chloé Dawson, the prior employee of J.T. Daly's, would be opening the store at ten the next morning, along with Megan and Jasmine. The others assigned to opening day would arrive in staggered shifts to ensure coverage until nine tomorrow night.

Once everybody was gone except Megan and Jasmine, he cornered Megan in the conference room. "Hey, did you know that Chloé Dawson had worked for J.T. Daly's?"

She nodded. "She has great experience. I think that's why Jasmine is having her open with us tomorrow."

"You're not concerned?"

"Of course not. It was Jasmine's decision to hire her but I applaud it. We should never turn our back on great talent."

"You don't think it's an odd coincidence?"

"No. I think it was nice happenstance that she was available when we were hiring."

"I'm going to add her to the list of people that we run background checks on."

She rolled her eyes. "I'm suddenly very glad that we paid a set fee for your services. If it was by the activity, I might go broke." She looked at her watch. "We need to get going. I have to change before dinner and then we'll go directly from there to the cocktail party. Like I said earlier, no black tie tonight."

"I'm still trying to get over the disappointment," he said.

"The use of silverware, though, is required," she said, her tone teasing.

"I've been practicing."

Chapter 9

Dinner was with the executive director of the Downtown Association and his wife and the mayor's chief of staff and her husband. Both the executive director and the mayor's chief of staff had been very persuasive when the opportunity to buy the struggling group of stores first came along. It was amazing to think it had been over a year ago that they'd first started having conversations.

Seth did not eat his peas with a knife or tuck his napkin into his shirt collar. Just the opposite. His manners were flawless and he was charming. Once they found out that he was former military, they had a thousand questions. Seth offered up fun anecdotes about his years in the air force without making it look like anything but what it was—serious and difficult work being done by serious and committed people.

They left dinner and drove directly to the cocktail reception, which was in a private room at a hotel. Seth was noticeably quieter in the car. "I thought that went well," she said.

"Nice people," he agreed.

"Is something wrong?" she asked.

"Nope. Just thinking about the next event."

She supposed she should be happy that he was so focused on providing security for her. But it was a stark reminder that while dinner had been fun, from his perspective, it was all part of the assignment.

They did valet parking and once inside the hotel, found their way to the party. Jasmine and her husband were already there and a couple other people she didn't recognize. Six steps in, a cocktail server approached.

"I'll have a glass of chardonnay," she said.

"Water with a twist of lime," he said.

When the woman left to get the drinks, she turned to him. "You can have a drink," she said.

He shook his head.

"Do you not drink?" she asked.

"Not when I'm working."

There it was again. Work. "Right." She offered up a smile as Jasmine walked over, her hand on a man's arm. She didn't think she knew him.

"Hello, Megan."

She immediately recognized the accent and knew who he was. Weston Marberry. His firm had negotiated the leases on the Sedona, Albuquerque and Colorado Springs properties and the purchase of the Vegas building. She'd spoken to him several times on the phone and had enjoyed his accent. *He's from Australia*, Jasmine had confided after the first call. Her manager had known him since they were in college and had, in fact, recommended his firm for the job.

"We finally can put a face to it," she said, extending her hand.

"And a gorgeous one it is." He ignored her hand and leaned in to hug her. "No need for formality. I feel as if we're best buds," he said.

He'd pulled her close enough that she could smell alcohol on his breath. And he held her a minute too long. "Of course," she said, taking half a step back. His firm had done excellent work and to date, he'd always been very professional. "Allow me to introduce you to Seth Pike, an associate of mine. Seth, Weston Marberry. Weston's firm negotiated our lease arrangements."

The two men sized each other up. She wondered what they were thinking. They were both handsome, fit, smart. Successful. Then she thought about Seth, in his underwear, umbrella in hand, flinging the snake across the room. And how fast he'd reacted when their cab was being shot at.

Advantage, Pike. Definitely.

"An associate," Weston said, repeating her introduction. "What is it that you do for North and More Designs?"

"Security."

Weston nodded. Looked thoughtful. "Well, that's certainly a necessary evil these days."

"As are lawyers," Seth said.

The air seemed to sizzle with a dangerous energy. She put her hand on Seth's arm. His head jerked up and she realized that it was the first time that she'd initiated contact. "There's someone I want you to meet," she lied. "Weston, we'll catch up later. So glad that you're here."

When they were five feet away, Seth leaned close. "We weren't going to come to blows."

"Testosterone is a dangerous thing," she said.

He smiled. "I think he's had a few pops tonight."

"I think you're right," she said. "Hopefully, he'll find the buffet and get some food in him."

"Is there really somebody you want me to meet?" he asked.

"No."

"Okay. Then I'm going to find a spot where it's easier for me to watch the room and the door. Please don't leave this area without letting me know."

"Okay." He was trying to accommodate her request that he not hover and cause a distraction or a need for a thousand explanations. So why, then, did she feel so alone when he walked away?

Because she was an idiot.

Who needed to keep her head in the game. She drew in a deep breath and pasted a smile on her face.

The next ninety minutes flew by. Even so, by the end of the night, her feet hurt. But now, there were fewer than ten people left in the room. She could leave.

She looked across the room, at Seth, who'd spent his night on a stool at the far end of the bar, sitting at an angle where he could see the room but still rest a forearm on the solid wood. Every time she'd looked throughout the night, there'd been a clear-colored drink with a wedge of lime in front of him. A casual observer would have thought he was enjoying a nice vodka on the rocks.

Also, every time she'd looked, he'd acknowledged her with an almost imperceptible nod. *I'm watching*, it seemed to say. *All is well.*

And it had been enough that she'd had a really great time.

When she got close, she said, "Were you bored to death?"

He shook his head. "Did pick up a bartending trick or

two. I think I may invest in cranberries—lots going on with that juice."

"Did you try any of the food?"

He shook his head. "Wasn't hungry and it's hard to react fast if you've got a plate of shrimp in one hand and a chocolate-dipped strawberry in the other. Both of which, by the way, looked delicious."

"They did, didn't they?" she said, happy that everything had been just perfect. "But my feet are telling me that it's been a long day."

"You don't have to turn the lights off?" he asked, insinuating that she needed to stay to the bitter end.

"Nope. Jasmine and I already discussed that she'd close out the event. I do need to make sure she knows that I'm leaving." She looked around the room and saw her very talented manager. "I'll go do that and find the ladies' room and then we're out of here."

"I'll meet you by the front door," he said.

Jasmine and her husband were chatting with another couple, and Megan, not wanting to intrude, decided to visit the ladies' room first. On her way out, she ran into Weston Marberry, who was exiting the men's room. They would have collided. Instead, they both awkwardly veered and he wrapped a hand around her bare arm to steady her. "Careful. Or you're going to need a good attorney. How'd we keep missing each other all night?"

His accent was a little more pronounced. "I don't know," she said, which was a lie, because she'd very carefully avoided him all night, not wanting to have exactly this moment. Throughout the night, she'd seen cocktail servers bringing him lots of fresh drinks.

She'd enjoyed her working relationship with the man and didn't want that to change.

She pulled her arm away and he let go easily. But then

he took a step forward, backing her up against the wall. He was tall enough that when he extended his arm from his shoulder and flattened his hand against the wall, he effectively trapped her in.

He wasn't touching her but was definitely in her space. "Great party," he said.

"Thank you." She was rapidly clicking through the best ways to delicately extricate herself when Weston's body suddenly jerked backward.

"Hey," Weston puffed.

"Hey," she echoed, her eyes on Seth, who had pulled Weston back and still appeared to have a death grip on the back of Weston's neck.

"Everything okay here?" Seth asked. In a second, his eyes traveled from her face down to her toes and back up again.

"Fine," she said.

Seth nodded and let go of Weston, who still looked a little stunned.

"What the hell?" Weston said.

Seth said nothing.

Megan had the feeling that if Weston was waiting for an apology, he was going to need a chair because it might be quite a while before hell froze over. She locked eyes with Seth. "We should go," she said, pushing away from the wall.

"Megan?" Weston said.

"We'll talk soon," she said. "Good night."

She could see Seth's body stiffen at the words but he didn't say anything. She saw Jasmine across the room, waved to get her attention and motioned that she was leaving. Jasmine nodded and smiled in return.

In minutes, she and Seth were outside and the valet had brought their car around. She got in the driver's seat and had pulled away from the curb before Seth finally said something.

"I'm sorry if I interrupted a moment."

"There was no moment," she snapped, irritated that she was now going to have to explain something that she hadn't initiated or even fully participated in. "He's drunk."

"Would have been a shame if he'd puked on that expensive suit. Is that the guy you want representing your legal interests?"

"He's been so professional on the phone. I don't know what happened tonight. It was…well, really just super awkward," she admitted. "I guess I'm thankful that you barged in."

He turned to look at her. "I do not barge. I stealthfully approach."

She smiled. "Is that a word? *Stealthfully?*"

"In my world."

"Then I stand corrected. No barging, only stealth." She ran her hand through her hair. "Listen, let's just forget about it. I need some sleep before tomorrow."

"I've got the directions to the hotel on my phone," he said.

It took them just under fifteen minutes. When they pulled in to the parking lot, she thought they might be out of luck because every space seemed full. But then she spied a spot at the end of a row that would work.

Inside, she started to pull her credit card but stopped when he put a hand on her arm. "I've got this," he said.

She closed her purse. Five minutes later, they were on their way to the seventh floor. Like before, he checked her room first and made sure the connecting door was unlocked. "What time do we need to be at the store?" he asked.

"We open at ten. I'd like to be there by nine thirty."

"Running in the morning?" he asked.

"Yes. Same place as this morning?"

"Probably not. But I'll find us a spot."

"Are we changing it up for a specific reason?" she asked.

He shrugged. "I just think that we don't need to be too predictable."

Different hotel. Different running path. He'd probably have her change the location of the boutique if it wasn't impossible. "Okay. I'll meet you in the hallway at six thirty. That should give us enough time for a run and a shower before we leave here at nine fifteen."

"Got to fit breakfast in, too."

She wasn't going to win this one. "Six, then. Good night."

When Seth got to his room, he sat on the bed and read through the emails that had come in from Wingman Security. The background checks on Gillian O'Day and Evan Chevalier were in process. So far, the basics had been verified.

Gillian O'Day had graduated from college six years earlier, with a master's degree in fashion merchandising. He reread that sentence. If she had an advanced degree, why was she working in an administrative capacity to Megan and Abigail? There could be a number of reasons, he supposed. Maybe she liked the administrative side of the business. It wasn't a red flag, but perhaps a yellow, and worthy of some follow-up. Evan Chevalier had an undergraduate degree in business management and had joined the investment company that his father worked at as a junior adviser. It reeked of nepotism but certainly wasn't illegal.

He clicked out of his mail and dialed Royce's number. "Hey, Seth," the man answered. "How's it going?"

"I spent my afternoon at a fashion show and my evening at a cocktail party where most of the conversation was about fashion."

"Are you still sane?"

"I'm not confident of that. I can talk to you about washable silk fabrics if you'd like."

"Don't threaten me, Seth," Royce said.

"Listen, I appreciate the quick work on the O'Day and the Chevalier backgrounds."

"No problem. We split the assignment up. Trey was taking on Gillian O'Day and Rico had Evan Chevalier. They'll get into the weeds tomorrow. More info to come." He paused. "Did something happen to initiate these checks?"

Seth told him about the snake and the person in the hallway. "We have no idea if this is some kind of hoax but I'd really like to understand what this guy's game is. There's been some other weird things happening in her life that make it seem as if she might have a stalker."

"Does all this have anything to do with the shots fired at the Periwinkle?"

"It might. We don't know. I do have another name for a background check. Chloé Dawson. I'll text you her details tomorrow."

"I'll watch for it. I have to say, Seth, that this assignment is going a little differently than I imagined. I was worried that you'd be bored with boutique life," he said.

"I'm not bored. Megan is..." He didn't want to say too much. Wasn't ready to yet. "Let's just say that I want to help her with this."

"You sound...fond of her."

"There's plenty of appeal," he admitted. "You should see her underwear."

Royce coughed. “You have?”

“Extensively,” Seth said. Let him stew on that. “Good night.”

The morning went as planned. Good run. Hot shower. Decent hotel breakfast that they were just finishing up.

The night had been uneventful. Well, that is, if one discounted the importance of sleep. He’d tossed, turned and ended up watching an old Western on television. Finally, he’d slept.

He’d awakened before his phone alarm sounded, slipped out of bed and opened the connecting door.

She’d kicked the covers off sometime during the night. No doubt because her room was too warm. She was on her stomach, with one arm under her pillow, the other thrown above her head. Her nightgown had ridden up in the back, giving him an excellent view of one of the panties that he’d pawed through the day before.

They looked even better on.

Her legs and butt were firm from the miles she jogged. And silky smooth. And he couldn’t seem to take his eyes away. But then she’d rolled over.

Like a turtle retreating back into his shell, but significantly faster, he’d ducked back into his room. She’d have felt real safe if she knew that he was ogling her.

Now she was pretending to eat a cinnamon roll and a few grapes. “Pretty psyched, huh?” he asked.

She nodded. “This has been two years in the making. Long before we had the locations, we had the idea. So many meetings,” she said, dragging the word out. “Long meetings. Short meetings. Hallway meetings. Meetings before the meeting. Meetings after the meeting. Virtual meetings.”

“I get it,” he said.

"I'm a little freaked out," she said, her voice soft. "I really, really want this to be successful. So much so that I'm feeling a little sick right now. It might have been easier to simply work for somebody else."

He nodded. "Leave the office at five and not take any of the headaches home."

She shrugged. "I've worked for a couple different companies. I never left at five and many nights, I lost some sleep trying to solve a problem."

"Is it the money?"

"Maybe." She laughed nervously. "Of course that's part of it. I mean, we've sunk a lot of our personal resources into this and borrowed more. So, yeah. I'd hate to lose that."

"But it's something else," he said, finishing up his coffee.

"I've been designing clothes under other labels for ten years. This is the first time that it will be my own label. Abigail believes in it. I think I do. I don't want us both to be wrong."

"I doubt you're wrong," he said.

She looked at her hands. "Abigail and I have the resources to do this because of our parents. They were big believers in life insurance."

"I suspect they'd be very proud," he said.

"I hope so," she said. "At first, I was reluctant to use the money. But Abigail convinced me that it would make them really happy to know that the money was being used to build a future for both of us."

"No pressure, right?" he said. "Look, I know less than nothing about fashion. But based on what I saw at the fashion show yesterday, I think people are really excited about your store. I think you're going to be a great success."

"I've been dreaming about the day that we'd open the North and More Designs boutiques. Of course, I always envisioned that it would be me and Abigail. Definitely hadn't seen you in the picture."

"Your dream is coming true," he said.

"Oh, I hope not. Most of the time, my dreams have been terrible. Something is always wrong. Everything from the store has no clothes to the cash registers won't open to the place is flooded with customers but somehow, someway, we're not able to help any of them."

"Just nerves. You know that's not really going to happen."

"Last night I dreamed that every single customer who tried on an outfit was unable to zip or button said outfit—it didn't matter what size they tried. On the hanger, the clothes looked as if they'd surely fit. However, once the customer pulled the clothing on, it shrank, to a size appropriate for a toddler."

He laughed, then quickly sobered when he saw that she was dead serious. "There's not much in life that I'm absolutely certain of. But I'm going to go out on a limb and guarantee that nothing similar to that will happen. There may be trouble with zippers and buttons but clothes will not miraculously shrink."

"I hope you're right. Nor spontaneously combust, I hope."

"You dreamed that, too?" he asked.

"Just once." She pushed her half-eaten cinnamon roll away. "Look, we should be going."

"You didn't eat much."

She waved a hand. "I'll eat later. I've got some sandwiches getting delivered to the boutique. Wishful thinking that we won't have time to get out for lunch."

"That's better—half-full thinking."

"Don't say half anything. One of my dreams was that we unpacked boxes and somehow every piece of clothing got sliced in half."

He smiled. "You know what I think your problem is?"

"I have no idea."

"You're creative. And you just can't shut it down. Even when you sleep."

"What's the opposite of creative?" she asked.

"I don't know. Noncreative. Dull."

"I want to be dull. For eight hours every night."

Nobody who looked like she did in bed would ever be accused of being dull. "Good luck with that."

Chapter 10

The sandwiches arrived just after noon. Megan scribbled her name on the charge slip and carried them back to the break area and slid them into the fridge. But she was way too busy to eat.

Most of the women who had been in the fashion show came. And they brought friends. And other people came, smartphones in hand, with their 20-percent-off coupon at the ready.

Chloé worked the cash register and Jasmine greeted people as they came in and offered up dressing rooms. That allowed Megan to chat with and help those customers interested in the North and More Designs collection.

At two, when there was finally a small break, she felt a tap on her shoulder. Seth. Who'd managed to be fairly unobtrusive although she suspected that every woman in the store had noticed the handsome man. "You should eat something," he said.

"I probably could now," she said, looking around. "Let

me make sure that Chloé and Jasmine have had something."

"They have. It's your turn."

"If you'll come with me," she said. "You've got to be starving."

"I could eat," he admitted. "It seems to me that almost everybody who has come in has bought something."

"I know. That's the goal. When Abigail and I went to market, we tried to always focus on quality first and then once we had that, we also made sure that we could offer merchandise at three different price points. A less expensive, a moderate, and then…well…pricier. The two-hundred-dollar sweater isn't right for everyone; I want people to know that there's something here for them."

"Smart," he said. "'Went to market,'" he repeated. "What's that?"

"There are major fashion shows each year, in various cities, where vendors have booths and product samples. Vegas is actually one of the biggest. Abigail and I attended multiple shows last year and purchased the merchandise that you're seeing hanging in the store today. Going to market is exhausting. You're looking at clothes and accessories all day long and then going back to your hotel at night to make decisions. Most markets last a week or so and may be spread out over multiple locations—clothing here, and two blocks away, accessories. The key is to wear good walking shoes. You're trying to be part fortune-teller and know what people are going to want to wear six to nine months down the road. Of course, I'd spent years already as a designer, which takes the same luck or ability to predict a trend."

"Is it the chicken or the egg?"

She frowned at him.

"As a designer, do your clothes come first and then fashion trends follow? Or is the trend happening and as a designer, you've got to make sure that you're in lock-step with that trend?"

"Probably a little of both."

"A chegg. Chicken and egg."

She smiled. "That's me. A chegg."

She was halfway through her turkey sandwich when Seth, who a second before had been sitting in his chair, looking very relaxed, moved fast, to get between her and the door.

She looked around him and saw Weston, who had opened the door and now stood in the entryway. He put his hands, rather sheepishly, she thought, in the air. "I come in peace," he said. "Jasmine said you were back here."

"Come in," she said.

Seth turned to give her a look. She ignored him.

Weston pulled out a chair and sat. Seth had yet to return to his spot. Nobody said anything.

It was ridiculous. "Uh, Seth, could you give us a minute, please?" she asked.

She thought he might say *hell, no*. Instead, he simply said, "I'll be right outside the door."

Weston waited until the door closed behind Seth before saying, "Should I consider that a promise or a threat?"

Megan smiled. "Probably a little of both."

Weston leaned forward, resting his forearms on the table. "I want to apologize for last night. I understand from several people that I wasn't at my best."

"Never really what we want to hear."

"Indeed. And while several details are a little sketchy, I think I owe you an apology for stepping over the line of attorney/client privilege."

This was the charming Weston that she'd encountered on the phone. "No harm done," she said.

"I think I may be lucky that I'm not here with a broken nose," he said, pointing toward the door.

"Seth was just doing his job," she said.

Weston seemed to consider that. "While it's no excuse, the woman that I'd been dating for the past eight months suddenly called it off yesterday. I consoled myself with too much whiskey. It was stupid and definitely unprofessional given that I was at a client event."

"It's done," Megan said. "Apology accepted. We don't need to discuss it again."

Weston's face relaxed. "So I didn't screw up our working relationship?"

"Not one bit. What do you think of the store?"

"It looks great. Good day so far?"

"Better than I think we even hoped for," she admitted. "And everything is going really smoothly."

"Excellent. If you've got a minute, I've had a call from one of the tenants in the Vegas building. It was kind of odd and I was hoping to discuss it with you before I responded."

"Of course."

Seth did not think that Weston was a threat to Megan. At least not in the traditional sense that he intended to harm her. But he was good at reading people and Weston was interested in Megan.

Now, maybe he cared about all his clients.

But Seth didn't think so.

Which was why he was going to give him another five minutes.

He saw Chloé Dawson coming his direction, her arms full of clothes. "Heading this way?" he asked, nodding his head toward the inventory room.

"Yes."

He opened the door for her and she walked past him.

"Thank you," she said, turning her head to look at him. She smiled. "Crazy day. One of our early customers asked me to put these aside for her daughter who can't get here until this afternoon and this is the first chance I've had. I almost just sold one of them by mistake."

"How's this work experience compared to what you did at J.T. Daly's?"

She looked surprised. "How did you know I worked there?"

"You mentioned it yesterday when we were doing introductions."

She nodded thoughtfully. "That's right. You're a good listener. Not a quality I associate with most men."

It was a bit of a backhanded compliment. And maybe an effort to avoid the question. "What store was it that you worked in?"

"In Scottsdale. It was their flagship store," she added. As if that had been important to her.

"Lucky for Megan that you found your way to Sedona, to this store."

"Fortunate for both of us, I hope. I know I'm certainly grateful."

She was saying all the right things. But there was a look in her eye. Maybe she wasn't all that impressed with Megan's little boutiques.

He was glad that he'd initiated a background check on her. Megan had found a spare minute to slip him Chloé's employment application and he'd texted her name, address and social security number to Royce. That was all he'd need.

Chloé returned to the cash register and Seth stared at the closed break room. He was just about to knock when Weston opened the door and came out. He ignored Seth.

Seth waited until the man had cleared the front door. “What did he want?” he asked Megan, who now stood next to him.

“Well, to apologize, for one thing.”

“For being an ass?”

She tilted her pretty little chin down. “For being overserved. And I’m grateful that he did. It cleared the air.”

“Right. I don’t like him.”

“You don’t know him.”

Seth just shrugged.

“I’ve appreciated his counsel,” she said. “Like just now, he brought me a request from an existing tenant at the Vegas property and together, we determined a response.”

“Is there a problem?”

“Not exactly. But they’re requesting a ten-year lease.”

“And what’s your position?”

“I’m not interested. I’ve met Mr. Precco and he’s nice enough, but a ten-year lease ties me up for too long. I may want to do something else with the space at some point. I’m just not sure yet.”

“Which tenant is this?”

“The one right across the corridor from the boutique. They have the antiques store.”

“That’s right,” he said. Not only could they see the antiques store from the Wingman Security windows, he’d also been inside with his mom on a couple occasions. She liked that kind of thing. “I’ve been in their store. I didn’t get the impression that merchandise was flying off the shelves.”

“They must do well enough. When we did our due diligence on the property, we checked the payment history of the current tenants. They always pay on time.”

“Maybe they’re asking for a longer lease because they’re concerned about the building having a new owner.”

"I'm sure they are concerned about me—I'm an unknown to them. That's why I made a point to meet every single one of the other five tenants after the purchase was finalized." She sighed. "Unfortunately, we have already lost one business. I think we'd owned the property for about ten days when the tea shop owners came to me and said that their lease was up for renewal but that they wouldn't be executing it."

"Do you know why?"

"I asked them specifically if it was because of new ownership of the building and they said no. But they didn't give me any other reason."

"Could be a thousand things," he said.

"I know. And it turned out to be a stroke of luck. We used their space to enlarge the existing footprint of the prior boutique. We could have gotten by but the extra square footage is allowing us much more display space."

He studied her. "Well, if Marberry is helping you with this, then maybe he's not a total ass. You've really dived headfirst into the deep end of entrepreneurship."

"At times, I feel as if I'm only treading water."

"Not so," he said. "You're doing the fifty-yard freestyle in just over eighteen seconds."

"I know nothing about competitive swimming. Is that good?"

"I think so. It sticks in my head as useless information I've learned along the way."

"Alright then. I'm going to sidestroke up to the front and check in with Jasmine."

If he'd been with his partners, he'd have figured out a juvenile way to interject breaststroke into the conversation. They'd have counted on it.

But now he just kept his mouth shut and took his spot in the back, leaning up against the wall.

Damn. She wasn't the only one worried about keeping a head above water.

He was sinking fast. She had him watching his words.

Chapter 11

Gillian O'Day's background check offered up nothing of interest. She had some student debt and a reasonable amount of credit card debt for someone her age. She had lived in the same apartment for three years and dated the same guy for two years. They were engaged with a wedding date set for next spring. She was planning to wear a North and More Designs original bridal gown.

Seth wondered when Megan was going to find time to make that happen.

Megan's brother-in-law, Evan Chevalier, had a more colorful report. He apparently liked fast cars and had several tickets to prove it. Also had one disorderly conduct charge for an incident in a bar. His passport had gotten twelve new stamps in just the last two years and based on his credit card changes, there'd been skiing in Switzerland, big-game hunting in Zimbabwe and sunning in Belize.

And then it had ended about six months earlier. Probably about the time that he'd found out about Abigail's pregnancy.

There was absolutely no reason to think he might want to harm Megan.

Seth sent his thanks back to Wingman Security and asked them to add Weston Marberry to the list.

At four, Megan walked past. "Time for us to get on the road to Albuquerque."

Where they would do this all over again. "Ready when you are," he said. "Happy with the day?"

"Very. How about you? Must have been kind of boring for you."

"Again, you don't hope for something bad to happen. And I was a little concerned when those two women both went for the same dress."

She smiled. "That was fun, wasn't it? Especially since it was one of my designs. Very good for my ego."

"You handled it like a pro. Got the dress in the hands of the person who looked good in it and convinced the other woman that ponchos were going to be the accessory of the year."

"You were listening."

"That's how I know useless swimming information."

"Are you saying that my fashion advice is useless?"

She was pretending to be outraged.

"Don't put words in my mouth," he said. "My mom's birthday is coming up. I'm going to put all this knowledge to use."

"I'll help you get her the perfect thing," Megan said. "I'm going to let Jasmine know that we're leaving."

"Is she coming for the opening, too?"

"Yes. She'll open here again tomorrow and then fly to Albuquerque tomorrow afternoon for the staff meeting and then spend two full days in Albuquerque."

"So, you don't hold your staff to the *no fly* rule?"

"Of course not. She's an adult. She can make her own decisions."

He could barely bite back a groan. It was a five-and-a-half-hour drive. Across desert.

Torture.

In his plane, he could easily fly it in about two hours.

"Lucky her," he whispered as Megan walked away.

They didn't get out of the store for another forty-five minutes. Even if they drove straight through, it was still going to be past nine by the time they rolled into Albuquerque. Fortunately, there'd been a bunch of sandwiches left over and Megan had grabbed those as well as some water. They ate those during the first half hour.

After they finished, Megan glanced over at him. "You'd rather be flying," she said.

"Was I that obvious?"

"You just sighed and looked up at the sky."

"Sorry." He paused. "Did you always dislike flying or did that just start after your parents died?"

"I was never a big fan but I had flown many times. Family vacations and things like that."

"Did you fly with your fiancé?"

"Yes," she said. "Before the accident," she clarified.

"But never after?"

"No."

"Are you afraid to fly?" he asked.

"No," she said. "I just don't want to do it. Don't want anything to do with it. It's too painful."

"It was a bad thing that happened to your parents," he said. "A bad thing for you and Abigail. You both lost parents. And you, well, you lost…the opportunity to stay at college, to be young without responsibilities, to be wholly focused on yourself at a time when that's really what you're supposed to do."

She pressed her teeth together so tightly that she wouldn't be surprised if she didn't crack a molar. What the hell was she going to do about Seth?

He wasn't like her family or her friends, who had been tiptoeing around her for years. Never pushing too hard.

He was a damn glacier and she was the *Titanic*, taking on water.

"I'm just saying—"

"Stop," she said, interrupting him.

To his credit, he did just that. She drove for several minutes. Then slowed the car to the point that she could pull off onto the shoulder of the busy highway. She turned to him. "I think we should limit our conversations to business."

Cars whizzed by them, rocking the vehicle. "That sounds boring as hell."

She let out a loud sigh. "How about business and anything travel- or tourist-related. Including food and weather."

"Oh, weather. Be still my heart," he said, patting his chest. "Love a good discussion about humidity or lack thereof."

"There's always dew points," she said. She tried for upbeat but it came out sounding sad.

"Listen, if I overstepped, I'm sorry," he said.

She pulled back. "Wow. I wasn't anticipating an apology."

"You know what I said about Wingman Security—we like to under-promise and over-deliver."

"Whatever. But I do appreciate the apology. And I'm sorry I snapped." She drew in a deep breath. "We don't need to talk about this anymore." She put on her turn signal and carefully pulled back onto the highway.

After twenty minutes or so, Seth said, "So what would be the business part?"

"What?" she asked. Her head was a jumble of thoughts, jumping back and forth fifteen years in seconds.

"You said we could talk about business. Help me define that."

"Well, anything about the stores or fashion in general."

"Oh, yeah. I've got a lot of questions on that."

She smiled. "You're really ridiculous, you know that?"

"I *do* know that," he said.

They drove another twenty miles before he straightened up in his seat. "I'd be happy to drive," he said. "I'm a good driver. Accident-free. You can call my insurance company and verify that information if you want."

She'd love to let someone else take the wheel. She was tired and it was an effort to stay alert. "I'm okay," she said.

"Just know that the offer stands," he said, turning his face to look out the window. There wasn't anything to see. Just desert and rock.

Four hours later, she was absolutely exhausted by the time they pulled in to the hotel parking lot. It was a smaller property than the one they'd stayed at the prior night. "Is that a lake?" she asked, pointing behind the hotel.

"Yeah. Man-made, according to the website."

Still, it was lovely. It was too late to explore tonight but maybe tomorrow. All she wanted to do was sleep now. But she knew that he was probably hungry. If only the idea of going to a restaurant wasn't enough to take her appetite away.

She popped the trunk and opened her car door. It was a warm evening in Albuquerque, probably at least eighty-five degrees. It felt very warm after the air-conditioned vehicle.

Once they got checked in, they took their key cards to the third floor and as before, Seth checked her room before opening his own door. "Hungry?" he asked.

"Sure," she said. She felt as if she could fall over but she couldn't expect him not to eat.

"I've got an idea," he said. "I saw a pizza place just two blocks down. I'll bet they deliver here. How about I call something in and we can eat in one of our rooms."

That sounded heavenly. "Anything but anchovies," she said.

"Then I think a sausage, mushroom and black olive thin-crust pizza works," he said.

If she'd been ordering for herself, that was exactly what she'd have chosen. "I'll take a salad, too. Balsamic vinegar dressing on the side."

"Rabbit food," he said, smiling.

Given that she felt as if she might have hopped the whole way from Sedona, it was fitting. "Here. Take my credit card."

When he hesitated, she wiggled her hand. "Come on. Our food is a business expense."

He took it without another word. "I'll get it from the lobby once they deliver it and bring it upstairs."

"Fine. I'm going to shower in the meantime."

"Feel free to put your jammies on," he said.

She gave him a sideways look.

"Just want you to be comfortable," he said, picking up his cell phone. "It's not like I haven't already seen them." He walked through the connecting door, into his room, shutting the door behind him.

She flopped down on the bed. She closed her eyes and didn't open them again until there was a sharp knock on the connecting door. Still on her back, she pushed herself up onto her forearms. "Come in," she said.

He opened the door, holding a very large pizza box as well as a white sack. He put everything on the desk. From the sack, he pulled paper plates, plastic silverware and her salad.

The last thing from the sack was two bottles of water.

"Dinner is served," he said. "But you never changed."

"Don't worry about me," she said. She swung her legs over the bed. "Smells delicious," she said. When she got closer to the desk and saw the size of the pizza box, she looked at him. "Are we feeding the people next door, too? Because if we are, they have to turn down their television first."

"Nope. All for us. I like pizza," he said. "And if the television isn't down by the time you want to sleep, I'll start pounding on the walls."

She opened her salad and took one piece of pizza. "It probably won't matter. I think I could sleep through anything tonight."

"What are they watching, anyway?" he asked.

"I think it's a *Jeopardy!* marathon."

"Alex, I'll take 'Irritating Habits of Hotel Guests' for a hundred, please," he said.

She took a bite of her pizza and smiled in appreciation. "Alex, I'll take 'Best Pizza in the World' for two hundred."

He lifted the lid of the box and looked at the receipt. "Who is Maidlin's in Albuquerque, New Mexico?"

"Ding, ding," she said. "Seth Pike is in the lead. What's your final wager?"

Seth picked up his second piece, already having devoured the first one. "All of it," he said, waving a hand carelessly. "Easy come, easy go."

She chewed. Leaned her head back. Swallowed.

"Be careful," he said. "If you choke to death, I'm going to have a whole lot of forms to complete."

"I would hate to be a burden."

"Want another piece?" he asked.

She shook her head. "All yours. But let me just get this warning out there. I don't think the cardboard is edible. Or that little plastic thing that kept the lid from squishing all the cheese."

"Sticks and stones. Real men enjoy their pizza." He kept eating and finally finished off the last piece. Stood up. Patted his stomach, which was still flat and tight. It really wasn't fair. If she ate like that, she'd have to squeeze sideways through the doorway.

He gathered up the garbage. "Want to keep the rest of your salad?"

"Nope." She was going to bed and she didn't intend to have it for breakfast.

He cleared off the desk. "Want me to check the closets," he said, his tone teasing. "Under the bed, maybe?"

She shook her head. "I'm not worried about right now. At three in the morning, it will be a different story."

He studied her. "First of all, there's no way for anybody to know that we're at this hotel. And just in case, when I was waiting downstairs for the pizza to arrive, I had a little talk with the night manager. Got her assurances that nobody was getting your room number."

"I'm going to stuff a towel under the door," she admitted.

"Can't hurt," he said. "Want a wake-up knock in the morning?"

She shook her head. "I'll set the alarm on my phone."

"Are we running again?"

"I'd like to," she admitted. "Maybe at six."

"No problem. Got some pizza to work off. Good night, Megan."

He left through the connecting door, taking all the garbage with him.

She undressed for bed and put on the nightgown that she'd worn the previous night. Too tired to shower, she washed her face and brushed her teeth and then stuffed the used towel as tightly as it would go under the door. It made her feel marginally better.

But her gut told her that it wouldn't be another snake. The next attack would be different, something she wasn't expecting.

Seth undressed for bed, listening all the while for any unusual noises from Megan's room. He lay down on the cool sheets, grateful to stretch. All the hours in the car were getting to him. And he knew that if he was tired as a passenger, Megan had to really be feeling it as the driver.

It was the reason he'd suggested pizza. Well, that and he truly did love a good pizza. And tonight's had been very decent. But not as good as he could make.

And he suddenly had a very clear vision of him in his kitchen, rolling out a pizza crust, a glass of red wine close by. And when he looked over his shoulder, Megan was sitting at his table.

Wearing her pretty white nightgown.

Which she might be wearing right now.

And the sheets that had felt cool now seemed way too warm, as if his body was putting off heat.

Alex, I'll take "Best Ways to Fall Asleep" for three hundred.

Oh, that was a mistake. He knew the answer.

Sex.

It wasn't going to happen. He was everything that she didn't want.

Which totally pissed him off.

He didn't want to be summarily dismissed by the one woman who quite frankly interested him more than any other woman he'd ever met.

He thought about calling one of his partners. Any one of the three could probably offer up some good advice. After all, they'd all fallen hard and fast when the right woman had come along. But he didn't want to talk about it. Not yet.

In a way, it reminded him of when he'd made the decision to join the air force after college. He hadn't told a soul until he'd signed on the dotted line and there was no going back. Then he'd gone to see his mom. She'd been wonderful about it, had said she'd thought it was only a matter of time. That his dad would be so proud.

What would she say now if he confessed? *Mom, I think I've fallen hook, line and sinker for a woman who likely thinks I'm the worst choice in the world.*

What he didn't think she would say is to give up. That hadn't ever been her message. No, it would probably be something along the lines of *Well, you'll just have to work harder to show her that she's wrong.*

But first things first. He'd been hired to keep her safe.

But to protect her, he needed to be sharp. He needed sleep.

He deliberately slowed his breaths. Relaxed his muscles. Closed his eyes.

And he didn't wake up again until six the next morning. It was still dark outside.

Ten minutes later, he heard her alarm. Then her tentative knock on his side of the door. "Yeah," he said.

She opened the door. "Good morning."

"Morning," he said.

"I wasn't sure if you were awake."

"I was about to make coffee," he said.

"I'm going for a run," she said. "Outside, I think. There's a path that goes around the lake."

"Okay. Give me five," he said.

He was waiting in the hallway when she opened her door. She'd pulled her long hair up into a high ponytail and it swung behind her. Her leggings were black, as was her T-shirt. He did not want to speculate on her underwear.

Even this early, she was really fabulous. And she'd told her sister that he was "an easy traveling companion." The only thing that might be worse was "an easy traveling companion who drooled." He might as well be a Saint Bernard.

They were out the back door of the hotel and on the path within minutes. The sun was coming up over the horizon and the morning sky was a combination of reds and oranges on a palette of deep blue. "That's Sandia Peak," he said, pointing off to the east.

"Gorgeous," she said. "I'm glad I got up to see this."

"I took the tram to the top and hiked a couple years ago. It was fun."

"Maybe I'll come back to New Mexico sometime," she said.

I'll bring you. He'd almost said it out loud. But the idea of watching a whole lot more sunrises and sunsets together was appealing.

They'd been running for about ten minutes when he heard a cell phone ring. It took him a second to realize the noise was coming from her. "You're ringing," he said.

"Oh." She slowed down fast and reached behind her back. She pulled up her shirt and he saw a pocket closed with Velcro in the waistband of her leggings. She pulled her cell phone from it.

"Didn't know you had that," he admitted.

"I would never run without a cell phone," she said, her tone absent. She was looking at the display number. He knew immediately when it registered because she yanked the phone up to her ear. "Who is this?" she demanded.

"Put it on speaker," he mouthed.

She did. He caught part of the sentence. "…matter who this is. Just listen. I've got information about the crash that killed your parents. Meet me at the Laundromat behind Marta's Deli today at 10:00 a.m. This will be your only chance."

Chapter 12

Seth reached for the phone but the caller had already hung up. He redialed the number. It rang and rang. "Pick up, you bastard," he said, his teeth gritted.

It continued to ring until it switched over to voice mail. "You've reached the voice mail of Marta's Deli. Our hours are 7:00 a.m. to 2:00 p.m., Monday through Saturday."

The phone disconnected. He checked the time on his watch, confirming that the time on Megan's phone matched. "Los Angeles is an hour behind us. That means it's just five thirty there. Marta's Deli doesn't open for another ninety minutes."

"I suspect there are cooks there, prepping for the day?"

He shrugged. "You would think so."

He tried the number again. Got the same results. "We could call the police," he said.

"I should have let it go to voice mail. At least then I'd have a recording of it."

"I heard it," he said.

"It doesn't matter," she said, sounding weary. "Even if I call and we both tell them what the caller said, I don't think it's a crime to offer to tell somebody something. I just can't see the Los Angeles police giving a damn." She stopped.

She was right. Even if they found somebody who would listen to the whole story, it was unlikely that they would put any effort into this. "Do you think it's legitimate?"

"I have no idea. The crash was fifteen years ago. Why now?"

He didn't know. "Do you want to be at the Laundromat at 10:00 a.m.?"

She turned and started walking back to the hotel. "It doesn't matter what I want. It's impossible. It's a twelve-hour drive from Albuquerque to Los Angeles."

"We could rent a plane. There would be some delay at the airport, I suspect, but I'd call ahead, try to get through as much of that as I could while we're driving to the Albuquerque airport. If we push it, we might be able to make it," he said.

She shook her head. "I'm not flying. And it's a moot point, anyway. It's already almost six thirty here. We have the meet and greet at nine and the ribbon-cutting ceremony after that."

Again, he was struck by the possibility that whoever was making those calls had access to the schedule. The first time, they'd called and left a message when she wouldn't have been able to answer her phone. Now they were asking her to be somewhere that she couldn't possibly be. "You could cancel today. Say that you're ill."

She shook her head. "That would be so irresponsible of me. If you're so interested," she said, waving a hand as if she couldn't care less, "you go."

"I stick with you. But you're onto something. How

about I ask one of my partners to go for us? From Las Vegas, they can easily fly to Los Angeles and be in place by ten."

"If it was a legitimate call, which I'm not even sure it was, then the person will be looking for me. None of your partners can pull that off."

"But if they see somebody there, they might be able to identify who's making the calls. They could talk to people at Marta's Deli. Try to figure out who made a call this morning before the place even opened up."

She stopped walking. He had her interest now. They were less than a hundred feet from the back door of the hotel. Another set of early-morning joggers were approaching and she didn't say anything until they passed.

"I'd be okay with that," she said. "I would pay them for their time, of course."

He nodded. "We can figure that out later." Now that they had a plan, he felt better. They had a chance to catch this person. And then they would figure out if he was legitimate and if so, whether his goal was to be helpful or not.

"Done with your exercise for today?" he asked, opening the hotel door for her.

She nodded. "Yeah. I'm just going to shower and get some emails answered before we go to the meet and greet."

"You want some breakfast?"

She shook her head. "No. Not really. I'll have coffee in my room."

He was going to argue with her but it would be like kicking a puppy. "Okay. I'll meet you outside your room at eight thirty. That should give us enough time to drive to the meet and greet. I mapped it yesterday before I made the hotel reservation. It's less than fifteen minutes away."

"Fine," she said.

They were back to *fine.* It made him want to slam his fist into a wall.

Once they were back to their rooms, he quickly checked hers before going to his own. He sat on the bed. Vegas was on the same time as Los Angeles, which meant it was pretty early there still. He sent a quick text and when he got the response he had hoped for, he dialed Royce, who was on call for the week.

"Morgan," he answered.

"Were you sleeping?" Seth asked.

"No. Lucky for you, Grace likes breakfast around five."

Good. That meant that Royce had already had some coffee and would be operating at full speed. He only wanted to explain this once. "I need a little help."

"Okay. What?"

"It's a long story so I'm going to give you the abbreviated version. Megan North's parents died in a plane crash about fifteen years ago. She has gotten two calls in the last few days, insinuating that it wasn't an accident. The male caller this morning indicated that if she wanted the truth, she needed to be at a Laundromat that sits behind Marta's Deli in Los Angeles at ten this morning. We're in Albuquerque, New Mexico, right now and we could make it there in time if we flew but we would miss some key events. She won't cancel and anyway, it's a moot point because she won't fly."

"Ever?" Royce asked. It wasn't the important part of the conversation but he would know that it was important to Seth.

"I guess," Seth said, not wanting to state it as fact.

"And you want one of us to be in Los Angeles at the Laundromat at ten."

"Yeah."

"I can do it," Royce said.

"It won't likely be much of a meeting but at least if you can get a look at the guy, maybe get a license plate number, something that we can go on. A photo would be super. Also, the call originated from Marta's Deli this morning at five thirty California time. They don't open until seven. When I tried to call the number, it went right to voice mail and gave me a standard after-hours message. I want to know who made that call."

"I'll call now to see if I can get a flight."

"Don't worry about a flight. I've got a friend who flies out of the North Las Vegas Airport. I've already sent him a text and he'll be ready to be in the air as soon as you can get there. I'll text you the info as well as the website info on Marta's Deli so that you have an address."

"That will all be helpful. I'll do my best."

"Thanks. I appreciate it."

"I know you do. Be careful, Seth. In all ways."

He hung up before he got sloppy on the phone and confessed that Megan had him in knots. He thought maybe Royce would understand, given that he'd secretly been in love with Jules Cambridge for years.

He undressed, shaved and brushed his teeth. Fifteen minutes later he was showered and dressed. And he still had some time to kill before he needed to meet her outside the room. It was time he read the NTSB report on her parents' accident. He knew the victims' names, the approximate date and that it had occurred in California. Plenty of information to be able to find it.

He was expecting to see a preliminary report done just days after the accident and then a final report completed much later. That was exactly what he found. The preliminary report, indicating cause of crash as pilot error, had been completed within three days. It was brief. Didn't tell him much more than what Megan had already said. There was a little additional information about weather conditions, visibility, witnesses on the ground and such but she'd summed it up pretty well. The final report had been completed fourteen months later. He skimmed the fifteen pages. There was nothing substantially different in the final report.

The pilot had been flying for only three years and had logged less than two hundred hours in each year. It wasn't much. He'd had one prior accident, where he'd been alone and experienced a hard landing. He'd walked away from that one with bumps and bruises.

His injuries, which were part of the report, had indeed been serious this time. Seth suspected he still felt some aches and pains all these years later. If he was any kind of decent person, he likely suffered a hell of a lot of mental anguish as well, in that he'd been flying an aircraft that had crashed and somebody had died.

He'd ultimately lost his fiancée over the accident.

Lost Megan.

It was a wonder the man had been able to go on.

But the years had gone by. And now, what new information could there be that would prompt somebody to contact Megan? Or if the information wasn't new but simply hadn't surfaced before, then why now?

Megan had quickly closed down the possibility of contacting Logan Lewis. And that made Seth's head spin a little. Was it even possible that she still harbored feelings toward the man? Was that why she'd never married anyone else?

Well, she might be adamantly opposed to reconnecting with her ex-fiancé, but that didn't mean that his hands were tied. He closed out of the NTSB website and in seconds had sent a message to his partners. "Need background info on Logan Lewis, ex-fiancé of Megan North."

He knew the last part would make them wonder, but it was necessary info so that they made sure that they were looking at the right Logan Lewis.

He hung his phone on his belt, slipped on his sport coat and went to stand in the hall. Five minutes later, Megan opened her door.

Today, her dress was a deep purple and she wore a white, navy and purple flowered scarf. Her hair was once again on top of her head and she looked lovely, as usual.

"How's it going?" he asked.

"Did you get something to eat?" she asked, avoiding his question.

He shook his head.

"Now that makes me feel bad. Just because I didn't eat doesn't mean that you can't."

"I'll just have an extra tea sandwich," he said. "I mean, one generally fills me up but I'll go for two."

"Maybe there will be doughnuts at the meet and greet," she said as they walked down the hall.

"Don't tease me," he said. "Who exactly are we meeting and greeting?"

"This event is sponsored by the local junior college. Probably a few administrator types, a few faculty and hopefully at least half the crowd will be students. There were fifty tickets in total."

"But it's not a fashion show?"

"No, we wanted to mix up the type of events a little. We were able to get some press interest in offering an informal meet and greet focusing on the intersection of textile design and entrepreneurship, both curricula offered at the college. I'm going to do a short presentation followed by a Q and A session."

"Sounds very smart. Who is your marketing genius?" he asked.

She smiled. "Me."

"And the woman with one head wears yet another hat."

Her eyes sparkled. "Let's hope it's the start of a new trend. Hats for all!"

"And the event afterward?"

"Ribbon-cutting at the store. Then we'll do the rah-rah meeting with the staff late afternoon along with another small cocktail party. We'll fall into bed and open the store tomorrow."

"Was there a reason that these store openings all needed to happen within two weeks? It's a pretty tough schedule."

"I know. But social marketing and trending topics have changed everything. We need the buzz of having multiple store openings in several cities. If we'd staged this over a couple months, we were concerned that we'd lose good energy. It was a risk that we weren't willing to take."

"Got it," he said. "Onward, then?" he asked, motioning to the door.

"Onward."

They took the elevator downstairs and walked outside to their car. A wall of heat knocked them back. It had to already be ninety degrees, which was very hot for an Albuquerque morning. Once they were seated and she'd started the car, he turned to her. "Aren't you going to ask what my partner said?"

She stared straight ahead. "I wasn't going to."

"Why?"

"Because I can't think about it. I can't be distracted by it. Attendees at the meet and greet have a right to expect me to be at the top of my game."

"I get that. And it is damn unfair of somebody to lay

this at your feet. But they did. And I just want you to know that Wingman Security is on it. Royce will be at the Laundromat at ten. He's also going to do what he can to find the person who could have called from Marta's Deli this morning." If Marta was simply going to tell Royce that it was impossible that somebody had called from there, it wasn't going to be good enough.

He didn't tell her that he had initiated a background check on Logan. If he found something interesting, he would. Until then, there was little use in discussing it.

She supposed that she was grateful that Seth had so easily picked up the ball and arranged to have someone at Marta's Deli. To have one of his partners there was as good a solution as any. She couldn't be—for so many reasons. First of all, she needed to fulfill her commitments in Albuquerque. Second, it was impossible to get her head around the idea that there could be any new information about the crash after all this time.

The first message had been rather cryptic. *Your parents were killed. It wasn't an accident. You better wake up and start smelling the roses.*

The second call had been much instructive. A simple quid pro quo arrangement. You do this and I'll do that. You come to Marta's Deli at 10:00 a.m. and I'll tell you something important about your parents' plane crash.

She supposed the only good thing about the second call was that it had come in this morning when she was sharper, versus last night, when she'd been almost too tired to form a complete sentence. She'd managed to get a very decent night's sleep, which had surprised her. But eating pizza with Seth had been…fun. And she'd gone to bed relaxed. Enough that she'd managed to put aside her worries and had simply stretched out in the big bed.

"Take a right here," Seth said. He was navigating off his phone.

She did. It was a big parking lot with lots of cars but she found a space pretty quickly. In minutes, they were in the right building. Like most buildings on a college campus, there was a big map inside the door and she quickly located the auditorium. When she started to walk away, Seth stopped her.

"Hang on a minute," he said.

He was staring at the map.

"It's right there," she said, pointing.

"I see that."

She waited. "What are you looking for?" she asked finally.

"Three other ways out of the building," he said. "This wasn't online," he said. "Otherwise, I'd have done it earlier." He studied the map for another minute before turning to look at her. "I think I'm good. Now we can go."

She wanted to be irritated that he was so compulsive in his need to be prepared for any eventuality, but she realized it was exactly this that had allowed her to sleep restfully the night before.

She opened the doors of the auditorium. There was a lone man sitting on the stage. He was wearing faded blue jeans with a sport coat and a button-down shirt. She guessed early fifties. He sprang up. "Ms. North?" he asked.

"Yes."

"I'm Dr. Scott. It's a pleasure to have you here."

"The pleasure is mine," she said. It was true. While the fashion show in Sedona had been fun, she really loved the idea of talking to professors and students. "This is my associate, Seth Pike." There was no need to say more.

The two men shook hands. "Got your laptop?" Professor Scott asked.

"Yes." They'd discussed her presentation at least twice.

"Okay." He waved to a person in the production booth at the rear of the auditorium. "Rory will take care of everything you need."

Twenty minutes later, she was confident that the presentation would come off without a hitch. People had started arriving and she introduced herself to as many as she could. Seth stood near the front of the room, watching everyone who entered.

Then it was time for Dr. Scott to introduce her. His opening remarks were brief and she slid into her presentation. Was on slide twenty-three of sixty-four when a jarring ring sounded and the lights started blinking.

Fire alarm.

Dr. Scott jumped up. "We need to exit," he announced. He pointed toward the rear doors. "That way."

People groaned at the unexpected interruption but got up and stared filing out the back entrance of the auditorium. By the time she'd reached for her purse that she'd stored on the interior lectern shelf, Seth was standing next to her. "This is fun," she said glibly.

"We're going this way," he said, pointing to the left of the stage.

"But..." Everybody else was going out the back.

"Follow me," he said.

He led her down a narrow hallway, made two right-hand turns, and then it was down a flight of steps. They exited on the side of the building. There was nobody else around.

"Hold this," he said, motioning to the still-open door.

In a second, he'd grabbed a stick from the ground and used it to keep the door from shutting. She could hear the sound of approaching sirens. Fire or police, maybe both. She looked for signs of smoke but saw none. "False alarm?" she said.

"That's what I'm thinking," he said. He didn't sound happy about it.

"We'll resume once this gets sorted out."

"Uh-huh," he said, as if he wasn't convinced. He put a hand under her elbow and gently guided her to the corner of the building, where they could see the people who had gathered out front. There had to be at least two hundred people. Not all from the meet and greet, because there were other classes being held in the building. Nobody seemed too concerned—most were on their cell phones and she imagined the social media posts that were popping up. It was a warm summer day and certainly not a hardship to be outside for a few minutes.

"It's like an impromptu lawn party," she said. "If only there was a beer cart..."

He didn't respond. He was scanning the crowd.

"What are you looking for?" she asked.

"Anything that doesn't look right," he said.

"It's just a fire alarm," she said. "These things happen all the time. It could have been a planned drill."

Again he didn't answer. Two fire engines and one cop car pulled up in front of the building. Six firefighters went into the building.

"We should probably join the group," she said. "It looks as if Professor Scott might be looking for me." The man had his hand up to his forehead, shielding his eyes from the sun. He was turning in a 360-degree circle. "He's going to think that I've abandoned the meet and greet."

"Let's just wait until the firemen clear the building," he said, still watching the crowd. "You don't see anybody who looks familiar?"

"Like the blond man?" she asked.

"That or anybody else. If we only focus on the blond man, we run the risk that we're going to shut our minds to the possibility of somebody else. That could be a problem for us."

"Of course." It wasn't that nice to think that there were multiple people wanting to cause her problems. "When will we hear from your partners about Marta's Deli?"

"As soon as they know something. Remember, they're an hour behind us. It's not even nine thirty there."

"Time's a-wastin' here," she said, feeling as if she was losing control of her morning. She could not be late to the ribbon-cutting at eleven thirty. She let out a sigh when she saw the firemen exit the building and the crowd starting to go back inside.

"Come on," he said. But instead of leading her around the building, he pointed at the still-propped-open door.

She didn't hesitate. And within minutes, was back on the stage. She could see Professor Scott's face relax when he saw her.

"I lost track of you," he said.

"Just happy that there's no fire," she said, not wanting to give any more of an explanation. And within five minutes, the auditorium had settled and she was back in full swing, although truth be told, she felt a little unsettled. She attributed that to Seth because she knew he wasn't happy about the interruption. At one point, during the presentation, she saw him quickly pull out his phone and type something and she knew it likely had something to do with her, because Seth wasn't the type to do casual correspondence when he was working.

At the end of the program, they still had fifteen minutes for questions and she could tell the audience was engaged. But she ultimately had to close it down so that they wouldn't be late to the ribbon-cutting.

When they were in the car, she turned to him. "Did you hear something from the Sedona police? I saw you looking at your phone."

"No. I was sending a message to my friend in the Vegas Police Department, asking him to make inquiries about the fire drill."

"Because?"

"Because that building had cameras everywhere. If somebody pulled an alarm, they are going to know it."

"Why didn't we just ask Professor Scott to look into it?"

"We're keeping the circle small."

She stopped for a red light and turned her head to stare at him. "In other words, you don't trust anybody."

"Not true," he said. "I trust the guy I sent the message to. I trust my partners." He paused. "I trust you."

Heat flooded her face. And she was glad when the car behind her honked.

She faced the road again and pulled forward with a jerk.

"That's not a bad thing," he added, sounding amused. "That last part," he clarified.

"Of course not," she said.

They rode in silence for several minutes. "Here's where you say," he said, "that it's reciprocal, that you also trust me."

She pulled in to the parking lot that was a half block from the boutique. They were right on time. "I wouldn't have signed the contract with Wingman Security if I didn't trust you."

He sighed. "There's trust and then there's trust. But no worries, we'll keep working on it."

"I'm not sure I understand the difference," she said.

"As they say, 'Houston, we have a problem.' But let's not worry about that now. Let's go cut a ribbon."

Chapter 13

Megan used a key to unlock the storefront. If there had been brown paper in the windows, somebody had already removed it. Two big windows facing the street allowed enough light in that he could quickly see that the Albuquerque store looked very much like the Sedona store—about the same square footage, and the paint colors and flooring were exactly the same.

Jasmine Pajo had not yet arrived in Albuquerque but it was just minutes before other staff showed up. He could tell that Megan had not met them before but she was immediately welcoming and told each person how happy she was to have them on the team. Then the mayor and a couple people from the city council arrived.

He stayed back, away from all the introductions. He wasn't too concerned while they were inside the store but he wasn't super excited about being outside on the sidewalk for the ribbon-cutting. His gut told him that the fire alarm during her presentation hadn't been by chance.

That's what had prompted him to send a quick message to Bobby Bayleaf, who had responded that he was on it.

Seth was also watching the clock. It was almost ten thirty in Los Angeles. Royce would check in as soon as he knew something and Seth told himself to be patient.

When it was time to string up the grand opening banner, which doubled as a ribbon, it was Megan holding a giant pair of scissors, with the mayor, the city council members, the chamber of commerce president and the neighborhood association vice president. She was in the middle of the group, her back to the entrance of the boutique, facing the street.

Seth stood off to the side, scanning the small crowd, looking for someone around five foot nine and a hundred and fifty pounds. There were a couple women who fit the physical description but no men. None of the women were blonde.

He glanced up and down the street and at the windows of the four-story building across the street. Saw a shadow pass in front of one window on the third floor and tensed but when the shadow passed back and forth a couple more times, he realized they weren't looking down, but rather forward, as if they were simply pacing a room.

The ceremony started. The mayor spoke first, then the chamber president and finally Megan said a few words. Her voice was strong, she was articulate and again, Seth was impressed with her professional demeanor. He had a feeling that North and More Designs was going to be a great success.

Within twenty minutes of the ribbon-cutting ending and the dignitaries leaving, lunch arrived and Megan and her employees were gathered around the break room table. They were just clearing the debris when his cell phone buzzed.

Royce.

"Hang on," he said, by way of greeting. Then he caught Megan's eye and motioned that he was stepping out of the break area.

He went all the way to the sidewalk and stood in front of the door. Nobody could get past him without him seeing them. "Talk to me," he said.

"I don't have much to tell you," Royce said.

Seth fought the wave of disappointment. "Let's have it," he said.

"I was at the Laundromat behind Marta's Deli at 9:46, staring at the dryers, waiting for my clothes to dry."

"Acting as if your clothes were drying," Seth clarified.

"No. I brought along a bag of wet towels."

With anybody but Royce, he'd have said they were lying. But Royce, knowing he was going to a Laundromat, would have brought along the right props. It was all part of his "have a plan, a backup plan and an it's-going-to-hell plan."

"Anyway, there was one woman already there, reading a book. She didn't seem to be paying much attention to me when I loaded my towels in the dryer. While I was there, she moved her clothes from the washer to the dryer and I really believe she was there just doing laundry. I stayed for an hour. During that time, one other individual arrived, carrying a large laundry basket."

"Describe him," Seth said.

"Midtwenties. Dark hair. Dark eyes. Six-two. Two hundred pounds. Gray towels. White sheets. Boxers, not briefs."

Seth almost smiled. Royce was always very thorough. He'd have gotten all that without the guy even knowing that he was looking.

"Nobody loitering outside."

"Nope. I went outside three times for a smoke."

"You don't smoke."

"I did today. Nasty things. They used to taste better when I was eighteen. I mostly let it burn down but it gave me a chance to look around. There were people coming and going from Marta's Deli but nobody who gave the Laundromat a second glance."

"Somebody could have been watching from a distance."

"Absolutely. But there's nothing close that would have given them a good view. With the right equipment, there's a couple six-story apartments a few blocks away that might have worked."

But if somebody had really wanted to make contact with Megan, they likely wouldn't have wanted to be blocks away when she arrived. They'd be risking the chance that she'd get frustrated and leave. Although they did have her phone number. He supposed they could deal with that by simply giving her a call and telling her to come back.

"I spent some time inside Marta's Deli," Royce said. "No men working in the kitchen. I pretended that I was looking for an old friend of my wife's and that I'd heard he was working at Marta's. My waitress said she'd worked there for over a year and there hadn't been any male cooks during that time. There was one waiter but he'd been out with the flu for more than a week. She wanted to know the name of the man I was looking for and I told her I thought it was something like John Johnson but I wasn't confident. Like I'd hoped, she offered up that the waiter's name was Ross Lewis."

The name meant nothing to him. But he let it roll around in his head. *Ross Lewis. Ross Lewis.*

Megan had said that her fiancé's name was Logan

Lewis. "Royce, I sent a text earlier asking for a background check on Logan Lewis, Megan's ex-fiancé."

"I recalled that. So, I found Ross Lewis's address, which was less than fifteen minutes away from Marta's Deli. I made a quick trip there but nobody answered the door."

"Too sick to get out of bed?"

"Don't think so. He lives in a duplex. I knocked on the neighbor's door and the man living there didn't think he'd seen Ross for over a week. Said they shared a garage and he also hadn't seen the motorcycle that Ross drives."

"Maybe he's got vacation flu."

"Maybe. I asked him if Ross had a brother but he had no idea. Same last name could just be coincidence but..."

"Hardly anything is ever just a coincidence," Seth said, finishing his partner's sentence.

"Megan would probably know if Logan had a brother," Royce said.

True. But he wasn't sure he wanted to ask her. "Who is heading up the Logan Lewis background check?"

"Trey. I'll follow up with him. Sorry I don't have more to report."

"No problem. I appreciate you being there. The caller might have chickened out when he didn't see Megan or maybe it was a hoax to begin with."

"How's the assignment going otherwise?"

"Just did a ribbon-cutting and now we're on to a staff meeting and then another cocktail party where I'll sip water with a slice of lime."

Royce sighed. "Chin up, my friend."

"Absolutely." Seth hung up. It wasn't as bad as he'd made it sound. He got to watch Megan in a pretty dress work her way around the room, charming everyone. Got to take her back to the hotel.

And then take a really cold shower.

Yeah, this assignment pretty much sucked.

Megan was relieved when Jasmine arrived just as they were clearing the remains of lunch. She was wearing North and More Designs, and the purple-and-black tunic top and wide-legged pants were stunning on her. She was a wonderful walking advertisement.

Jasmine'd done all the hiring for the Albuquerque store so she knew everybody. Still, they did introductions so that the group could get to know one another. Megan knew that Seth, who was back in the room, was listening carefully, based on his comments after the Sedona meeting that Chloé Dawson had been an employee at J.T. Daly's.

She didn't hear anything that would get his attention but knew that she was really only half listening. When he'd returned to the room, he'd given her a brief shake of his head and said, "Nothing to report." She'd wanted to take him outside and demand details but right now, her priority had to be on establishing a connection with the Albuquerque staff and getting them ready to open a store tomorrow.

Jasmine's remarks were a bit different than in Sedona and Megan realized that even in the short time the Arizona store had been open, there had been some early lessons learned that would help them in Albuquerque. She knew that was one of the real benefits of having common management over several stores. It was hectic in these early days but would ultimately pay off.

When it was time for her rah-rah speech, she spoke about the joy of helping customers find clothes that made them feel confident and beautiful and the fun of showing a customer that one perfect accessory that was going to turn the nice outfit into a knockout look.

It wasn't just words to her. She believed it. She hoped Jasmine had hired people who did, too. She ended her spiel with a reminder that they were all invited to the cocktail party. Finally, it was time to go. She gave Jasmine a hug, told her they'd catch up later, and she and Seth walked to the rental car. His door was barely shut when she pounced. "What did your partner say?"

"He was there in time. Didn't see anybody who fit the physical description of your blond friend and saw nothing unusual, as in somebody obviously looking for somebody else. At Marta's Deli, he verified there are no male cooks and one male server, who has been out with the flu for about a week. His name is Ross Lewis. I wonder if that might mean something to you."

Ross Lewis. Of course that meant something to her. "Logan had a younger brother named Ross."

"How much younger?"

"At least ten years. When Logan was twenty, he was probably nine or ten."

"Which would make him midtwenties now?"

"I guess. But why would he call me? After all these years? With that kind of message?" She simply could not get her head around what he was telling her.

"I don't know. What kind of relationship did Logan and Ross have?"

She shrugged. "There was such a big age difference that they were in different worlds. I'm sure they loved each other. But I haven't seen or heard anything about Ross since Logan and I broke off the engagement. I…I wish I knew more."

"Don't worry about it. Royce went to his apartment and the neighbor verified that Ross and his motorcycle haven't been seen for about a week. But don't worry. Now that I know for sure there is a connection, we're going to find him and talk to him."

"Who is *we*?"

"It depends of where he's at. Either I'll do it or one of my partners."

"I want to do it," she said.

He stared at her. "Before we make that decision, let us gather some background info on him. I don't want you walking into a dangerous situation."

"Maybe I should call Logan and ask him what the heck his brother is doing?"

Seth shook his head. "No. Earlier when we discussed calling Logan, I didn't have strong feelings. Now that we know there's a connection between him and Ross Lewis from Marta's Deli, I think it's the wrong move. We don't know what kind of relationship the two men have, don't know what one would do to protect the other."

She rubbed her temples. "Well, at least Marta's Deli makes some sense finally. If he works there, it's a place where he could easily use the telephone and would feel comfortable asking me to meet nearby." She started her car and pulled away from the curb.

"It's not smart," Seth said. "Not smart to use a telephone where you work because everybody knows about caller ID. Not smart to want to meet near your work because it's logical that people might start to snoop around and discover your identity that way. In the second call, he told you the Laundromat was behind Marta's Deli. So of course, that is going to lead you to Marta's Deli."

"So, he wants me to know that it's him? Then why doesn't he simply just tell me who he is when he calls?"

"I don't know. But we will. Once we find him."

"I don't think he's the blond guy who has been following me," she said. "Logan and Ross both had dark hair, olive skin. And the blond guy was older than Ross would be."

"Then that's still a mystery."

"One that I can't worry about right now. When we get back to the hotel, I've got an interview with a local magazine and a conference call with the contractor working on the Vegas property. Then it will be time to get ready for the cocktail party."

"And here I was, hoping for a nap."

She gave him a quick look. "You don't strike me as the nap type."

"Then you've never seen me on a warm Sunday afternoon, after a big lunch."

The idea of him stretching out across a couch was an appealing one. "Television on or off?"

"Old movie on, one that I've seen many times."

"Blanket or no blanket?"

"None. I run hot."

She just bet he did. There was no escaping it. Seth Pike was a very handsome, sexy guy. At both the Sedona and Albuquerque staff meetings, she'd seen the appreciative glances that her team was sending his direction.

Anybody in her situation would be attracted to him.

Even if he was all wrong.

A pilot, for goodness' sake.

"That maybe came out wrong," he said.

She kept her eyes on the road. "I understood what you meant." *Still didn't stop me from getting a little heated up myself, however.*

When they got to the hotel, she had less than fifteen minutes to get ready for the interview with the local magazine. They did the interview in the lobby. She was grateful when Seth stood off to the side, near the entrance. She didn't want to have to explain his presence to the journalist. Certainly didn't want it getting reported that she traveled with her own security.

Once that was over, she went back to her room and made her call. Then she took a quick shower and changed her clothes. By the time she was ready and opened her door, Seth was waiting in the hallway. "You're never late, are you?" she said.

"Never is a long time. But not usually. And I'm pretty psyched about this next event."

She smiled. "No, you're not. This can't be fun for you. You're in a room full of strangers and you don't let yourself eat or drink."

"I'm looking on the positive side. Weston Marberry won't be there."

Chapter 14

At twenty minutes after seven, the bastard proved him wrong.

Tonight's cocktail party was in a private room at the back of the Peacock Restaurant. There was a rear emergency exit, which probably met fire code, but didn't allow for access from the outside. Seth appreciated that because it meant he had to watch only one entrance.

It was a smaller room and more crowded than in Sedona. But other than that, much the same. Bar in the corner of the room, appetizers being served by waitstaff. Tall round tables offered guests a place to put their plates but there were no chairs.

Things had been going well until Weston Marberry walked in. He stood near the doorway, his eyes searching the room, holding steady when he saw Megan. Then he made a beeline toward her.

Seth had to practically hang on to the railing behind him in order to keep from intercepting the man and tossing him out on his ear. Instead, he watched Megan. Relaxed when he realized that she was just as surprised as he was. She hadn't been expecting him.

Was the guy drunk again? Seth didn't think so. His gait had been steady.

He watched as Megan introduced Marberry to the couple she'd been speaking with before he'd interrupted her. Then, within minutes, the two of them drifted off to the corner of the room. Too far away for him to hear. Not at the right angles for him to read their lips.

Screw it.

It took him four seconds to cross the room. "Everything okay here?" he asked, coming up on Megan's left.

"Yes, yes, of course," Megan said hurriedly. Her face was flushed. With excitement? Nerves? He had no idea.

He turned to Marberry. "I didn't think we were expecting you."

"I'm kind of an impulsive guy," Marberry said. "Just didn't want to miss my favorite client's grand opening."

"Do you bill your travel time?" Seth asked.

Megan let out a puff of air and put her hand on his arm. "We were just in the middle of something here, Seth."

In other words, get your nose out of my business. Fine. He stared at her. "At least he's not slurring his words tonight."

He went back to his wall and surveyed the room, making sure that nobody new had entered while he was shooting off testosterone. His remarks bordered on juvenile but damn it, couldn't she see that this guy wasn't right for her?

And how could he be so confident of that?

Easy.

He was right for her. He liked Megan North. A lot. More than he'd ever liked any other woman. She was smart and funny and she kept him on his toes. Being gorgeous didn't hurt. But it was more than that. It was how she interacted with her employees, making each one of them feel special, no doubt leaving them feeling as if they'd made a very wise decision to join North and More Designs. It was how she cared so much for her sister that she had changed her whole life to take care of her.

It was how she looked in her pajamas, standing in the middle of her bed, one hand up to her mouth, the other pointed at a snake.

Priceless.

He used his phone to send a text, asking for an update on the background checks on Chloé Dawson and Weston Marberry. He got a reply almost instantly. Ms. Dawson had twelve years of retail experience, six of that at J.T. Daly's. She had been an average student, earning an undergraduate degree in business from the University of Phoenix. Never married. No children. Lived in an apartment. Reasonable amount of debt. All in all, there wasn't much there.

He thumbed down to look at the next report. Weston Marberry had been born and raised in Australia. Family had come to the states his junior year in high school. After graduation, Weston had taken a gap year and traveled throughout Europe. He returned and entered the University of Colorado, where he'd earned a bachelor of arts in political science. He'd attended law school at Arizona State University and it had taken him two tries to pass the bar. He'd used family money to open his own law practice in Sedona upon graduation. His shingle had been hung out for the last thirteen years and he was generally regarded as competent and fair. He was active in Sedona and sat on two not-for-profit boards. He had never been married but dated extensively and had had several long-term relationships with women. He had no siblings and would be the sole heir to his parents' estate, which was estimated to be in excess of five million.

It was no wonder that he wore thousand-dollar suits.

For the next forty minutes, Marberry clung to Megan. Perhaps not literally. He kept his hands off her but he was never more than a few steps away. They looked as if they were a couple. And by the time the event was over, Seth was hanging on to his temper by a thread.

He forced himself to relax when Megan finally broke away from Marberry and approached. "How's it going?" she asked.

"Fine," he said, picking up on her word that meant everything was indeed not fine.

She didn't seem to notice. "Weston and I are going to get a bite to eat after this. You can take the car and I'll grab a cab home."

No way, no how. "Get a table for three. I was hired to provide security and that's what I'm going to do."

"You're being ri…really somewhat difficult."

He was pretty confident that she'd started to say that he was being ridiculous but at the last minute, had softened her words. He didn't care. He excelled at ridiculous. Damn badge of honor.

"I don't want to have to pull rank but I am the client here. I hired you."

"That's true. And you signed a contract, which it appears you may not have read in its entirety. That document clearly states that you agree to comply with reasonable requests to ensure your ongoing security."

She sighed, sounding weary. She had to be tired. She'd been "on" all day. But he wasn't simply being a jerk. He certainly wasn't convinced that the danger was over.

As recently as this morning that surprise fire drill still seemed suspicious. He would know for sure once the tapes were reviewed.

And even if there wasn't any danger, the idea of giving Marberry a chance to get up close and personal was, well, simply a little crazy. He might be a lot of things, but crazy wasn't one of them.

"If I have to have a babysitter, then I'm just going to tell him that something has come up and I can't go," Megan said.

"That works. There's a restaurant at the hotel where we can get some food." He looked around the room. It was clearing out nicely. "Same arrangement as last night? That Jasmine will close out the event?"

"Yes."

"Then I think it's time we make our exit." If Marberry saw them leave together, that would give the lawyer something to stew on.

"Fine."

He watched Megan cross the room and speak with Marberry. Her back was to Seth, which meant that Marberry was facing him. The man's reaction was controlled—he was probably good in a courtroom. He smiled at Megan, leaned in for a hug that might have lasted a second too long to be considered impersonal, and turned to leave. But at the door, he hesitated and turned to give Seth a stare.

Seth gave him an index-finger wave.

He was pretty sure Marberry didn't see it as being friendly. The man's ears turned beet red. So red that even across the room, they were a version of Rudolph's nose.

Maybe he could feel them heating up, because he turned quickly and left the room. Seth casually made his way over to a window that looked down on to the street.

He didn't relax until he saw Marberry get in a car and drive away.

His cell phone buzzed. Before looking at it, he checked to make sure Megan was in sight. Then looked at his phone. Trey Riker. He'd sent a text to him while Megan was doing her interview in the hotel lobby, asking him to call when he could.

Seth moved to the back of the room, away from everyone. "Hey, Trey. Thanks for calling."

"No problem. Would have gotten to you earlier but I was on a plane."

"How's Kellie?"

"Good. I'm a wreck about these babies and she's very Zen. She's really just amazing."

"She is," Seth agreed. "Hey, I wanted to follow up on a conversation I had with Royce."

"I just got done talking to him, too. He told me about his visit to Marta's Deli and that Ross Lewis is the lone male employee of the deli. He mentioned the possibility the Ross might be related to Logan Lewis. I confirmed that I already knew that to be true. I'd come across it in the background information. But the brothers, if not estranged, aren't buddies. We got information from a couple of Logan's friends who didn't even realize that he had a brother."

"Any reason for the distance between the two of them?"

"I don't know," Trey said. "There's an age difference of ten years, but I suspect it has more to do with the fact that Ross hadn't ever held a job for longer than six months and has a couple short-term jail stints for nonviolent crimes. He apparently isn't very good at stealing things. Logan is definitely more settled. He's a middle manager at a bank in Cincinnati, Ohio. Has a house in the suburbs. Still has a pilot's license although he doesn't regularly fly. Is married with two preschool daughters. His wife stays at home with them."

Logan Lewis had moved on. It didn't make Seth like him.

"I want you to talk to Logan," Seth said. "First of all, we need to know if there's new information about the crash. If there isn't, then we need to know what kind of game his brother might be playing." It killed him to ask Trey to handle the task. He wanted to be the one in the room with Logan, to get a sense of whether he was telling the truth. But to do that he'd need to leave Megan and there was no way in hell that was happening.

Face it, he wanted to see the man whom Megan had been willing to leave.

"Will do," Trey said. "I've got a meeting in Vegas tomorrow but will catch a flight to Cincinnati tomorrow night and talk to him the next day."

"Thanks," Seth said, and hung up. Ten minutes later, he and Megan were on their way to the hotel. It was a quiet drive. He did not intend to tell her yet about his conversation with Trey. Didn't want to catch her up on her ex-fiancé. Didn't want to have another conversation about Ross Lewis or Marta's Deli again. He didn't want her worrying about one more thing.

For her part, she didn't seem interested in talking to him, either. In the parking lot, she found a space and pulled in. She turned the car off with a quick flick of her wrist and reached for her door.

"Just a minute," he said.

"What?" she asked, sounding irritated.

"There's a man by the door," he said. "He's got light hair and he looks the right height and weight."

"Oh." She turned in her seat to get a better look. "I didn't even see him when I pulled in," she admitted.

"That's my job," he said. "Does he look familiar?"

The man was smoking a cigarette and talking on the phone. "I never saw my guy smoking."

"Your guy," Seth repeated.

"I guess that's how I've come to think of him. My stalker guy. And I really have only seen him from a distance, but this guy has a really thin face and that's not what I recall. My guy had a rounder face, almost a baby face."

"Let's get out. But stay on my left side, a half step back."

"Okay."

It was forty-three steps to the front door. Seth watched the man as they approached. He didn't appear to be paying any attention to them. They were six feet away when the man tossed his cigarette to the ground and looked at them.

Seth saw no recognition on the man's part. He simply stepped another foot away from the door, as if he didn't want Seth and Megan to hear his phone conversation. Still, Seth made sure that he stayed between Megan and the man, all the way through the automatic front doors. He put his hand gently on the middle of Megan's back, to guide her toward the restaurant.

Her steps faltered. "I'm not eating dinner with you," she said, her voice low. "I mean, I appreciate all this, your thoroughness in evaluating every possible danger, but I'm still…"

"Mad?"

She walked over to the elevator. Stabbed the up button. When the door opened, she stepped in. Finally, she turned to look at him. "Mad seems rather childish. Kids get mad when their parents tell them no. When they have to make their beds. When they're grounded. You know what, maybe I should be mad."

The door closed, leaving the two of them alone. "Are

you implying that I treated you like a child?" he asked. He could feel his own temper spiking and worked to maintain control.

"Maybe," she said. She ran her hands through her long hair. "I don't know."

The bell dinged, signifying the third floor. When the door opened, he went first, checking the hallway. Then reached for the key card in her hand. Their fingers connected and he could feel the zing run up his arm.

He opened the door. Quickly searched the room. Made sure the connecting doors were unlocked. "I'm not going to apologize for doing my job. I guess I didn't realize how much you wanted to go to dinner with Marberry. What the hell was he doing there, anyway?"

"I don't know." Now she was yelling.

It was the first time he'd ever heard her raise her voice.

She threw her hands in the air. "I didn't invite him."

"But you didn't seem too upset about it. The two of you were practically linked at the hip once he arrived." Okay, maybe he was exaggerating.

She stalked toward him, pushed the heel of her hand into his chest. "We were not."

Her eyes were big, her face was flushed, her hair was wild. She was fabulous. He wrapped his hand around her wrist.

If their fingers touching had sent a shock up his arm, his hand, her wrist—it was a direct hit below the belt. And her trembling lips told him that she might be feeling something similar.

For days he'd put aside his feelings, tried to temper his reactions. But it had cost him. "Megan," he said, pulling her toward him.

She lifted her face. He bent his head.

It was a scorching-hot kiss, full of frustration and need

and want. And when it ended, her back was against the wall and he was pressed up against her, his hands full of all that glorious hair. Her arms were wrapped around his neck.

They were both breathless.

"Megan?" he whispered.

She kissed him again. And when it ended, he was pretty confident that he had his answer. But he had to be sure. "I want you in my bed."

"Then take me."

He rarely needed someone to repeat important directions.

They didn't make it to his bed. Hers was closer.

Once there, it was a frantic scrambling of getting naked. The undoing of zippers and buttons and snaps on a bra strap. Need. Want. So difficult to tell the difference.

Energy clung to them, then slipped away, to hover above them as skin touched skin and breaths stretched out, finally calming.

"You're so beautiful," he said.

And she felt as if she truly was.

They lay on their sides, both now fully naked. He was magnificently made, so strong, so male. She ran her hand up his arm, across his chest and laid it flat on his heart. It was beating fast. She bent her head and kissed one flat nipple.

And when he groaned and his body literally jerked in response, she felt superior. She was the cause of all this heat and desire, and it made her feel deliciously female. And when he cupped her breast with the palm of his hand and flicked his thumb across her nipple, she felt the response settle between her legs.

One hand on her hip, he gently pushed her to her back.

Then crowded up next to her, so close that their bodies were touching almost everywhere. And then he started kissing her. His mouth was warm and wet and she welcomed his tongue.

As fast as it had ignited, now that the path had been chosen, he seemed to want to take his time. To meander about.

He worked his way down her body. Soft kisses to her neck, shoulder, breast, rib, stomach. He spread her legs. Oh…

She couldn't think, couldn't speak, could only take. Until finally, she pulled at his shoulders. "Do you have a condom?"

In response, he reached for his pants. When he had the condom in his hands, she helped him put it on his pulsing length. "I want you inside me," she said.

And when he slipped inside, it seemed as if it was perfectly right, that there had never been anything as wonderful as that moment.

He'd had sex before. Good sex. But it had never left him shaken. But now, as he tucked a sleeping Megan into his side, he had to admit. He was just about undone.

Her skin was so silky and it smelled so good. And when he buried his head between her legs, her taste had thrilled him. And he'd wanted to make her come with his mouth, but when she'd begged to have him inside her, no man could have resisted that.

Hot. Tight. So damn good that he'd been afraid that he might not make it last. But they'd moved together as if they'd been doing the dance forever, each seeming to know just what the other wanted and needed, until she'd come and he'd quickly followed her over the cliff.

Anybody would say that he wasn't a man prone to poetry. But if he'd started spouting verse, it might not have surprised him. His damn heart had simply felt full.

He pulled her long hair to the side and kissed her neck. She stirred, stretched, but did not open her eyes. "Megan," he said softly.

"Mmm-hmm."

"Can we talk about this?"

To her credit, she didn't simply ignore the question and pretend that she was sleeping. Instead, she opened her eyes slightly, looked over her shoulder and said, "No."

Then she closed her eyes again and in ten minutes, he was pretty confident that she was indeed sleeping. He wondered if he'd ever sleep again. Felt as if he could maybe do a 5K and then a twenty-mile bike ride. Energy was coursing through his veins.

He watched the clock. And some time toward morning, finally fell asleep. Woke up instantly when her alarm went off and she slipped out of bed. "Hey," he said.

She was standing next to the bed, holding the sheet up in front of her. "I'm going to go for a run," she said.

He stared at her. Her hair was tumbling around her face and the sheet wasn't quite covering everything. Her right breast was visible and it was all he could do not to reach out. To touch. "How do you feel?"

"Great. Really good."

It sounded forced but it was a definite improvement over *fine*. He patted the side of the bed. "Now can we talk about this?"

She shook her head. "No."

His chest started to burn. "Ever?"

"Maybe not. Is it enough if I tell you that I don't regret it?"

Damn sure better than her saying that it had been a mistake. "Glad to hear it." He lay back on his pillow.

"Are you running with me this morning?" she asked.

"I was thinking that we could get our exercise another way." He tossed back the covers, showing his naked body. Showing her exactly what kind of exercise he was hoping for. What he was ready for.

She stared at him. And her cheeks turned a delicious shade of pink.

"Let go of your sheet," he said.

It took her a minute, but finally her grip loosened and the sheet fell to the bed. Her breath was coming fast. "Do you have more condoms?" she asked.

He was already moving. "In my shaving kit," he said. "Don't move," he added, headed for the connecting door.

She didn't. When he got back, she was still standing next to the bed. He came up behind her, stood close, close enough that they were touching. "What time do you need to be at the store?" he whispered, his mouth close to her ear.

"By nine thirty."

That gave them four hours. "I've got three more condoms. If we run out, I'll call room service for more." And then he bent her forward over the bed.

Chapter 15

Over scrambled eggs and bacon, in the hotel breakfast area, she decided to set some expectations. "About earlier," she said.

He looked up from spreading jelly on his toast. "Which time?" he asked, so innocently.

Except that she was never ever going to buy innocent from him again. Not after…well…all that. "All of the times," she hissed. Why did there have to be so many other people eating breakfast?

"I'm listening," he said. He took a bite.

How could he eat? Her stomach was a wreck. "I want to reiterate that I have no regrets."

He cocked his head. "If this is the *start with something positive* approach to giving feedback, I think you can do better."

"Okay, new rule. You don't get to talk."

His eyes told her what he thought of that rule. But he said nothing.

"I just need you to know that I'm not looking for anything serious right now. I have a lot on my plate and a relationship isn't in the cards."

He had no change of expression. But he'd stopped eating. His eggs were likely getting cold.

"I am also a very private person and I don't really want people knowing about this. Especially Abigail. She has to be a hundred percent focused on having her baby. She cannot be worrying about me getting myself into something."

"You make me sound like a patch of poison ivy."

"No talking," she reminded him.

He pressed his lips together.

"So nothing can change about how we interact with each other in public. We are business associates. You are consulting on security."

She stared at him, looking for some sign of agreement. But it appeared that if he couldn't verbalize his thoughts, she was just going to have to guess what was going on in his thick head.

"What I'm looking for is light and easy. Just light and easy. No pressure. No commitments. No drama."

She let out her breath. Picked up her coffee, which was now too cool to drink. Set the cup back down. "I'm sorry that I said you couldn't talk. That was juvenile of me. Of course you can talk."

But still he said nothing. Just looked at her.

"What?" she demanded.

"Fine," he said.

"'Fine' as in how I say fine but I don't really mean that it's fine or 'fine' it's really fine."

"Could you repeat that?"

"No. You know exactly what my question was."

"'Fine' as in last night and this morning was pretty

terrific. I'd like to think that you thought so, too. That's about it. Ask anybody. I'm not terribly complex."

Was he telling the truth? Had it just been good sex to him? She fought off the wave of disappointment. She should be happy. He was offering exactly what she had said that she wanted. Exactly what she really thought she wanted.

"Okay, well, I'm glad we got that settled. We should take off. The store opens in less than an hour."

"Ready when you are," he said, shoving his half-eaten breakfast to the side.

Light and easy. The words pulsed in his head as she drove to her boutique. He was pretty sure that's how she'd described the fabric of one of the dresses at the fashion show. Or maybe that had been light and breezy. In any event, he didn't like the sounds of it.

It sounded inconsequential. Unimportant. Not memorable. Fluff.

Not how you wanted something that had shaken you, maybe even changed you forever, to be described. But if he'd articulated that, two things might have happened. She might have been amused, which would have been bad, or she might have been scared off, which would have been much worse.

He could do light and easy. And somehow convince her that a relationship with him didn't have to be heavy and complicated. A stone around her neck. He'd be a veritable pebble, skipping across a calm lake.

When they got to the boutique, Jasmine was already there. He walked through the store and followed his nose to the coffee that was brewing in the back room. On the table, there was a gift basket, still wrapped up tight, with a colorful ribbon cascading from the top. Megan had followed him back, to stow her purse in one of the cabinets, and she stopped when she saw it.

"How pretty," she said. "Oh, it's from Abigail," she said, looking at the card. She pulled at the bow and peeled back the layers of cellophane.

Inside was a chocolate bonanza. A huge box of assorted milk chocolate candy. A tin of hot chocolate mix. A bag of chocolate cookies. Chocolate-covered pretzels. And more stuff underneath that layer. While he wasn't a chocolate connoisseur, he recognized many of the brands. He watched as Megan picked through everything. When she was finished, she looked a little puzzled.

"What's wrong?"

She waved a hand. "Nothing. It's just that Abigail knows that I don't eat any chocolate besides dark chocolate and there's none in here. But that's fine. It's the thought that counts. It will be a great treat for the staff." Megan started to unwrap the large box of assorted chocolates.

"Stop," he said. "Put it down."

Now she looked really confused.

"Text Abigail and thank her for the basket," he said.

"Right this minute?" she asked.

"Yeah." He had a bad feeling about this.

"Fine," she said, pulling her phone from her purse. She keyed in the text and pressed Send. Almost immediately, her phone dinged with a response. She read it. Then handed her phone to him. It said, I didn't send a basket but it sounds divine. Hope you enjoy.

"I don't understand," Megan said.

He glanced at the two-by-two card. Blank except that Abigail was typed, right in the center. "Do you know any other Abigails?"

"No."

He continued to stare at the name. Typed. As if it had

been ordered from a vendor and they'd prepared the card. But what was weird about that was that it was an assortment of brands. He'd ordered a few of these baskets over the years, sometimes for his mom, sometimes for a girlfriend, but almost always they came from a particular vendor and all the chocolates were produced by that vendor. This looked as if someone had accumulated items and put them in a basket—a do-it-yourself kind of deal. But then why go to the trouble of typing a card? Why not just scrawl a name?

Because they suspected their writing might be analyzed, was the easy answer.

"I'm not exactly sure what's going on but clearly, somebody sent this and wanted you to think it was from Abigail. I can't think of too many reasons to do that unless there's something wrong with the items in the basket."

"A bomb?" she whispered.

He didn't think so. She'd already picked up every single item and nothing had exploded. "Can you ask Jasmine how this got here?"

"Sure." She left the room and was back within a minute. "It was outside the door when she arrived. As if someone had dropped it off."

The camera outside her door might be helpful. "Call your landlord. Ask him if he can provide us a copy of the security tape."

"He's going to want to know why."

"Tell him the truth. Some of it. That a basket was left without any identification and you're attempting to figure out who left it."

"Don't you think he'll think that I'm making too big a deal out of it? I mean, I barely know this man. Weston has done all the negotiating on the leases."

"He might. And if he balks, let it go. The police can

always ask for it. But maybe it's just the push of a couple buttons on his phone and he can send it over to you."

"The police?" she asked. "We're calling the police?"

"Yes. We need to have these things looked at. I'll call them while you get the store ready to open." He could tell she was upset and he didn't want her hearing him explain the situation to authorities.

"We open in forty-five minutes. Having police cars out front is not going to endear me to customers."

"Yeah, well, I'm not sure that's your biggest problem."

She nodded. "I guess you're right," she said dully before she turned and walked from the room.

He picked up his cell phone and dialed his friend Bobby Bayleaf.

"Bayleaf," he answered.

"I need a favor," Seth said.

"You've needed a few of those lately," Bobby said good-naturedly.

"I know. And the requests just keep getting odder." Seth explained the situation to Bobby, who listened carefully.

"Make sure nobody else touches it," Bobby said when he finished. "I'll make a call to the Albuquerque PD and see if we can't expedite a lab test."

"Thanks, my friend."

The boutique was set to open in ten minutes. He went to find Megan. She was behind the cash register, chatting with Jasmine. Two other employees had arrived as well and they were talking near the front window.

It all looked very normal.

And maybe he was making a big deal out of nothing. He hoped so. After all, the box of assorted chocolates had been wrapped in clear film and Megan surely would have noticed if it had appeared to have been previously opened.

But if it had, easy enough to fix, his head told him. For somebody with bad intent and plastic film. He should have examined the package closely before Megan unwrapped it. If he had, maybe he'd have seen something.

He waited until he caught Megan's eye and then motioned to her. Then he took his spot along the back wall, where he could see the entire store. She joined him. Her posture was tense and her jaw was tight—so different from the relaxed, sated woman he'd held in his arms this morning.

But he took a deep breath. Her perfume was the same. And just that little thing made him feel as if not everything had changed. "Did you get a hold of your landlord?"

"He didn't pick up the phone so I sent a text."

"Let me know when he responds."

"Are the police coming?"

"I hope so. Bobby Bayleaf is reaching out to them."

"Even so, I can't expect that they'll hop right on this."

"Maybe. Maybe not. I suspect he'll tell them that it could be related to an open case in Vegas that may be attempted murder."

She jerked her head back, almost knocking it into the wall. "Murder?"

"If one of us was the intended victim of those gunshots at the Periwinkle, that's the charge that could get levied."

"It's a harsh word."

"It's a harsh crime."

"I guess so. And it makes more sense, then, why the Albuquerque police might take an interest."

"You let me worry about the police. Jasmine is unlocking the door. You've got a boutique to open. Do your thing. Let me do my thing."

She smiled at him, looking again like the woman that he'd made love to. "Super Security Man."

"Maybe I'll get it printed on a T-shirt."

"Maybe I'll design it for you," she said softly. "Thanks for being here, Seth. Thanks for keeping me and others safe."

Super Security Man. He could make a joke. Instead, he reached for her hand, careful to do it in a way that no one else would see. He gently squeezed it. "Your being and staying safe is important to me, Megan. Nobody is going to hurt you. I'm not going to give them a chance."

It wasn't a declaration of love—because everyone knew that wasn't light and easy. But he hoped she understood. What was happening between them wasn't inconsequential or unimportant. It wasn't fluff.

It was real.

The police arrived about an hour later. Megan saw them enter, looked over her shoulder to make sure that Seth had also seen them, and went back to helping her customer. The boutique had been busy since they'd unlocked the doors. Like in Sedona, they were doing hourly drawings for prizes and that seemed to really bring people in. The idea of winning something had universal appeal.

None of the shoppers seemed overly concerned that the police were in the store and within twenty minutes, they were gone. One of the officers, wearing gloves on his hands, carried the chocolate basket, which had been placed inside a big clear plastic bag.

She completed the sale with her customer, put the woman's items in a pretty sack and held the door for her. Then she walked to the back of the store and stood next to Seth. "They weren't here long," she said.

"Nope. They will let me know once the lab tests are complete. I told them we'd requested the camera feed from the front door and they asked me to share that with them if there was anything of interest. They said they'd do their best to see if there is any other available footage from nearby neighbors and street cameras."

"I guess that's that," she said. "If there's nothing wrong with it, I'm going to feel bad about giving it away. The staff here would probably have really enjoyed it."

He said nothing. The door opened and two more women entered. "Duty calls," she whispered.

And for the next ten hours, she worked. She was grateful for the business. The online presence they'd generated in the last few weeks combined with the promotional giveaways and the events that they'd sponsored had been enough to drive traffic to the store. And every customer who purchased something was given two coupons, one for themselves and one for a friend, offering 20 percent off on one item at their next visit. Hopefully, that would bring them back.

She had gulped down a quick sandwich at lunch after Seth had insisted that she eat something. He had to be as tired as she was. He never sat, just stood and kept a careful watch on everything that was going on in the store. He'd spotted a shoplifter midafternoon and alerted her to the fact that a woman had slipped several bracelets into her purse.

"Want me to shoot her?" he'd asked quietly from the corner of his mouth.

"Let me try this first," she'd said. Then had walked up to the woman, smiled, looked at her purse and said, "I think something may have fallen into your purse."

The woman had paused, then opened her purse and said, "Oh, I don't know how that happened." Within minutes, she'd left the store.

It was after eight before they finally got to do the same. Fortunately, they did not have to travel. They had another night in Albuquerque and then tomorrow would make the five-hour drive to Colorado Springs.

"I want a steak," Seth said, sinking into the passenger seat.

"Find a place," she said. And then followed his directions to a small restaurant two miles away. It was a one-story stone building with a big arched doorway and a heavy door. Inside, it was dimly lit, smelled like freshly baked bread and when the hostess led them to a booth in the corner that offered them some privacy from the other diners, Megan thought she might never leave.

"I may sleep here tonight," she said.

"I'm sure you're tired. It was a good day, right?" he asked.

"Again, better than we expected. It will make up for the days when there are a total of five customers in the store. I'm not crazy enough to know that those days aren't coming." She opened her menu, found a baked fish that she'd like and closed it. His menu was already at the edge of the table.

"Bottle of wine?" he asked.

"Since I've already decided to sleep here, why not?"

When the server arrived, they ordered. And when the wine was delivered, he tasted it and nodded his approval. Glasses were poured and when Megan took a sip, she almost sighed in appreciation. "This is good," she said.

He clicked the rim of his wineglass to hers. "To the great success of North and More Designs."

She smiled. "Two down and two more to go. But at least for the last one, we'll be back in Vegas. On your home turf."

"If you want to save some money," he said, his tone casual, "we could forgo the hotel in Vegas and stay at my house."

She put her glass down. "I pictured you as an apartment guy."

"I was. But then my mom fell in her yard. I promised that I'd move in to her house, which is the house I grew up in, if she would agree to move to a retirement village. So I guess you could say that I've come full circle. Grew up in the house, left it for college, then the air force, then lived on my own for many years and now I'm back. Mowing the same yard I mowed when I was twelve."

"Same lawn mower?" she asked.

He shook his head. "I upgraded last year. And did some work to the house. It had good bones but the kitchen and baths needed updating. All the carpeting got tossed and hardwood flooring installed."

"I'm sure it's lovely," she said.

"I'd like for you to see it," he said.

The words hung in the air. She would love that. But...

"You're thinking that I've crossed the boundaries of light and easy," he said.

It was exactly what she'd been thinking. "I just..."

"You seem to be having trouble finishing your sentences," he said finally.

"I just don't want us to go too fast," she said.

He drummed his index finger on the table. Drank his wine. Said nothing for a few minutes. The server delivered salads but neither of them picked up silverware.

"I guess I'm just going to have to ask the question," he said. "Is it because I'm a pilot who flies his own plane? Is light and easy the only acceptable arrangement because of that?"

"I don't know," she said. "I've been trying not to think of that," she added, deciding that it was time to be brutally honest. "Fifteen years ago, it was a deal breaker," she said.

"You were just a kid."

"I was so angry. So very angry that my parents were dead, that the life that Abigail and I had enjoyed was gone. I was grateful that Logan had lived, of course. But then, when he wouldn't stop flying, I was even angrier. How did he not understand that the crash had absolutely torn my world apart? How could he contemplate making me live through that again? What if there was another crash?"

"All kinds of dangers in this world," Seth said.

"I know that," she snapped. Then held up her hand. "I'm sorry. Of course there are. Look at me, I could have been seriously injured when that car blew the stop sign. I had some time to think about that when I was trapped inside the vehicle, waiting for the ambulance. Listen, can we just talk about something else?"

"Will you tell me more about the car accident?"

"Not much to tell. It was a four-way stop. I'd stopped and was proceeding through the intersection. The car coming from the right didn't stop and hit my passenger side. Hard enough that my vehicle flipped to the side."

"Tell me about the driver?"

"A woman. She looked to be early fifties."

"You would have gotten her name and address?"

"We didn't exactly exchange information at the scene. I had to be extricated from the vehicle and then I was taken by ambulance to the hospital. After a CT and an MRI, I was pronounced healthy enough to leave and I got a cab home."

"You didn't call Abigail," he said knowingly.

"No way. There was no reason for her to be upset."

"Of course. Was there a police report?"

"Yes. That did have the woman's name and address."

"Was she local?"

"Actually, no. Her permanent address was in Vegas.

There was a note on the police report that she'd recently relocated to Carmel but was temporarily living in a hotel."

He looked puzzled. "Vegas, huh? You don't think that's odd?"

"What?"

"Her being from Vegas," he said.

"You're from Vegas," she said. "I don't think there's anything strange about that."

"What was the driver's name?"

"I'd have to look it up. I don't have the paperwork with me."

"Where would it be?" he asked.

"In my office in Carmel."

"Can your assistant, Gillian, find it?"

"Yes, she would have filed it. But I don't understand where you're going with this."

"I'm not sure where I'm going," he said. "But around the same time that you're being followed and odd things are happening, a women rams into your car. And she's from Vegas, where our journey together started and where it's going to end. I don't like it. And when I don't like something, it gets my attention."

She let out a breath. "Fine. I'll text Gillian. She can get me the name."

"Have her scan the whole accident report and email it to me."

"It will be tomorrow, when she's back in the office. Anything else?" she asked. At least he seemed willing to let the discussion about him being a pilot go.

"Nope," he said, as the server came back with steaming plates. She set them down and left. "We should eat because I don't think they're going to let you sleep here," he added, reaching for his fork.

She knew where she wanted to sleep. And it wasn't in

this booth. She reached her arm out, resting her fingertips against his hand. "I want to sleep with you. Your bed, my bed, I don't care. But don't ask me to think beyond that. I just can't do it right now."

He swallowed, hard enough that she could see the muscles of his throat working. "Did you see that they had dark chocolate mousse on the dessert menu?"

It wasn't the response she'd expected. "I did," she answered carefully.

"You're not the only one who likes chocolate."

"Okay."

"We're getting a couple to go," he said. "No plates needed."

"Because…"

"Because I'm going to eat you up, darling."

Chapter 16

They were both quiet on the drive from the restaurant to the hotel. In the elevator, they stood a foot apart, as if afraid to get too close. She carried the desserts so that his hands would be free.

He unlocked her room, checked it and motioned her inside. Then very deliberately locked the door and turned. She was still standing in the same spot, just feet inside the room.

The air in the room was warm.

And more heat was pouring off him.

He wanted her badly.

"Don't move," he said. He used the connecting door to get to his room, made sure it was clear, and then took his gun from his waist holster. Returned to Megan's room and carefully placed the gun in the drawer of the night-stand. Sat down on the edge of the bed. With his index finger, he motioned for her to come close.

She took small steps and his heart was hammering in his chest by the time she reached him. He reached for the sack in her hand and set it on the nightstand. Then used one finger to slide the strap of her purse off her shoulder and down her arm. He tossed it toward the chair in the corner. Heard it hit.

Every sound, every touch, every breath—it was all exaggerated.

So like he felt every time he'd suited up and climbed into the cockpit of his F-16.

He pulled her closer, between his thighs. With her still standing, he reached under her dress, ran his hands up the backs of her strong legs, settled them on the cheeks of her butt. Could feel her sexy underwear. "What color?" he asked.

"Pink," she whispered.

"Very girlie," he said. He edged his hands around, feeling her hips, the front of her thighs. He slipped his thumbs under the lace and pressed hard into her center.

She gasped and arched. "Oh, God," she said.

He slipped two fingers inside her. Moved them. Finding the spot.

Her head was back, her breath was coming in spurts and she bucked on his hand. Reaching blindly, she grabbed for a shoulder.

"I've got you. You won't fall," he said. He held her tight with his leg muscles. "I promise."

But minutes later, she did tumble. Over the edge, her inner muscles clenching and unclenching, over and over.

And when she was spent, her head hanging, she pushed her hair back from her face and smiled at him. "I guess we're eating our chocolate mousse with spoons after all."

He moved fast, almost flipping her onto her back on

the soft bed. “Not so. That was the appetizer. Dessert comes after the main meal.”

“What’s for dinner?” she asked, a bit weakly.

He laughed.

“You, darling. Just you.”

Megan missed her morning run for the second day in a row but she didn’t mind. It was after eight when she finally woke up, feeling as if there wasn’t an inch of her body that Seth had not explored. And enjoyed.

She felt as if her brain had been emptied and filled with straw. It had matched the boneless exhaustion that had consumed her before they’d finally slept. Now she saw that he was already up, showered, dressed, with coffee made. He was sitting in the chair, looking at his phone.

“Good morning,” he said.

His eyes were warm but there was something in his tone. She sat up in bed, pulling the sheet up to cover her. “What’s wrong?”

“We have two bits of news. One, the Albuquerque police have a report back from their lab. The candy in the assorted box of chocolates was tainted. With a laxative that you can purchase over the counter. They suspect a syringe was used to insert the laxative into each piece. It likely wouldn’t have killed anyone who ate it but they’d have been…let’s just say, incapacitated for a period of time. And two, there is confirmation that an alarm was pulled to initiate the fire drill. By someone wearing white pants, a white lab coat and a white baseball cap.”

She rubbed her forehead. “Can I have a cup of coffee, please?”

“Of course.” He poured it and brought it over to the bed. But he didn’t sit down. Instead, he returned to his chair.

She sipped. Tried to think it through. "It seems… I don't know, it all seems kind of lame."

"Agree. Which has made me reflect on the pattern of things that have occurred. The first odd thing was you noticed the blond man following you, once home from work and once on the Fourth of July. He watched your apartment one night but he never approached. Then it was hang-up calls and annoying door buzzers. I'd put all that into the lame category."

She nodded.

"Then you overhear a scary conversation between a man and a woman, both with some accent, about the best way to kill a person. That ratchets up lame into threatening. Then you have your car accident, which we're going to get more information on this morning. You and Abigail travel to Vegas and you think you're being followed. Back to lame. But then we're shot at."

"Maybe the shots were purposely fired over our heads. Could be lame," she said. "More scare tactics."

He shook his head. "That shot came from some distance. And most people are not that good with a gun. If we were dealing with former military, then maybe. But I really think they fired that gun with some seriously bad intent. So for my money, it almost seems as if somebody was acting upon that conversation you heard underneath your window."

"It was a man and a woman. If we assume the man was the blond guy, then the woman is the new player. She's… not lame…" Her voice trailed off.

"Oh, she's probably pretty lame but it does look like she's bringing more serious toys to the party," he said. "Then we go on the road and there's the call about your parents' plane crash and subsequent no-show at Marta's

Deli, the snake, the fire alarm, and now candy that would have kept you and your employees in the bathroom all day. All lame."

"Irritating," she said.

"Definitely. I remember you using the word *unsettled.* A series of things, even when they are lame, is damn unsettling."

"I still think that I should call Logan," she said. "He would know if there was new information about the crash. He would know why his brother would be contacting me."

It was time to tell her the truth. "Trey Riker is going to be talking to Logan today."

"What? When was this decision made?"

"The night before last. I had a conversation with Trey when we were at the cocktail party. He was already working on Logan's background check so he seemed like the logical one to have the conversation."

"Oh." She stared at him. "Did he tell you anything about Logan that was interesting?"

He felt a pain in his gut and recognized that it was likely jealousy. Was it possible that after all this time she still cared for the man? "He's married with two kids and works at a bank in Cincinnati."

She said nothing. That unnerved him.

"What do you think about that?" he asked.

She shrugged. "I think it sounds as if he's got a nice life."

"You could have had that life." Now he was really poking at her.

"But I don't," she said. "Because I made a choice. The best choice for me."

The burn in his gut intensified. "I'm just wondering if you ever have any regrets." He wasn't generally a chicken but he was clearly not able to man up. What he should have asked was whether she was willing to make the same ultimatum again, live with the same consequences again. Was she going to push him away by giving him unacceptable options?

She said nothing for a long moment. "I have no regrets," she said. "Now, I'm going to get up and shower and then I think we should get on the road. We've got a long drive to Colorado Springs today."

She wasn't answering his unspoken questions. Fair enough, he supposed. Damn frustrating, though. Was it possible that she didn't realize what he was truly asking? He didn't think so. She was too bright, too perceptive. But she'd asked for light and easy, and the conversation he was edging toward would be none of those things.

"I can be ready in fifteen minutes," he said, deciding to back off. They had a few more days together. He wasn't going to risk that by pushing her too hard.

"Give me thirty," she said. "And please, when you hear from Trey, don't hide the information from me. I want to know what Logan has to say."

"Okay." It was a fair request. "But I need you to do something before you shower. Get a hold of your assistant. I want information about the driver who hit you. Have her send it to both of us."

She picked up her phone. "On it."

Megan's assistant was efficient. Both of their phones chimed, indicating new emails, while they were eating breakfast. The email from Gillian was succinct: As you requested. He clicked on the attachment and studied the notes the responding officer had made.

Female driver, age forty-eight, claimed that she didn't

realize that she was approaching a four-way stop. When she saw another vehicle crossing the intersection, she tried to stop but was unsuccessful. Driver of the second vehicle, female, age thirty-five, was extricated from the vehicle and removed from the scene by ambulance.

Pretty much what Megan had said. But it still made his blood run cold. She could have been killed.

He found the driver's name. "Nadia Vitron," he said. "That was the other driver's name."

Megan also had her phone in her hand. She'd pushed her half-finished poached eggs and English muffin aside. "Yes, that's right. I remember now."

"Doesn't mean anything to you?"

"No."

He forwarded the email on to Royce and added a message. Need information on Nadia Vitron ASAP.

"Royce will be on it," he said.

She shook her head. "I suspect that none of your partners realized that doing business with North and More Designs was going to be a full-time job *for everybody.*"

"They're fine with helping out," Seth said. "That's what we do for one another."

"You're a lucky group of guys to have found one another. Not everybody gets that at work."

Luck probably had something to do with it. But they all worked hard at the friendship. He knew how much he'd miss it if it ended. Probably a little like she missed having Abigail on this trip. "Once Abigail has the baby, will she be more involved in North and More Designs?"

"I imagine so. We'll play it by ear. She's actually doing a great deal for the Vegas opening. She's getting everything ready for the fashion show and making sure the boutique is ready to go."

"You don't have Jasmine to see to things there."

"No. It's enough for her to oversee the three other boutiques, with site managers reporting to her. We have a manager hired for the Vegas store. She'll report directly to me, as will Jasmine."

"And you'll work from your office in Carmel?"

"I'll likely divide my time between Carmel and Vegas to start."

"Going to stay at the Periwinkle?"

"No. That would be kind of pricey. I'll get an apartment."

"I do have that extra bedroom," he said, his tone light.

"We had this conversation," she said. "When you offered your place for the Vegas opening."

"We had limited conversation about it," he said, "before we moved on to other topics. I don't recall a decision ever being made."

"That's right. I'm not making *any* housing decisions on this trip."

Read between the lines, Pike. Discussions about sharing a living space did not fall into the light and easy category. "Okay. Just wanted to make sure you were aware of your options. If you're done, we should get on the road."

They were an hour outside Colorado Springs when she heard Seth's phone buzz. "It's Trey," he said.

"Can you put it on speaker?" she asked.

"Hey, Trey," he answered. "I've got you on speaker and Megan is here."

She wasn't offended by the disclaimer. After all, the man had been talking to her ex-fiancé. Logan had been very angry at her when she'd broken off the engagement. Perhaps during the years, he'd mellowed. Perhaps not.

"Hi, Megan. How are the grand openings going?"

"Good. Two down and two to go."

"Kellie is all excited about your Vegas store. Said that once she has these babies, she gets a couple hours there."

"That will be great," Megan said.

"I didn't see any short black skirts or white shirts," Seth interjected.

Huh?

Trey laughed. "Not to worry. Ordered a lifetime supply of those already."

"He's got a slight fetish for the outfit that Kellie wore when she was a cocktail server at Lavender," Seth explained. "So what do you have for us?"

"I met with Logan Lewis this morning. There's three things that I'm pretty confident of. He didn't know anything about Megan getting anonymous calls regarding the crash. There is no new information about the crash. And three, he doesn't have a clue what his brother is up to. Hasn't seen him for four years."

"Did he say why?" Megan asked.

"Not in detail but I got enough to know that four or so years ago, Ross visited Logan in Cincinnati and when he left, Logan was missing about a thousand dollars in cash and his wife's jewelry box had been depleted of anything of value. Ross evidently has a drug problem."

That was sad. But if they'd had no contact for four years, what would cause Ross to suddenly make up a story that there was new information about the crash? That really made no sense.

"Did you tell him that we're trying to find Ross?" Seth asked.

"I did. I told him that he was most recently living in

the Los Angeles area and that was news to him. He's not going to be any help to us."

Megan glanced quickly at Seth.

"Did he say anything else?" Seth asked.

"He…asked about Megan?" Trey said. "I told him that she was well and he seemed happy to hear that."

Megan could feel her face get warm and adjusted the vent so that the air-conditioning was aimed there.

"Okay, we got it," Seth said. "Thanks very much."

"No problem. See you when you're back in Vegas."

Seth put his phone down. "Well, that's that."

"Now that we know this, is it even important to find Ross? Logan confirmed there's no new information."

"I want to find him," Seth said. "There's a couple things that bother me. Ross has had no contact with you for fifteen years and no contact with his brother for four. But something motivated him to pick up the phone, two times, to call you. And his message was guaranteed to cause you angst. So why and why now? I want to understand that motivation. And maybe equally important is that Ross doesn't sound like an upstanding citizen. I don't like those types to be unaccounted for."

"What should I do if he calls again?" she asked.

"We need to force his hand. So call him by name. Let him know that you know there's no new information. Ask him why he's calling you. We might get lucky and he'll offer something up that will be helpful. Tell him that you want to meet with him in person, for old times' sake, if nothing else."

"I have to tell you," she said, "I hope he just doesn't call again."

"I'd be okay with that, too," he said, "if I only knew where he was."

* * *

It was a warm August afternoon in Colorado Springs with the thermometer hovering around eighty. They got to their hotel and entered the air-conditioned lobby.

"Checking in for Megan North and Seth Pike," Megan said.

The clerk clicked some computer keys. "I see your reservation for two rooms."

"We just need one," Megan said. "Can we cancel the other?"

"Of course, Ms. North," the clerk said, and in minutes, they had a room key and directions to the elevator. They were the only ones going up. Once the doors had slid shut, she turned to him. "I didn't see any need to keep up the pretense."

"Agree," he said, grateful that his voice didn't squeak. For most of the drive, in his head, he'd been kicking his own ass for stepping over the light and easy line that morning. Had wondered what he might do to convince her to let him back into her bed, because staying out of it simply wasn't an option.

"We should probably eat an early dinner," she said.

"Whatever you want," he said.

She smiled like a cat. "Really?" She leaned forward, put her mouth close to his ear. Whispered exactly what she wanted.

He could feel the burn start in his toes and spread upward.

"I'm thinking that you might want a steak," she said.

And maybe an ambulance, just in case. But hell, what a way to go.

Chapter 17

The Colorado Springs cocktail party was black tie. She'd enjoyed watching Seth get ready and when he was done, he looked magnificent. "I think you should wear a tux every day," she said.

"I think that might be more for the likes of the Weston Marberrys of the world."

She knew why he was bringing it up. Weston had surprised them at the Albuquerque cocktail party.

"If he shows up tonight, I'm not going to be my cordial self," Seth said, slipping his gun into his waist holster.

"I don't think he thought you were all that cordial on the other occasions."

"I'm serious, Megan. Things are...different."

No doubting that. After arriving at the hotel last night, they had the early dinner they'd discussed and then had fallen into bed together. Because there hadn't been any morning events, they'd basically slept until noon because quite frankly, there hadn't been a lot of sleeping until well into the night. Then they'd had the rah-rah meeting with the Colorado Springs staff and a walk-through of the store, which again, was almost identical to the Sedona and Albuquerque stores. She'd congratulated Jasmine following the meeting. The woman had done an excellent job of delivering upon their brand of upscale yet relaxed shopping for the woman who might want something slightly different.

She'd done another media interview, this time with a local television station, after the meeting and then they'd returned to the hotel to change for the cocktail party.

And at every moment of the day, she'd been intensely aware of Seth. Had practically memorized the shape of his head and the deceptively relaxed-looking way he stood. He was right. She wasn't exactly sure what it was between the two of them but it certainly was different. "I'm not expecting him," she said.

"I think that's what you said in Albuquerque."

It had been. But she'd exchanged a couple business emails with Weston earlier and while she wasn't comfortable asking him outright if he was going to surprise her, she was fairly confident that he was still in his Sedona office midafternoon, which would make an appearance in Colorado Springs that evening difficult.

Thus far the drives between the cities had been four to five hours. But it was a twelve-hour drive from Colorado Springs back to Las Vegas. They would have to cross the mountains in Colorado, then go down through Utah and finally Nevada. Seth had yet to mention the upcoming trip but she knew he was very aware of the mileage and the time. There was no way she could do the entire drive by herself in one day. She'd fall asleep behind the wheel.

They'd have to stop halfway. He'd taken care of cancelling their existing hotel reservations in their destination cities and making more. She needed to make sure that he'd done the same for their layover night as well.

"If he shows, I will tell Jasmine that her only task for the evening is keeping him occupied," she said. "They're old friends. It won't be a hardship for her. And it will likely keep him alive."

"I didn't say I was going to shoot him. Just that I wasn't going to be cordial."

"Right. We should go."

The Colorado Springs cocktail party was in a hotel that offered stunning views of Pikes Peak. As she mingled with her guests, she kept an eye on the door. Didn't really relax until the night was winding down. Weston was a no-show.

Once they were back at the hotel, she noticed that Seth was more quiet than usual. "I thought you'd be happy. No Weston."

"That's all good. I guess I'm waiting for the other shoe to drop. Nothing has happened here in Colorado Springs. No weird phone calls, no fire drills, no tainted candy."

"No shots fired," she said.

"Exactly."

"Maybe it's over. Maybe the person got tired of tormenting me."

"Maybe," he said.

He wasn't convinced. But she couldn't worry about that now. Tomorrow they would have the grand opening in Colorado Springs and then they would travel to Vegas, where she'd have decisions to make. Decisions that she wasn't ready to weigh in on yet. She crawled into the bed. "Come here," she said.

"Got another list?" he asked, referring to what she'd whispered in his ear the night before.

"That first night at the shower for Trey and Kellie and Rico and Laura, you said that you speak poker at Wingman Security. Let's just say that tonight, it's dealer's choice."

"Who's dealing?"

"We'll take turns. You go first."

Several hours later, when it was again his turn, he had her flat on her back, naked, when his cell phone rang. It was across the room, charging. She glanced at the clock. It was two in the morning. She immediately reached for her own phone on the nightstand, to make sure that Abigail or Evan had not been trying to reach her. But there were no calls.

He was out of bed, looking at the display. "Royce," he said to her.

She knew it could not be good.

"Hey, Royce," he said. Then he listened for a minute or two. "I'll be there as soon as I can," he said. Then he hung up. Turned to her.

"My mom has been transported by ambulance to the hospital. Arm and chest pain. She was feeling faint and called the Everpark emergency number. They called 911 and Royce."

"Heart attack?" she whispered.

"Not yet," he said. "The paramedics did an EKG and it was normal. But they weren't taking any chances."

"Of course not. You have to go."

He didn't answer. Was busy typing something into his phone. Finally looked up. "There's a flight out of Colorado Springs into Vegas at five this morning."

"You can make that," she said.

"I'm not leaving you."

"Yes, you are. Don't be ridiculous. I'll do the grand

opening here and then leave for Vegas. I'll be there by late the following day."

"No. Unacceptable."

He wasn't wasting any time. He was pulling on clothes, then his shoes. His suitcase was out of the closet and on the bed. Items going in.

Her head was whirling. She could miss the grand opening. It wasn't ideal but Jasmine would be there, had already successfully handled the other two. Could she fly? She hadn't for more than fifteen years.

He'd told her how safe commercial flying was. She hadn't needed the lecture. After her parents' crash, she extensively studied crash records. Almost always, it was small planes.

She wasn't afraid to fly on a big plane. Had simply chosen not to. There was a difference.

He zipped his suitcase. Looked up. "Please don't make me choose between you and my mother," he said.

If he chose his mother, she would understand. But she was awfully afraid that he would choose her. And that he would never forgive her for that. And while she didn't know where this was going, she didn't want something like that forging a divide between the two of them.

She swung her legs over the bed. "Fine," she said.

He shook his head. "No. No room for equivocation. 'Fine' as in 'I'll do this but there's going to be a big price for you to pay, Seth Pike,' or 'Fine, I just need ten minutes.'"

"Neither. I only need five minutes."

He stared at her, then stalked toward her. Kissed her hard. "Thank you," he said.

They dropped off the pretty blue rental car at the airport. They got inside, through security, in record time.

Of course, at that time of the morning, it was basically deserted. At the gate, he reached for her hand.

She hadn't made him choose. And he was grateful. Royce had said that his mom was getting additional tests at the hospital and they'd know more by morning. He wanted to be there when any news was delivered to his mom, wanted to be able to help her with any decisions that needed to be made.

"How are you?" he asked.

"I'm fine."

"Not angry about not being at the opening?"

"No."

"Not angry about getting on a plane?"

"No."

"Not angry because you've had less than three hours of sleep?"

"Maybe a little," she admitted, letting her head drop to his shoulder.

He slouched down in his chair to make it more comfortable for her. "If you're worried about anything at any time, just tell me."

"I'm planning to sleep on the plane."

"There's this thing called the mile-high club."

"Shush, Seth," she said gently, closing her eyes. "You've used up your quota of favors."

The flight was uneventful and she did sleep for most of it. When they were on the ground, she sent a quick text to Abigail, letting her know the change of plans. Got an immediate response. Let me know if there's anything that Evan or I can do.

They took a cab from the airport to the hospital and the front desk directed them to the cardiac floor. The door to his mother's room was partially open and they entered quietly. She immediately saw the resemblance between Seth and his mom, who was a lovely older woman. She was watching television with the sound very low.

She turned and smiled when she saw Seth. "Royce told me that he called you," she said. "I'm fine. You didn't need to run home."

Seth gathered his mom in his arms. And held her.

Megan stayed back, blinking her eyes fast so that nobody would see that she was this close to bawling. Seth Pike was Super Security Man who unabashedly loved his mom.

Seth pulled back. Patted his mom's leg. Turned to Megan. "I want to introduce you to Megan North," he said.

"Good morning," Megan said, taking a step forward. "It's a pleasure, although difficult circumstances."

"A big fuss about nothing," his mom said. "Dr. Kahla was in very early this morning and she said that she should have the results of the tests I had last night by midmorning. I'm convinced it's nothing. I probably overreacted when I called the office but all I could think about was how upset Seth would be if I didn't call."

"That's right," he said.

"Pull up a chair and tell me about your boutiques, Megan. Seth sent me a few pictures and I can't wait to see your Vegas store."

The next two hours passed quickly. Seth and his mom both seemed to be relaxed but when the doctor came in, she wasn't sure which one of them tensed up more.

But the news was good, according to Dr. Kahla, who was tall and slender, midfifties probably, with a lovely face and gorgeous thick silver hair that she pulled back in a turquoise clip. There had been no heart attack and she suspected that it might have been a case of mild acid reflux. "I'll prescribe something for your mom to help with that and we'll get her discharge papers ready."

Seth extended his hand. "Thank you, Dr. Kahla."

The woman turned to Megan. "I saw some very nice pictures this morning of your boutique. You don't happen to have a card with you?"

"I do," Megan said, fishing one out of her purse.

The doctor took it. "Excellent. Hope to see you there." She left the room.

Seth's mom was practically beaming. "When I saw her shoes, I knew she'd like what you were selling. I figured if I had to be here, I might as well try to drum up some business for you."

Seth was shaking his head. "You amaze me."

"Whatever you want from the boutique," Megan said. "It's yours. On the house."

"No, no, no. That's not how you make any money. But I will drop by for your grand opening."

"Would you like to come to the cocktail party that we're having the night before?" Megan asked.

"Everybody from Wingman Security will be there," Seth said.

"You know, I think I'd like that."

It was hard to believe that she'd left Vegas a week and a half earlier and she and Seth had been virtual strangers. Now they were as intimate as two people could be. But she wasn't ready for that to be public knowledge.

"I thought we'd agreed that it was a waste to rent two hotel rooms," Seth said as their cabdriver waited at a red light.

"You let me worry about that," she said. She let her head fall back. "What a relief about your mom."

It had taken a while for the discharge paperwork to arrive and then she and Seth had accompanied the woman back to her home. Seth had wanted her to come to the Periwinkle, since that was where he'd be staying, but she only laughed. "I want to sleep in my own bed," she'd said. "Don't fuss over me, or the next time I won't call you." Seth had evidently figured she was serious because he had stopped badgering her about it.

"I was scared," he said.

"It was a climactic way to top off some pretty crazy days."

He shrugged. "Days were okay. I liked the nights better."

"Shush. It's those kinds of comments that I don't want Abigail to hear. She's got enough to think about with this baby. I don't want her worrying about me."

"Maybe she won't worry. Maybe she'll think I'm perfect."

He was. But it had been so fast. What would Abigail think when she found out that Megan had jumped into bed with her security guard? A pilot, no less.

She'd think that she'd lost her mind. Megan wasn't so sure she'd be wrong.

If Abigail had questions, Megan wasn't going to be any help. She was still trying to sort it out in her own head.

"I can't wait to see her," Megan said. "Evan is traveling, so she'll be solo. I told her she could spend a couple nights."

"Great," he said, his voice flat.

"If it makes you feel any better," she said, almost wanting to laugh at his disappointed face, "I'm going to miss you in my bed."

He cocked his head. "Really? What will you miss the most?"

She pretended to consider. "It was all rather lovely.

If it had been the Olympics, I'd have given you a 9.8 on technique, a 9.9 on artistic impression, and a 10 on..." She smiled. "Stamina."

He narrowed his eyes. "What's wrong with my technique?"

She smiled. "I knew that would drive you crazy."

"Are you planning to stay in for dinner or go out?"

"There are a couple nice restaurants at the hotel. We can eat at one of those. That makes it easy." The driver pulled up to the Periwinkle. She took off her sunglasses and carefully put them in their case. "I have to admit, I'm torn. I want to see Abigail but I don't want to expose her to...whatever it is that is dogging me. While I'm taking heart that Colorado Springs was without incident, I keep thinking about your comment that you're waiting for the other shoe to drop."

"You know," he said, "now that we're back in Vegas, you have the expertise of the entire Wingman Security organization at your disposal. Nothing is going to happen to you or to Abigail."

She reached out and placed her palm on the side of his face. His skin was warm from the taxi, which didn't seem to have working air-conditioning. Or, as he'd said, maybe just because he ran hot. "Or to you," she said softly. "Don't be a hero."

Neither of them said anything for a long moment. They simply stayed connected, her palm on his cheek. Finally, he pulled away. "Absolutely not," he said. "I have to be around to work on my technique. A 9.8 is simply not acceptable."

Abigail was already in the hotel lobby when Megan and Seth walked through. Megan carefully wrapped her arms around her little sister. "Oh, my God, I'm so glad to see you."

"I know," Abigail said. "I missed you so much." Abigail turned her head to the side and smiled at Seth. "Afternoon, Seth. Thanks for watching over my sis. And I'm glad the news about your mom was good."

"It was my pleasure and yeah, a big relief," he said.

"And the trip was uneventful, nothing out of J.T. Daly's?" Abigail asked, stepping back from Megan's embrace.

"Not a peep," Seth said.

He was telling the truth. Neither one of them thought this had anything to do with J.T. Daly's. "Let me look at you," Megan said. "Your tummy is even bigger than when I left."

"Babies gain weight fast during the last month of pregnancy," Abigail said. "And supposedly I've dropped, although to me, I can't really tell. All I know is that I'm about as round as I am tall."

"You are beautiful," Megan said. And Abigail was. But in truth, she also looked a little tired. "Are you getting enough rest?"

"Plenty of opportunity," Abigail said. "But sleeping isn't all that comfortable. But just about three more weeks."

"North and More Designs baby clothes, here we come," Megan said. Out of the corner of her eye, she could see Seth carefully watching the lobby. "Let's go to my room," she said. "We can have a couple hours of girl time and then Seth will join us for dinner. I wish Evan were here."

"Me, too. But it might be good that he got away. I swear, he is so nervous about this baby. Telling him that women have babies every day in all parts of the world that are significantly less ideal than a highly rated hospital doesn't seem to matter."

"Give Seth and me a second to check in," Megan said. "We'll be right back."

This time, their rooms were on the eighth floor. Adjoining, of course. But there'd be no sneaking in tonight. That thought was almost enough to make her regret inviting Abigail to stay. She would miss him. She'd been lying about the 9.8 in technique. He was a solid 10.

Once they took the elevator upstairs, Seth opened the door and checked the room. Then he unlocked the connecting door. "I'll see you two later," he said. "Knock if you need anything before that."

"Thanks, Seth," Abigail said. "I'm looking forward to dinner and getting a chance to talk."

Seth just nodded.

Megan waited until he'd left before saying, "What did you mean by that?"

"Nothing," Abigail said innocently. "I guess I'm just interested in the man who makes my sister stammer."

"What? He does not," Megan protested.

"He does. Every time we talked, when the subject came around to Seth, you got a little tongue-tied." Abigail sat on one of the queen beds.

Megan sat on the same one. She didn't want to have to yell across the room. There was no way she wanted Seth to hear this. "He's a really good man," she said.

"You weren't crazy about the idea of traveling with security," Abigail reminded her.

Megan wasn't going to tell her that she'd needed it a couple times. "I know. But we developed an understanding of sorts."

"In bed or out of it?" Abigail asked.

Megan stared at her sister. "How did you know?"

"Because you're my sister. My best friend. I knew from our phone conversations and then it only took one look at you to know something was very different. You're absolutely radiant. That's not generally what a road trip will do for you."

Megan groaned. "The sex was amazing. Knock-your-socks-off amazing."

"I remember sex," Abigail said good-naturedly. "And if it was that good, I'm not sure I understand what you're moaning and groaning about."

"He's all wrong for me. You know he's a pilot. Has his own plane."

"There are worse things."

"I know. It seems...well, it seems a little hypocritical of me, doesn't it? I mean, I gave Logan an ultimatum. That he give up flying or me."

"It was so soon after Mom and Dad's accident. Your nerves were raw. And secretly, I think you were hoping that he'd choose flying. It made it easy for you to walk away."

She didn't know what to say to that. "You were fourteen. I don't think you might have understood it all."

Abigail didn't seem offended. "I didn't. At the time. I was too wrapped up in my own misery. But it's been fifteen years. And I've fallen in love myself. As I think back to your and Logan's relationship, I'm not sure that the two of you loved each other. Liked, certainly. Cared deeply about. I think so. But loved?" Abigail shook her head.

Did she love Seth? Was it even possible to love someone after such a short time together? "I'm not sure where it's going," she said honestly.

"You got on a plane with him," Abigail said. "I think that says something. Were you scared?"

"I might have been, if I had been by myself. But when Seth is there, it...it just seems as if everything is going to be okay. I'm glad I did it. Not because I had something to prove. There was no way I could make him endure a car ride over the mountains when he was worried about his mom. That would have been horrible of me."

"You are definitely not a horrible person. Listen, tomorrow was going to be your travel day. Instead, we're going to the pool. We'll have to find an extra-sturdy beach chair that will support my weight and you'll have to promise to wear a cover-up the entire time so that I don't want to drown you, but you can decompress. Think things through."

"This is scary," Megan admitted.

"No, *this* is scary," Abigail said, pointing at her baby bump.

Megan reached for her. "We'll get through it together."

"Like always," Abigail said. "By the way, I stopped at the Vegas store yesterday. It looks fabulous."

"They've been sending me photos. The coffee bar turned out even better than I thought."

"I know. Love the furniture. I'm excited. I promised Evan that I wouldn't be on my feet too much but I want to do it all. The fashion show, the ribbon-cutting, the cocktail party."

"Well, there's lots of brand-new chairs for you to sit in when you get tired. And I'll make sure you do."

"Trust me on this. No one has to make me. I'm going with that suggestion quite willingly these days, although I prefer to lie down rather than sit. More space for the babe."

"Aren't a couple of those chairs recliners?"

Abigail smiled. "Love it when a plan comes together."

"Okay. Well, here's my plan. I'm going to take a shower and change before dinner," Megan said.

"Fine. I'll just rest here while you do that. Don't worry about me." Abigail leaned back against a pillow, waved a hand in the air and closed her eyes.

Megan smiled. She had been worrying about her for the last fifteen years. That wasn't going to change now.

Seth had not been expecting the soft knock on the connecting door. He'd assumed Megan and Abigail would talk until it was time for dinner.

"Yes," he said.

"May I come in?"

Abigail, not Megan. "Of course." He moved off the bed and went to open the door. "Everything okay?" he asked, looking over her shoulder. The room was empty but he could hear the shower.

"Yes, Megan is soaking the road grime off," she said. "I thought this might give us an opportunity to chat."

He wasn't sure that sounded all that great. "Want a chair?" he asked.

"I'll stand," she said. "But go ahead."

He was almost a foot taller and didn't want to tower over her. So he sat. And pressed his lips together. She'd called this meeting, she could damn well start. It didn't sit well with him that they were hiding the security threats that they'd encountered on the trip. Abigail was every bit as much the client as Megan. It went against his basic instinct to be anything but absolutely truthful and transparent.

"I understand that you're sleeping with my sister."

Chapter 18

Well, hell. Speaking of transparent. Evidently, Megan had been. He ran a hand across his hair. "Listen, Abigail. Neither one of us planned this. But we're caught up in something that..."

She stared at him. "That what?"

He was just going to say it. "That feels very right. Perfect."

"You know Megan hasn't had a serious relationship since she was engaged to Logan."

"I know that."

"She was too busy raising me. Then with her career, so that she could continue to provide for me."

"She considers it time well spent," he said.

"That's good to hear," Abigail said. "And I believe that she believes that. I know I'm certainly grateful. No one could have asked for a better sister. You know she's only six years older. Sometimes I forget that because she handles so many things well."

"She's amazing," he said.

"But she's really not very experienced in affairs of the heart. I guess I'm asking you to remember that."

"I've got no intention of hurting her," he said, a little irritated that Abigail had thought the warning was necessary. "I...love her," he admitted.

"Have you told her that?"

He shook his head. "She hasn't given me any indication that she's interested in hearing that. She wants to keep things 'light and easy,'" he said, putting the words in air quotes.

She smiled. "Oh, that so sounds like her. And you don't want that?"

"There's a time for light and easy. And there's a time to dig deep, to pull it out by the roots. To be honest. With yourself. With each other."

She opened the connecting door and took two steps back into her own room. "Don't let her push you away, Seth."

"I don't intend to. She may be amazing, but I'm a damn bulldog."

He could hear her laughing as she shut the door between the two rooms.

The next morning, Megan woke up and saw that her sister was already awake and sitting up on the other bed. It felt strange not to have Seth's big warm body spooned around her. How the hell had she gotten so used to that in just a few days? "Doing okay?"

"Oh, fine. I was just examining my ankles."

"Because?" Megan asked.

"Because I like to torment myself," Abigail said. "Maybe I shouldn't have had the French onion soup. But it was delicious."

"Dinner was fun," Megan said.

"It was," Abigail agreed. "I like Seth."

"What do you mean by that?"

Abigail smiled. "I mean, I like Seth. Seems like a nice guy. I enjoyed his stories about the air force. And he seems to love his mom very much."

"Oh." Megan threw back her covers. "I'm sorry, sweetheart. Didn't mean to jump at you."

"It's okay. When I was first falling for Evan, my emotions were all over the place."

"I didn't say I was falling for him," Megan protested.

"You didn't?" Abigail asked, her eyes deliberately wide. "Maybe I imagined that." She got out of bed and stretched. "I am a little surprised that he's coming to the pool with us," she said nonchalantly. "I thought he'd be happy enough to have a few free hours."

"He takes his responsibilities very seriously."

"I guess. But given that J.T. Daly's appears to be playing nice, it seems…I don't know…a little much."

"It's not," Megan said, automatically defending Seth.

"If you say so," she said, not sounding convinced.

"Listen, Abigail, there are things…that I haven't told you. And Seth has been spot-on in helping me deal with them."

Abigail sat back down on the bed, looking satisfied. "I knew it. Don't you think it's about time you tell me what's going on?"

Megan stared at her sister. She'd baited her brilliantly. "I think it is time. I'm sorry, Abigail. I haven't meant to keep secrets from you. I just didn't want you—"

"To worry," Abigail interrupted. "I'm a big girl, Megan. I can handle it."

"I know you can. Let me order room service and then I'll tell you everything."

And thirty minutes later, over ham-and-cheese omelets, she did exactly that. Didn't keep anything back. And when she was finished, Abigail reached for her hand.

"I'm so glad you told me," she said. "And I'm mad as hell that somebody is putting you through all this."

"We need to be watchful," Megan said. "But we also need to go on about our lives. Because to do anything else gives them too much power over us."

"Damn straight," Abigail said. "But I swear to God if I get the chance, I'm scratching somebody's eyes out. Ross Lewis. Blond stalker guy. Nadia Vitron. They better watch out for me. I've got an extra thirty pounds behind my swing now."

"I'll hold them down for you," Megan said, smiling. "Now let's go to the pool. I have a feeling that Seth Pike is going to look really good in a pair of swim trunks."

"I don't know why I don't do this more often," Megan said. She reached for the drink that Seth handed her. "What is this?" she asked as she relaxed back into her lounge chair.

"Frozen piña colada," he said. He smiled at Abigail, who was next to Megan. "Yours is a virgin."

"Still delicious," Abigail said. "We can drink to the success of the Colorado Springs opening. Megan talked to Jasmine this morning. It went well."

"Good to hear," Seth said.

"I'm going to take my beautiful drink and dangle my swollen ankles in the water for a bit."

He waited until Abigail was far enough away that she wouldn't hear their conversation. "Something is different," he said.

"She knows everything. I told her."

"What brought this on?"

"There were reasons," Megan said evasively.

"Tell me."

"She tricked me. Casually criticized you, that you might be hovering for no reason, and I jumped to your defense."

"You defended me?" he asked. *If you were only interested in light and easy, would you care? Wouldn't you simply let a little criticism roll right over you?*

"Of course I did," she said, as if that had been the only acceptable alternative. "Plus, there were other reasons. To keep her in the dark, I potentially endanger her. Especially now that we're back in Vegas. Forewarned is forearmed, right? She needs to be aware of what's going on around her. And two, she's an adult. Has been an adult probably since she was fourteen. You know people, you included, always remark that I took on an adult's responsibilities when I was just twenty. In her own way, Abigail did the same. But she was only fourteen. I suspect her teenage years might have gone far differently if my parents had lived. But at that young age, she somehow knew that we were going to have to hold it together some way, in order to stay a family. And she did her part. She made it easy for me."

"I think," he said, his tone very serious, "that the only conclusion we can draw from this is that both of the North women are extraordinary. Beyond comparison." He looked her in the eye. "Perfect, really."

She held his gaze. Then after a minute, a slow smile lit her beautiful face. "Perfect, huh?"

"Yes." He wasn't backing down from that. To him, she was.

She stood. "Come here then. I need to show you something." She reached for his hand. Led him toward Abigail.

"What?" he asked.

“Just wait.”

Five steps away from Abigail, she stopped. Pointed directly into the pool. “Right there.”

He looked and felt her slide her hand up his arm, settle on his shoulder.

“In the middle of the pool,” she urged.

He dutifully looked again just as she shoved him hard, straight toward the deep end.

He surfaced and Abigail and Megan were laughing like a couple of little girls.

“Now that,” Megan said smugly, “was perfect.”

Chapter 19

When Megan woke up the next morning, again Abigail was already awake. "Are you even sleeping?" she asked her younger sister.

"Some," she said. "And then I have to pee or I get a cramp in my foot or my sweet baby kicks me. Bits and pieces. They say it's to prepare a person for when after the baby is born, when there really will be no sleep."

"That's when you call Auntie Megan. I'll come over and watch the little terror so that you can rest."

Abigail rubbed her stomach. "She will not be a terror. She will be sweet and delicate and born with a complete set of manners."

"Perfect, then. Like her aunt." She'd told Abigail about Seth's comment.

"Oh, yeah. Ms. Perfect. You're lucky Seth was a good sport about getting pushed into the water."

"I was right about him looking good in a swimsuit," Megan said, her tone a little wistful.

"Hey, hey. Enough of that. I'm out of here tonight. Right now, I call the shower first. What time do we need to be at the fashion show?"

"By ten. And Seth is going to want to eat breakfast first."

"Of course," Abigail said. "Whatever Seth wants."

When her sister disappeared into the bathroom, Megan took a moment to breathe deep before she knocked on the connecting door. "Seth?" she said, as the door whipped open.

"What?" he asked, taking in the room.

"Do you ever stop working?"

"Once we catch your stalker," he said.

"I just wanted to tell you that Abigail and I'll be ready for breakfast by nine."

"Abigail in the shower?" he asked.

"Yes."

"She generally take long showers?" he asked innocently.

"Not that long," Megan said, laughing.

"Long enough for this?" he asked as he pulled her into his arms, bent his head and kissed her. And as if it was the most natural thing in the world, his hands bunched up her nightgown and one hand settled on her butt and the other on her breast. It was so good. Good enough to make her momentarily consider just how long Abigail's shower might take. But finally, she squirmed away and let her nightie fall back into place.

"Nine o'clock. Be in the hallway," she said, her breath coming in spurts. She could see that he was fully aroused. She stared at him. "I'm sorry about that."

"No problem," he said. "I'm getting used to it."

She stepped back into her room, closed the door and leaned up against it. Amazing sex. That's how she'd described it to Abigail. They were simply just incredibly hot for each other. It was a perfect affair.

If that's what she was interested in.

At breakfast, Megan was quiet. Seth chatted with Abigail about the day. She was excited to finally be part of a grand opening and had toured the space where the fashion show would occur.

It would be on the second floor of their building, directly above the boutique. Evidently, at one time, it had been a dance studio but that tenant had departed years ago. Megan's contractors had cleaned it up, given it a quick coat of paint and a red carpet of sorts had been fashioned. Chairs and a sound system had been rented. Tonight, most of the chairs would go and tall tables would be brought in so that the cocktail party could be held in the same space.

He was glad to be back in Vegas and happy that he'd see his partners and their wives and in Rico's case, almost wife. Megan had offered invites to the fashion show to Jules Morgan, Kellie McGarry and Laura Collins and all had responded that they'd be delighted to come. Royce, Trey and Rico would join them for the cocktail party in the evening.

Seth had talked to his mom early this morning. She'd said she was feeling good and looking forward to the cocktail party. He'd arranged for Trey and Kellie to pick her up.

Right now, Trey and Rico were out of the office, conducting a security audit for one of the casinos. Royce had said in one of his emails that he'd be in the office. Seth hoped to have a minute to swing by and say hello and get an update on the background check he'd requested on Nadia Vitron. He'd have to make sure Megan was in a safe spot, though. His gut told him that even though Colorado Springs had been without incident, the danger wasn't over. Both the snake and the tainted candy had had the potential to have serious consequences for her. She'd escaped unharmed. Would her luck continue to hold out?

He wished to hell he knew where Ross Lewis was. Even if he wasn't the blond-haired man, Seth was willing to bet his last dollar that he was involved in some way in Megan's troubles.

They finished breakfast and then drove to the boutique. The brown paper was still in the windows, but he'd seen photos of the inside and knew they were ready. They opened the main doors of the building and the boutique was off to their left. He glanced to his right and saw that the antiques store had a closed sign in its window. A plastic hours sign said it opened at ten and closed at six. It was too early yet.

Past the boutique was an elevator to the second, third and fourth floors. Across from the elevator were stairs that led to the same.

"I'm taking the elevator," Abigail said. "I'm assuming it will hold my weight."

Megan pushed the button and the door slid open. She pointed to the sign on the right side. "Unless all together we weigh more than 2,200 pounds, we should be okay."

He wanted a look at the stairs but he'd do that later. He'd studied the blueprints of the building on her computer. She'd gotten them when she was first considering purchasing the building. So he understood the layout, but it was always helpful to see it in person.

They got out on the second floor. Abigail pointed to her left. "That empty storage room at the end of the hall has been converted into a place for the models to change clothes."

"Can I take a quick look?" he asked.

"Sure," Megan said.

She unlocked the door. It was an empty room, maybe fifteen by fifteen. Two large mirrors on rollers had been brought in as well as a portable clothes rack with empty hangers.

"The outfits are still in the other room," Abigail said. "Laid out. I thought you'd want to see them in person." Abigail had been sending photos for days and Megan had been making small tweaks.

They left that space, passed by the restrooms, the elevator again and then got to the big room that was directly over Megan's boutique. Megan again used her keys to unlock the big double doors and once she pushed them open, it appeared the space was ready to go. Rows of chairs. A middle aisle where the models would parade. Microphone in the front.

Like moths drawn to a flame, Abigail and Megan immediately went to the clothes. Within fifteen minutes, the models started showing up and outfits were passed out.

As attendees started to arrive, he stood near the door, carefully watching everyone who came in. He'd memorized the latest photo of Ross Lewis that he'd been able to unearth and nobody looked remotely similar to that. There were also no blond men. Several blond women, but nobody with the right height and weight.

Jules, Kellie and Laura arrived together. Each woman hugged and kissed him on the cheek.

"So you've spent the last ten days shopping. I'm dying to know whether ankle pants are in or out," Laura said.

"Speaking of pants, Seth, do these pants make me look fat?" Jules asked, hands on her hips.

"Hmm," Kellie said, index finger up to her lips. "I'm

confused about my color wheel. Do you think I'm a summer?"

"I think I feel sorry for Rico, Royce and Trey."

"Seriously," Laura said, "you must be able to get us some sort of a discount."

"I'm going to tell her to add another 25 percent for you," he grumbled.

Kellie and Laura exchanged a high five.

"Was it horrible, Seth?" Jules asked.

"It was…just a job," he said.

The three women exchanged a look. "Nothing snarky to say about women, women's fashions or the cluster that occurs when those two things coincide?" Kellie asked, her tone thoughtful.

Laura reached for his forehead and laid her hand flat. "Oh, honey, are you sick? What happened to the *don't bother to ask me to conform to your social norms* Seth that we know and love?"

He certainly wasn't telling them the truth. That he'd fallen for a woman who only wanted light and easy. "You three should take a seat. The show's about to start."

He retreated to the corner of the room where he could see everything.

Once the fashion show started, nobody in the audience would have known that twenty minutes earlier, it had been chaos. As usual, Megan was engaging and informative, and he had a feeling that everybody who attended would be visiting the Vegas store sometime in the near future. It lasted a little more than an hour and by the time the models cleared out, it was almost noon.

He saw Jules, Kellie and Laura at the front of the room, likely congratulating Megan on a great show. He hoped that was it and they hadn't succumbed to the idea of interrogating her to see what was going on with him.

He waited until they and everyone else had left besides Abigail before approaching.

"Are you hungry?" Megan was asking Abigail.

"Of course. I'm eating for two."

Seth stepped forward. "How about the two of you come with me for just a quick stop across the street. I need to speak with Royce. And then I'll take you both to lunch."

"I'm in the mood for a greasy burger," Abigail said.

"If Evan hadn't already married you, I'd hope that you would consider me," Seth said.

Abigail laughed and patted her belly. "You don't want to take this on," she said.

"I wouldn't mind." He said it and then realized that Megan was staring at him.

"You want children?" she asked.

"Sure." He shrugged. "I'd love it."

"How many?" she asked.

"Less than a litter. Maybe more than one."

Abigail reached for the door. "Third wheel moving out into the hallway."

"No, no," Megan said, shaking her head. "It's fine. Let's go."

None of them said anything as they walked across the street and into the Wingman Security offices. Of course they hadn't talked about kids. Kids weren't light and easy. Kids were hard and scary and wonderful.

Inside the office, he motioned for Megan and Abigail to have a seat in the waiting area. "I'll just be a second."

He was barely down the hall when Abigail leaned forward. "Oh, my God, Megan. You have got to keep him. He's perfect."

Megan rubbed her forehead. "Because he wants children?"

"Yes. Because you'd be a fantastic mom. But more importantly, he adores you. His eyes follow you around the room."

"He's getting paid to provide security for me."

"He's not doing this for the money, honey. Stop kidding yourself."

Megan frowned at Abigail. "When did you get so smart? I'm supposed to be the one giving you advice."

"It feels good to have the shoe on the other foot," Abigail said. "Although I did feel a bit like a voyeur back there. The two of you need to talk."

"After we get the store open," Megan said. "Light and easy. That's what I need right now."

"Okay, I won't push it. Just don't mess this up."

Royce handed Seth the file. "Nadia Vitron was born in Vegas and has lived here her entire life. Up until last year, she was married to Malcomb Vitron, but they are now divorced. She continues to live in the house they owned, located on Crestmountain Drive. She got a ticket for the accident involving Megan but other than that, has a clean driving record. Her vehicle was totaled in the accident and she recently purchased, with cash, a new Cadillac SUV. I could not find any connection between Nadia and either Logan Lewis or his brother, Ross Lewis."

Seth nodded, leafing through the folder. He looked at the picture that Royce had found somewhere. A woman, her elbow on a bar, a cocktail in her other hand. "This her?"

"Yeah. She posted it on social media."

She was squeezed into a black dress that looked about ready to burst at the seams, and her blond shoulder-length hair had very dark roots, hinting that the color came out of a bottle. Suddenly, he looked up. "Wait. You said that she continues to live in the house on Crestmountain Drive. That doesn't mesh with what Megan was told. Nadia was supposedly relocating to Carmel but didn't yet have a permanent address, so she provided an address of a hotel."

Royce shook his head. "I took a drive by. The SUV was parked in the driveway."

"We need to talk to this woman. And I want to know where the hell she's getting her money. Her new vehicle is expensive."

"I know. Her house is nice but nothing special. And I couldn't find any recent employment records for her. The last earnings reported for her was several years ago when she worked as a commercial loan officer for one of the banks in the area."

"Do you have time to follow up on this?" Seth asked.

"I'll make time," Royce said.

Seth leaned forward, his forearms on his side of the desk, his hands clasped. "I saw your wife earlier."

Royce's eyes took on a look. He loved Jules to distraction.

"She can be a pain," Seth said. "Her and Kellie and Laura. All pains."

Royce smiled. "Did the three of them gang up on you, Seth?"

"Maybe," Seth admitted.

Royce considered him. "Did it have anything to do with Megan North?"

"Might have." Seth looked down at his folded hands. "I think I'm in love with her," he said.

Royce appeared to be considering his next words. "Because you saw her underwear?"

"That didn't hurt," Seth admitted. "But she could probably wear burlap and make it look good. She's...special. The real deal."

"So what's the problem?"

"She's only interested in light and easy," Seth said.

Royce scratched his head. "Megan took on a huge responsibility when she was barely out of her teens. Now she's opening four stores, buying commercial real estate, becoming a landlord. None of that is light and easy. Maybe she just needs a little time. Be patient."

"Were you patient with Jules?"

"I was an idiot with Jules. I let her go for eight years."

If he lost Megan for eight years, he didn't know if he could go on. "Patience has never been one of my strengths."

"That's the crazy part of falling in love," Royce said. "Nothing is really what it always has seemed. You'll find a way."

Chapter 20

Abigail got her greasy burger for lunch and Seth joined her. Megan ate a salmon salad and felt a little jealous. She stole some of their fries.

Now they were back at the boutique, getting ready for the ribbon-cutting and the midafternoon staff meeting. Seth had helped them remove the brown paper from the display windows and the place looked great. It was almost twice the size of the other three stores, allowing plenty of room for the coffee bar and comfortable chairs. For the grand opening, they'd have a barista there serving up drinks. On most days, the staff would make the specialty coffees, put them in carafes and it would be a self-serve operation.

Abigail was straightening a display of scarves and Megan was adding accessories to one of the mannequins. Seth was staring out the front door, at the antiques store across the hall. "Did you hear anything more from the people who owned the antiques store after you told them that you weren't able to offer them a ten-year lease?"

"Weston sent a text and said they were disappointed."

He turned to look at her. "You and Weston are texting?"

"He's my attorney. Yes, we text."

"Just business?" he asked.

"Yes."

"If he shows up tonight, I might shove his phone down his throat. He'll have to wait until it makes its way through his large colon before he can continue texting."

"Uh, gross. You're not serious, anyway," she said.

"I'm not?" Seth asked.

She wasn't sure. He was staring out her windows, across the hall. "What are you looking at?"

"Precco's Fine Antiques," he said, reading the writing on their window. "They still haven't opened for the day. Earlier when we arrived for the fashion show, that made sense. But it's hours later, and there's no sign of activity there. Yet the sign on the door says that they should be open from ten to six today. I mean surely they have to know that today is the ribbon-cutting. You had a banner across the window that faces their store. They had to have seen it a whole bunch of times. So this is an opportunity to have important local people in their building, maybe taking a few minutes to scope out their store, and they're a no-show. That doesn't sound right for people wanting a ten-year lease."

He was right. "I'll make an effort to get to know them better now that the store is opening. Once I get my apartment rented, maybe I can buy something from them. Or—" she paused "—maybe you can quiz them tonight. We invited all the tenants in the building to the cocktail party."

He guessed he didn't really care if they were terrible businesspeople as long as they paid Megan the rent on time and didn't cause her any problems. He just didn't like it when things didn't add up. Maybe he would take a minute tonight and check out Mr. Precco.

A half hour before the ribbon-cutting was to start, staff started to arrive. No Jasmine for this opening. Instead, he met Patrice Woodman, the manager of the Vegas store. She was midforties and had very short red hair. She didn't command the attention that Jasmine did when she entered a room but he had a feeling, after watching her for a half hour, that she was going to be very competent.

Once the ribbon-cutting was over, they had their staff meeting. More people were employed by the Vegas store because it was bigger. There were eighteen people in the room. He thought by now that he could have given Megan's rah-rah speech, but she surprised him. Today she talked about how grateful she was that the other three openings had gone so well and that she was confident that the Vegas store would be even bigger and better.

The cocktail party was again a black-tie affair. Back at the hotel, Seth showered and slipped on the tux he'd worn in Colorado Springs with a fresh white shirt. He hoped Megan might wear the same black dress that she'd also worn that night. He had fond memories of that dress and of taking it off her.

But when she opened her door to the hallway, he saw that she was wearing black but it was a different dress. This one was strapless, oh, yes, and came to the floor in what looked like layers of shimmer. Her hair was up. She wore earrings but no other jewelry, leaving her lovely neck and shoulders bare. She looked…like a princess.

If his partners ever found out that he was thinking crazy stuff like this, he would never live it down.

Abigail was also in black but it was to the knee, with the material hugging her baby bump. She wore more makeup than he'd previously seen her in and he suspected the sisters had had some fun getting ready.

"You both look very nice," he said.

"Thank you," Megan said. "You do, too. I'm excited about tonight. Last one. Biggest party yet. On your home turf."

He liked that. Tonight, it wouldn't be just him watching the room. Royce, Trey and Rico would also be there. Nothing was going to happen with the four of them on high alert.

She glanced down at her black high-heeled sandals. "I may regret these shoes because tonight I'll have to stay until the bitter end. Jasmine won't be here to finish out the night for me."

It would be a late night but once they came back, Abigail would be returning home with her husband and Megan would once again be alone in her room. It was going to take him about five seconds to abandon his room and find her bed.

"I'll stay until my back gives out," Abigail said, "or until Evan's flight gets in and he arrives to take me home."

Megan shook her head. "You, and Kellie McGarry, will take chairs when we get there. And if Evan doesn't arrive by a reasonable time, we'll find another way for you to get home."

Abigail rolled her eyes but didn't argue. The phone in Seth's pocket buzzed and he glanced at it. "Our car is here," he said. The memory of getting shot at while exiting the cab outside the Periwinkle was still too vivid in his mind so he'd arranged for a car service that Wingman Security regularly used in Vegas to pick them up and take them to the party. They would exit the hotel from a side door where the car would be parked at the curb.

He led the way down the hotel corridor, to the elevator and then out the door. The limo driver opened the car door and the three of them slid into the back seat. They pulled away from the curb without incident and he let out a breath. So far, so good.

When they got to the building, the company Megan had hired to valet park cars was already in place. The limo pulled in to an open space. "I'll text you fifteen minutes before we're ready to be picked up," Seth said.

"Very good, sir," the driver responded.

Once they were out of the car, Seth moved them quickly inside and into the elevator. When the doors opened, he saw that the space looked totally different than it had earlier that day. The lights were dimmed and there had to have been a hundred candles burning. All but a few chairs had been removed and tall bar tables had been brought in. There was music playing and two bartenders were already behind a portable bar that had been moved into one corner.

"It's gorgeous," Megan said. "Thank you so much, Abigail, for pulling all this together."

"It was the least I could do," Abigail said. "And I could do it all from my computer and my phone. I didn't have to go traipsing all around the country."

"It was a lot," Megan admitted. "But I think we did it the right way. I wouldn't change a thing."

Did that include him? He sure as hell hoped so. Hoped he could convince her that she should keep him around another forty or fifty years.

He'd told his partners to come early and they did. Royce and Jules were first, followed quickly by Trey and Kellie with his mom, and Rico and Laura. Abigail, Kellie and his mom declined the immediate offer of chairs but promised that they'd be careful to not overdo it.

He wanted to know what Royce had learned about Nadia Vitron but he didn't want Megan to hear him ask the question. She had plenty on her mind tonight.

He waited until other guests started to arrive. Then he found an opportunity to approach Royce. "Any luck this afternoon?"

"I went to Nadia Vitron's address but there was no one there. Her SUV was also not there."

That was disappointing. "Thanks for trying," Seth said.

"Yeah, well, I decided to pay her ex-husband a visit. He lives in North Vegas, not that far from your mom's place. And that was interesting."

"Why?"

"Malcomb and Nadia Vitron divorced over a year ago. He said that Nadia had an affair with her old boss, which precipitated the end of the marriage."

"Boss at the bank?" he asked.

"No. The boss years before that."

He waited. Royce was leading up to something.

"Her boss was Stout Precco. He owns Precco's Fine Antiques."

Seth could feel his heart rate accelerate.

"Evidently, six years ago, Nadia worked for Mr. and Mrs. Precco. At some point, Precco and Nadia had an affair and when Mrs. Precco found out, Nadia was out of a job. At the time, Nadia told Malcomb that business was down and they were cutting back on help. Malcomb said he didn't think much about it. Nadia got a new job and life went on."

"Fat, dumb and happy," Seth muttered.

"Exactly. Precco evidently swore to his wife that the affair was over. Except Malcomb now doubts that. He suspects they continued on, just a little more carefully. But evidently not carefully enough, because Mrs. Precco hired a private detective to follow her slimeball of a husband. And lo and behold, he's still ducking into hotel rooms with Nadia. Mrs. Precco blows a gasket, calls Malcomb to tell him what a bad girl his wife is and hires a divorce attorney."

"What did Malcomb do?" Seth asked.

"Hired his own divorce attorney. So both couples split up. I asked him if there was still a relationship between Nadia and Precco and he said that he wasn't sure but that Nadia was driving an expensive car after she wrecked her previous vehicle, and he was sure somebody else had paid for it."

The car she'd wrecked running into the side of Megan. He was more confident than ever that the accident wasn't simply bad luck. "Mr. Precco is on the guest list for tonight. All the tenants are," Seth said.

"I've got a fairly recent photo of him on my phone," Royce said, pulling his cell from the inside pocket of his tux jacket. He pushed a couple buttons and then handed the phone to Seth. The man was early fifties and losing his dark black hair in the front, making his forehead seem unnaturally large. "Malcomb said he didn't understand the attraction because Precco is a kooky crook. He laughed when he said that, like it was funny to call somebody that."

"'Kooky crook,'" Seth repeated. "Did he elaborate?"

"Nope. I asked but all he would say is that if I was interested, I should follow the money."

"What money?" Seth asked.

"I don't know. But the man warrants a closer look, especially given that he's one of Megan's tenants. And..." Royce hesitated.

"And what?"

"I don't know," Royce admitted. "I was confident that Malcomb Vitron was telling me the truth and I did have time afterward to verify both divorce transactions, and that all checked out. But there was something not quite right with the explanation. I can't tell you what it was, but I left there thinking that there was more to the story."

Royce had a very good gut about these kinds of things. "Keep thinking on it," he said.

"I will."

In the meantime, if Seth could prove that the car accident hadn't really been an accident, he was going to make sure that Nadia Vitron was charged with something a whole lot more serious than a traffic violation. "Can you pass his photo around to Trey and Rico so that they can also be watching for him? I want to know the minute he arrives."

"Of course."

Seth leaned casually against a wall. Because Wingman Security had done work for many of the community notables, Seth knew a lot more people at this party than the previous ones. When they came up to chat, it made it a little harder to watch the room without appearing rude.

But he managed to mostly keep one eye on the door, one eye on Megan and to make sure that his mom seemed to be having fun. And as the hours flew by and the guests finally dwindled down to a handful, he was hopeful that everything was going to go fine. Maybe Megan had been right. There'd been no trouble in Colorado Springs and maybe that meant the person responsible for creating it had gotten tired of the game or scared that he might get caught.

A couple times he'd seen Megan approach Abigail, who had taken a seat alongside Kellie at the edge of the room, likely to see if she wanted to go home. But across the room, he'd seen Abigail shake her head. He suspected she and Kellie were having fun catching up on the missed years.

Finally, it was just the ten of them in the room—Royce and Jules, Trey and Kellie, Rico and Laura, Megan, Abigail, and his mom and him. Even the servers and the bartenders had cleaned up and gone home. He texted his car service to let them know to come.

All in all, it had been a good night. No Weston Marberry. No Logan or Ross Lewis. Unfortunately, no Stout Precco. Tomorrow, he was going to find the man, come hell or high water, and get him to answer some questions about Nadia Vitron.

"Thank you so much for being here," Megan said to the group. "It was perfect having all of you with Abigail and me for this final event."

"Happy to do it," Royce said. "You need anything else before we take off?"

"No. We're done here," Megan said. "Just need to lock up."

"Thank you for inviting me," his mom said to Megan. "It was good to be out. I caught up with an old friend who works with the visitors' bureau. They're looking for some volunteers so we're going to chat next week."

His mom would be great at that. "I'll call you tomorrow," he said and hugged her.

Trey, Kellie, his mom, Rico and Laura went first, taking the elevator to the first floor. That left Royce and Jules, Abigail, Megan and him to bring up the rear. When the elevator returned to the second floor, they all got in. They got to the first floor and were five feet from the elevator when Abigail grimaced.

"I hate to do this but I really should use the restroom one more time before the ride home," she said.

"I'll open the store. You can use the one in there."

"I'll just run back upstairs," Abigail said. "Because I think I really have pregnancy brain. I pulled my phone from my purse to text Evan that I was getting a ride home and not to bother stopping here," she said, holding up her phone in her right hand. "But then I forgot to put it back in my purse and I left my purse in the room. My house keys are in it. Normally, Evan's parents could let me in but they are out of town."

"I'll go with you," Megan said.

Seth motioned that Royce and Jules should just keep going. "You two get home to Grace. I'll wait for these two and we'll be right after you."

"You're sure?" Royce said.

"Definitely. Good night."

They got back into the elevator and went upstairs. Abigail put a hand on her belly. "Pregnancy brain and an aching back," she said. "This baby cannot come too soon."

"Did you stand too much tonight?" Megan asked.

"I don't know. But my back does feel like somebody is kicking it every once in a while. I'm sure once I stretch out in bed, it will be better."

He saw Megan grip the door keys that she carried. She was worried about Abigail and trying not to show it.

They got off the elevator and he stood in the hallway, his back braced against the wall. Abigail and Megan were in the restroom for just minutes. As they passed by him to once again open the doors of the big room, Megan made eye contact with Seth and smiled. "Two seconds," she said. They stepped into the dark room.

Seth waited. Heard something light hit the floor. "Everything okay?" he asked, his voice loud enough to carry.

There was no answer.

A chill went up his spine. He reached for his gun. Edged around the corner of the room.

Saw Megan and Abigail, against the back wall, a purse on the floor.

Saw the man, gun in his right hand, pointed at the two women.

It was Stout Precco.

"Put your gun on the floor, Mr. Pike," Precco said, his voice high for a man. "And kick it toward me. Otherwise I'm going to shoot them."

Could he take the chance? His aim was generally good but there was a possibility that the man would get a shot off and his bullet would find a target. Too risky. He'd disarm the man another way.

"Okay, Precco," Seth said, bending forward. "I'm putting my—" He caught movement out of the corner of his eye. Whirled. But when a bullet knocked him back, he knew that he hadn't been fast enough.

He heard Megan's scream as his knees buckled and he went down.

Chapter 21

He fought through the searing pain in his right arm. The bullet had entered about three inches above the elbow. He was pretty sure it had cracked the bone but did not have any idea whether it had exited his body. However, based on the amount of blood that was spurting out, he was pretty confident that he had some arterial bleeding going on.

He searched out his attacker. Nadia Vitron. She was in the far corner, still with her gun pointed at him. A blond-haired man stood next to her. He also had a gun.

Unfortunately, Seth did not. He'd dropped his.

"Oh, Nadia. Do you always have to go too far?"

Seth heard Precco's words, tried to make sense of them. But the man seemed very far away. Seth was sitting, willing his legs to cooperate so that he could stand.

"Stop," he heard Precco yell.

Stop what? he thought. Bleeding? Dying? All good ideas.

"I'm not letting him bleed to death."

It was Megan. And she was running toward him. He stared at her. "Sorry about this," he managed.

"Shut up," she said gently. Then she yanked up the wide skirt of her long dress, separated one of the layers from the others, ripped it upward at a seam, then tore off a wide strip. She quickly folded it a couple times.

He looked past her, watching Precco, who had moved, likely so that he could continue to still have a shot at both Abigail and Megan. But he didn't look as if he intended to put a bullet through the back of Megan's head. Nadia had also moved, so that she was standing next to him. Precco was shaking his head at the woman, as if he was very disappointed with her.

Yeah, well, so was Seth. He didn't like getting shot.

And if Megan could help him get the bleeding stopped and he could get his damn head to clear, he was going to rip both of them apart. With his teeth if he needed to.

"Stay alive," he hissed. "I'll take care of the rest."

Megan didn't answer. She moved his arm so that she could wrap the homemade tourniquet around his biceps and he saw stars. "I love you," he said when he got his breath back.

She looked at him. Her eyes were very dark. Fierce. "Then *you* stay alive." She tied the tourniquet very tight. "And I love you, too," she whispered. "I don't care that you fly your own plane. None of that matters."

"Stop talking," Precco said. "The two of you need to come back over here. Right now."

The man was getting agitated. Seth didn't want him or Nadia firing off any more bullets. "Is the other guy your stalker?" he asked.

She nodded.

"Okay, help me up," he said.

It wasn't graceful but he managed to get to his knees. Then with her arm around his waist, he stood. Leaned heavily on her as they walked across the room. Once his back was up against the wall, he let go of Megan's shoulder, but not before giving it a squeeze. Then he rested. The damn room was spinning and he felt as if he might throw up at any minute. He could smell his own blood and he didn't like it.

"Sit down," Precco said. "All of you."

He slid down the wall, grateful to have a solid floor underneath him. Megan did the same. He glanced at Abigail, who was still standing. She was coming in and out of focus.

But when he heard Megan's gasp, he knew something was terribly wrong.

"Oh, my God," she said. "Your water broke."

"It's okay," Abigail said.

"It's not okay," Megan yelled. "She needs a doctor. Now."

"No doctors," Nadia said.

It was the first time Seth had heard her speak. She had an accent, maybe Eastern European, he wasn't sure. He saw Megan's head jerk up and knew that this was the woman she'd heard talking below her second-story window. The woman had been talking to a man and Seth was willing to bet his last dollar it had been the blond-haired man who was standing next to her. Megan's guy.

Megan had scooted close to Abigail and was helping her sister down to the floor.

He was going to need to get the three of them out of here sooner rather than later. Knew very little about babies being born or how soon it could happen after the water broke but he thought that it could be quick.

"I want your cell phone, Mr. Pike," Precco said.

He considered lying, telling the man he didn't have

one. But they'd probably search him and he wasn't ready for that yet. When he went after these three, he needed to make sure that Megan and Abigail knew what was going on so that they didn't inadvertently get in the way. "I'm going to reach into my pocket and get it," he said. He used his good arm to do exactly that. Tossed it on the floor so that it landed a couple feet in front of Precco.

"This is all your fault, Mr. Pike," Precco said. He kicked both the cell phone and the gun that Seth had dropped toward the blond man. He didn't pick up either one. Precco didn't seem to notice.

"How so?" Seth managed. He felt clammy and thought he was likely going into shock.

"Well, yours and Nadia's," the man said, as if he was willing to throw him a bone. "Nadia can be…impulsive." After he said the words, Precco leaned forward and kissed the woman on the lips. "Like when she rammed into Ms. North."

Mr. Pike. Ms. North. Precco was being awfully formal, considering that he was holding them at gunpoint.

But why? What had Megan done to put herself on the man's radar, other than buy the building where Precco rented space? She said that she'd made a point to meet the tenants, to express her hopes that they continued to be tenants. Had been disappointed when the tea shop had abruptly moved out.

"When Malcomb called," Precco said conversationally, as if Seth had come in to buy a lamp and they were simply passing the time, "and said that your partner had been to his house, I realized that you were getting close."

The husband had called Precco. Why the hell had he done that? Precco had been screwing his wife. That generally wasn't the basis of a good friendship. "You two tight?" Seth asked. There was a buzzing between his ears and it made his voice seem odd.

Precco and Nadia exchanged a glance. "He despises me. But," Precco added, "we both love the same woman. He saw your partner as a potential threat to Nadia and when push comes to shove, that trumps everything else."

Nadia giggled, like a young girl.

Royce's gut had been spot-on. Whatever was going on with Precco, Nadia and her ex, it wasn't right. Malcomb Vitron had spewed some venom about Precco and then picked up the phone to warn the man that somebody had been asking questions about Nadia.

He was pretty confident that Precco and Nadia both had a screw loose. And given that they both had guns, that was a very bad thing. With effort, he focused his gaze on the blond man. Needed to assess what kind of threat he was. "So, you finally show your face?"

The man showed no reaction. But Precco smiled. "Pardon my manners," he said. He waved in the direction of the blond-haired man. "This is Simon, Nadia's brother. I think he and Ms. North have had the pleasure."

"I don't think we've actually met," Megan said, her voice tight.

"I heard that the snake was particularly effective," the man said. His accent matched his sister's. "I wish I could have seen it. Had to be content hearing the story secondhand from that stupid woman at the desk."

"You got the room number from her?" Seth asked.

"People will do most anything for a hundred bucks," Precco said. "Simon is very good with computers," he added. "If it's any comfort, he said your security at your company is very good. Fortunately for us, your assistant, Ms. O'Day, does some work at home. She needs to upgrade."

It explained how they'd known Megan's travel schedule and hotel plans.

"You're all chickens," Megan said dismissively. "And bullies."

Seth appreciated her spunk but now wasn't the time to irritate any of them into doing something stupid. "What do you want?" he asked. It was never a good idea to negotiate with a nut but there weren't a lot of good alternatives right now. He was going to pass out, Abigail was going to have a baby and Megan would be left to deal with this alone. Like so many times before.

Not on his watch.

"I'm not sure," Precco admitted. "It's a bit of a mess that we've contributed to, certainly, but you," he said, pointing at Megan, "really started it all when you lied about wanting to keep your tenants. And then you pushed the tea shop right out the door, without a second thought. This might be a plaything for you but it's our lives, our livelihood."

"I didn't do that," Megan said. "They didn't want to renew their lease."

"That's not true," Nadia said, her voice shrill. "We were going to be partners. They had access to markets in countries that we did not. It would have been a good situation for both of us. I talked to them all the time about us being partners."

Things clicked in place for Seth. Malcomb Vitron had said to follow the money. Which would lead one to believe that Stout Precco and his antiques business might be making money in unconventional ways. Illegal ways. Maybe drugs if it was something the tea shop could have helped with.

Megan had said the tea shop gave no explanation. He had a feeling that if Nadia Vitron was talking to them all the time, that in itself would be reason enough to want to avoid renewing their lease. But they couldn't necessarily tell Megan that without pointing a finger at Nadia or Precco. Maybe they'd witnessed a little bit of their crazy and decided that it was better just to get away, as far away as they could. They'd told Nadia and Precco that Megan had pushed them out in order to pave the way for a painless exit.

"You showed your hand when you wouldn't give us the ten-year lease," Precco said.

"I…I couldn't commit to that. But I wasn't pushing you out."

"What were you doing in here tonight?" Seth asked. "Before we came back."

"We were waiting on the third floor for everyone to leave. We had keys to this room because the locks haven't been changed." Precco paused. Then laughed. "You look confused, Ms. North. You clearly don't know much about the building that you bought. When I realized that your contractors, who, by the way, were loud and annoying and horrible to have in the building, didn't replace the false ceiling in your space, I just knew what we needed to do." He held up a hand, motioning for Simon to do something.

What he did surprised the hell out of Seth. He started rolling back the rug. When he had about a third of the rug pulled back, he stopped, squatted and opened a square door in the floor. And Seth knew immediately what it was. Rico Metez had a very similar door in the floor of his Colorado cabin that allowed him to get to his basement without going outside. Rico's had a drop-down ladder that folded out once the trapdoor was removed.

It took just a minute to realize that this was much less sophisticated. No ladder. Just a thick rope that Simon was gathering up. When it was in his hands, Seth guessed it to be at least fifteen or twenty feet.

"There are three of these," Precco said, motioning around the room. "When this place was a dance studio, the dancers would shimmy down and back up—it was part of their strength training routine. Simon is not a dancer but he's in good enough shape that he could have gotten down, wrecked your store and gotten back up in no time. It was really the perfect crime."

Not really, thought Seth. It wouldn't have taken a good cop that long to figure out that the intruder had to have come from above if there were no visible signs of entry anywhere else. Once they'd have started looking, they'd have found the trapdoors. But consistent with Precco's and Nadia's other actions, they didn't really think things through the whole way.

"What were you hoping to do by terrorizing me?" Megan asked.

"You should be grateful that was all I was doing," Precco said, as if he was offended that Megan wasn't more appreciative. "Nadia and Simon wanted to kill you. But," he said, waving a hand, "that is how their people do things. I was finally able to convince them that we simply needed you to regret ever buying this building," Precco said. "So that you would be amenable to another offer."

"You were going to make an offer?" Megan asked.

"Of course not," Precco said dismissively. "But my friend has a daughter who had worked for J.T. Daly's. She now works for you."

"Chloé Dawson," Megan said, her voice flat.

"Yes. Isn't that fun? Anyway, she said that J.T. Daly's was still interested in the purchase and would be willing to take it off your hands at the right price. Something substantially less than what you paid. Chloé is confident that

J.T. Daly's won't have any issue with a long-term lease. They offer them to tenants all the time."

Seth felt ill. If Nadia and Simon had prevailed, Megan might already be dead. In some crazy way, he was almost grateful to Precco.

There was potentially one more player who wasn't in the room. Seth wanted to account for him. "What does Ross Lewis have to do with all this?"

Nadia giggled again.

"Yes, darling. You did a good job in finding him," Precco said, looking at the woman. Then he returned his gaze to his three captives. "He's nothing. A drug addict who would do most anything for his next high. When we started looking more closely at Ms. North, we found the story of her parents' deaths. At first, we considered approaching Logan Lewis—after all, he'd had a relationship with Ms. North. But then, with a little digging, Nadia found that his brother had a habit that we were ideally suited to respond to."

It was drugs. That was how they were making their money. Running the business out of the antiques store, which gave them a way to get the drugs into the country and a way to launder the money.

"For a little product, Lewis was easily persuaded to make a few phone calls," continued Precco. "We wanted to mess with your head, confuse the issue. Especially after we realized that you were reporting things to the police."

Seth was angry at himself. These three idiots had led them down a rabbit hole. "Where is Ross Lewis now?" Seth asked.

Precco shook his head. "Sadly, he got a bad batch. Probably died within seconds of it hitting his blood stream."

He'd been a loose end and they'd figured out a way to tie it up.

He felt his heart sink. They had already committed murder. There was no way for them to back away from this. They were going to have to kill again.

Chapter 22

Megan held Abigail's hand and squeezed it hard. "Is the baby coming?" she whispered. Nadia, Simon and Precco had stepped back and were conferring. Unfortunately, Precco was still facing them, gun pointed toward them.

"I…think…so," Abigail said. Her face was sweaty and her speech halted. "Seth needs a doctor."

"You both do." Seth was still conscious but he'd lost a great deal of blood. He had to be holding on by a thread.

Megan didn't want to scare Abigail but she had a terrible suspicion. She'd read at least ten pregnancy books. "Is it possible that the back pain you had earlier was really labor?"

"I guess anything is possible," Abigail said. "Oh, God. One's coming." She gripped Megan's hand even harder until the contraction passed. "Evan is going to go crazy when he can't find me," she said when she could talk again.

"We're going to get you to the hospital. This baby, my

niece, is not going to be born on a floor with guns pointed at her." She was furious. Abigail and the baby and Seth were all in precarious shape. She was not going to lose everyone who mattered to her. Not again.

She had to find a way to get the guns away from Nadia and Precco. She was twenty years younger and in much better shape. She could do this. But she needed to find a way to separate them.

"I have to go to the bathroom," she said.

"You'll have to hold it," Precco said.

"I can't. And what I need to do, I don't think you want me doing in here. It's going to be pretty unpleasant for everybody."

Precco, a man who dabbled in fine antiques, evidently found the topic distasteful. "Nadia, take her to the ladies' room. And you have my permission to shoot her if she gives you any trouble." He looked at Megan. "Nadia is actually a very good shot. The two of you were lucky at the Periwinkle."

Nadia used her gun to point at the door. Megan gave Abigail's hand one last squeeze. She did not look at Seth but could feel his gaze on her back as she crossed the room. She opened the door and headed down the hall.

Megan waited until they were past the elevators and almost at the restroom door. Nadia was about two feet behind her. Too far for Megan to turn and grab the gun.

She shifted, put all her weight on her left leg and lifted her right leg. She didn't go for Nadia's hand, in an attempt to dislodge the gun; she went right for her face. And hit her target with a satisfying *crunch*. The woman doubled over, her hand to her nose. Now Megan was close enough to bring a knee up hard into the woman's chin.

Nadia's head snapped back and she lost her grip on

the gun. Megan grabbed it and pointed it at her. "If you scream, I'll shoot you. We're going back in there."

That evidently gave the woman hope because she kept her mouth shut. Megan let her take about three steps before she brought the butt of the gun down hard on the back of Nadia's head. The woman fell to the ground, unconscious. Megan wasted no time in dragging her body into the bathroom.

Sometimes it was very good to be tall. And strong.

Her hands were shaking as she tightly gripped the gun. She'd never shot one before but she would do it—she would do whatever she needed to do to save Abigail and Seth. All she needed to do was go back into the big room and surprise Precco and Simon.

She quietly edged around the almost-closed door. Precco and Simon were still talking. Abigail was having a contraction and they were staring at her.

Seth was looking right at Megan. He held up a hand, as if to halt her.

Then very quietly, especially for a man who had to be light-headed from loss of blood, he stood up. "Cramp in my leg," he said, rubbing his thigh.

Precco and Simon ignored him.

She watched as he took a couple breaths, his chest rising and falling. Now his good arm was hanging at his side. He made a fist. Then released his index finger, keeping it flat against his pants, out of sight to everyone but her. Then added his middle finger. She got it. What had he told her? *At my count. On three.*

She could see him gathering his body. Remembered something else he'd told her.

There's trust and then there's trust.

She understood exactly what he'd meant.

He added his ring finger. *Three!*

She came around the corner at exactly the same time he launched his body away from the wall and somersaulted across the room.

"Put your hands up," she screamed, wanting to draw the men's attention to her.

Precco's gun swung toward her. "Nadia," he yelled. "Where—"

She heard the shot and Precco fell to the floor like a stone. Seth had retrieved his gun and shot him.

"You're next," Seth said, his gun pointed at Simon. And time seemed to stand still as the man, gun in hand, glanced between Seth and Megan.

Seth was literally swaying.

If Simon didn't cooperate, Megan would have to be the one to shoot him.

"Simon," Seth said. "Don't be a—"

"Police. Drop your weapons."

Megan spun and almost passed out in relief. It was a flood of police. And when they stopped, she saw Royce, Trey and Rico right behind them. And then Evan, who ran to Abigail's side.

"We need ambulances," Megan said. "And there's a woman in the bathroom." She ran to Seth, who was once again on the ground, his eyes closed, his breathing very labored. She gathered his head and shoulders up into her arms. "Hang on, damn you," she said.

"Paramedics already here," Royce said. He squatted next to her and wrapped an arm around her shoulder. He put his other hand on Seth's leg.

And the paramedics were in the room. Doing their thing. Pushing her away. Hurrying. As if to say that they, too, knew that time was short.

"How did you know?" she asked Royce as they were loading Seth onto a gurney.

"Car service called the emergency number for Wingman Security when you guys didn't show up. I was the one on call and I knew immediately that something was wrong. We called the police and they were able to ascertain that all the activity was occurring in this room. We were attempting to identify another means of entry, other than the door. When we heard the gunshot, all bets were off. We came running."

"You needed a rope," she said.

He looked at her oddly.

"Never mind. I'll explain later." They were wheeling both Seth and Abigail out of the room. "I'm going with them."

"Of course."

"Seth was so brave. So very brave."

Royce looked at the third gurney that had Nadia Vitron on it. She was conscious but clearly still dazed. Her smashed nose had stopped bleeding. "Who did that?"

"I did," Megan admitted, a little sheepishly.

Royce smiled. "I think you were both incredibly brave. You're going to make a good pair."

Epilogue

Sophia North Chevalier arrived at 1:17 a.m. the next day. She was a healthy seven pounds, three ounces and twenty inches long. Her mother could not seem to stop smiling.

Seth was in the recovery room. His humerus had been broken by the bullet, which had not exited his body. He'd had surgery; the bullet had been removed and two pins were inserted to help the bone knit back together. The doctor had told Megan that she'd likely saved his life with her tourniquet.

Now she sat quietly next to his bed. They weren't going to let her stay long. She could come back later, once he'd been assigned to a room. But she'd begged to be able to see him. Once she did that, she'd go and sit with his mom, who'd come to the hospital.

His eyelids fluttered and she could tell he was working to focus his eyes. "Hey," he said. He tried to use his good arm to push himself up on the bed.

"Settle down," she said. "Relax."

"You're not hurt?"

"Not a scratch."

"Abigail?"

"She and Evan are with little Sophia, who might be the prettiest baby I've ever seen."

He shook his head. "Our kids will be cuter."

"Our kids?" she repeated.

"The whole litter."

She smiled. "I never agreed to a litter. I don't actually remember agreeing to anything."

"Too late," he said. "A man takes a bullet for you, you've got to marry him."

"You could have just asked," she said, leaning down to kiss him lightly on the lips. "I love you, Seth Pike."

"And I love you, Megan North. But you need to get out of here. You've got a boutique to open."

"We've got a boutique," she said.

"And an airplane," he added, no doubt testing whether she'd meant what she said that she didn't care if he flew his plane.

"Indeed we do," she said. "You can park it in the backyard for all I care." He loved flying. She loved him. There were no choices that needed to be made.

He motioned for her to lean down and kiss him again. "It was fate," he said, "meeting you under that awning."

Fate. Luck. Some of both. "Get better," she said. "It's my deal in poker."

* * * * *

Headhunter Lila Adrian's career is on a roll, until she witnesses the murder of her latest target! Former SEAL Travis Hawkins is the only person who believes she's in danger, and together, they have to find the murderer and get out of Costa Rica alive—no matter what it takes.

Read on for a sneak preview of
New York Times *bestselling author Tawny Weber's first book in her new Aegis Security series,*
Navy SEAL to the Rescue.

"I think I might be pretty good at motivating myself," Lila confessed.

"Everybody should know how to motivate themselves," Travis agreed with a wicked smile. "Aren't you going to ask about my stress levels?"

"Are you stressed?" she asked, taking one step backward.

"That depends."

"Depends on what?"

"On if you're interested in doing something about it." His smile sexy enough to make her light-headed, he moved forward one step.

Since his legs were longer than hers, his step brought him close enough to touch. To feel. To taste.

She held her breath when he reached out. He shifted his gaze to his fingers as they combed through her hair, swirling one long strand around and around. His gaze met hers again and he gave a tug.

“So?” he asked quietly. “Interested?”

“I shouldn’t be. This would probably be a mistake,” she murmured, her eyes locked on his mouth. His lips looked so soft, a contrast against those dark whiskers. Were they soft, too? How would they feel against her skin?

Desire wrapped around her like a silk ribbon, pretty and tight.

“Let’s see what it feels like making a mistake together.”

With that, his mouth took hers.

The kiss was whisper soft. The lightest teasing touch of his lips to hers. Pressing, sliding, enticing. Then his tongue slid along her bottom lip in a way that made Lila want to purr. She straight up melted, the trembling in her knees spreading through her entire body.